Ricochet

Addicted Series

RECOMMENDED READING ORDER

Addicted to You (Addicted #1)

Ricochet (Addicted #2)

Addicted for Now (Addicted #3)

Kiss the Sky (Spin-Off: Calloway Sisters #1)

Hothouse Flower (Calloway Sisters #2)

Thrive (Addicted #4)

Addicted After All (Addicted #5)

Fuel the Fire (Calloway Sisters #3)

Long Way Down (Calloway Sisters #4)

and

Ricochet

KRISTA RITCHIE
and
BECCA RITCHIE

BERKLEY ROMANCE
NEW YORK

Berkley Romance
Published by Berkley
An imprint of Penguin Random House LLC
penguinrandomhouse.com

Library of Congress Cataloging-in-Publication Data

Names: Ritchie, Krista, author. | Ritchie, Becca, author.
Title: Ricochet / Krista and Becca Ritchie.
Description: First Berkley Romance edition. |
New York: Berkley Romance, 2022. | Series: Addicted
Identifiers: LCCN 2022015402 | ISBN 9780593549483 (trade paperback)
Subjects: LCSH: Sex addicts—Fiction. | LCGFT: Romance fiction. | Novels.
Classification: LCC PS3618.I7675 R53 2022 | DDC 813/.6—dc23/eng/20220413
LC record available at https://lccn.loc.gov/2022015402

Ricochet was originally self-published, in different form, in 2013.

First Berkley Romance Edition: October 2022

Printed in the United States of America
1st Printing

Book design by Kristin del Rosario
Interior art: Broken heart on wall © Valentina Shikina / Shutterstock.com

One

I fucked up.

That's the only thought I have when I digest my surroundings. A live DJ blasts music from wall-engulfed amps while people guzzle colored drinks. My youngest sister, Daisy, sips beer from a Solo cup, scouting her model friends. I fear that she'll pull a guy over and try to hook us up—to take my mind off Loren Hale. Five hours ago, I believed a house party would be a safe choice.

Not true.

So. Not true.

I should be chastely tucked beneath my comforter, sleeping through the New Year's riffraff at my place with Rose. Only days ago, Lo—my best friend, my boyfriend, literally a guy who encompasses my *entire* life—left for rehab. Rose and I spent a full Monday packing my belongings. And I sorted through pictures, knickknacks and valuables, bursting into tears in random spurts. Besides clothes and toiletries, what's mine was Lo's. I felt like I was going through a divorce.

I still do.

Only an hour in, Rose called movers and paid them to finish packing my old apartment and unpacking at our new house. She bought a four-bedroom villa near Princeton with five acres of sprawling, lush land and a white wraparound porch, black shutters and purple hydrangeas. It reminds me of the Southern homes in Savannah or the *Ya-Ya Sisterhood*. When I told her this, she stood with her hands on her hips, appraising the building with those powerful yellow eyes. Then she broke into a smile and said, "I suppose so."

The isolation from male bodies doesn't stop my flyaway mind from traveling to bad places. Mostly, I worry about Lo. I toss and turn at night only to have to swallow large doses of sleeping pills to rest. I miss him. And before he left—I never imagined a world without Lo here. My throat closed up at the idea, my heart dropped and my head spun. Now that the moment has arrived, I realize that he took a piece of me with him. When I told this to Rose, she patted my shoulder and said I was being irrational. That's easy for her to say. She's intelligent, confident and independent. Everything I'm not.

And I don't think . . . I don't think many people can really understand what it's like to be so invested in someone—to share every single moment and then to have them ripped from you. We have an unhealthy, co-dependent relationship.

I know this.

And I'm trying to change, to grow beyond him, but why does that have to be a stipulation?

I want to grow *with* him.

I want to *be* with him.

I want to love Lo without people telling me that our love is too much.

One day, I hope we'll get there. *Hope*, that's all I have to go on right now. It's my driving force. It's literally what keeps me standing.

The first few days in withdrawal tortured me, but it helped that I hid in my room. I refused to see the real world until I could push past the most fervent urges. So far, I've contained my sexual needs by drowning in self-love. I've thrown out half of my porn to try to appease Rose and to convince myself that I'm on the path to recovery like Lo. But I'm not so sure that's the case. Not when my stomach clenches at the thought of sex. But mostly, I want to have sex with *him*.

And I worry about that fifty percent chance where I'll drag another guy into a bathroom, where I'll pretend he's Lo for a single moment to satisfy my hunger. I shouldn't be here. At a house party. Distance from wild things has helped so far. This— this isn't even close to my wildest moments, but it's enough to push me someplace bad.

When Daisy called and invited me to a "house party," I imagined a few people mixing strong drinks and huddled around a television to watch music performances. Not *this*. Not an Upper East Side apartment crammed with models . . . *male* models. I can barely scoot an inch without a body part invading my personal space. I don't even look to see what kind of ligament brushes my skin.

I should have told Daisy no. I have many fears since Lo left, but my greatest one is failing him. I want to wait for Lo, and if I'm not strong enough to squash these compulsions before he returns from rehab, then our relationship will really be over. No more Lily and Lo. No more *us*. He'll be healthy, and I'll be stuck on a destructive turntable alone.

So I have to try. Even if something in my brain says *go*. I keep reminding myself of what waits for me if I don't wait for him. Emptiness. Loneliness.

I will lose my best friend.

As per Rose's knowledgeable instruction (she's been reading up on sex addiction—and so has Connor, but that's another story), I should be looking for a suitable therapist before I attend any social events that'll tempt me. Daisy has no idea about my addiction—that it surrounds the allure of hot guys and the high of a lay. Rose is the only person in my family who's aware of my problem, and it'll stay that way if I can help it.

Still, I didn't tell Daisy *no*. Even as I was trying to say it, she used the "I never see you" mantra to guilt me into submission. She topped it off by saying that I was oblivious to the fact that she broke up with Josh during Thanksgiving. (First mistake: asking "How's Josh?" on the phone this morning. And I thought I was being so sly remembering his name and all.) That's how "uninvolved" I am in her life. So not only was I processing her single status, I was feeling a torrential downpour of sisterly remorse. I had to say yes to make it up to her. This is Lily 2.0—the girl who is actually trying to be a part of her family's world.

That means spending quality time with Daisy. And worrying about her jumping back in the dating pool. Especially if these older models are flinging in their hooks to catch her.

So here I am. Obviously not prepared for this type of party. Although, I did ditch my sweats for black pants and a silky blue blouse.

"I'm so glad we're here together," Daisy exclaims for the third time. "I never see you." Her arm flings around my shoulder, pulling me into a tipsy hug. I almost eat her golden-brown, nearly blonde, hair. The feathery, straight strands flow past her chest.

We separate and I pinch one of her locks off my glossy lips.

"Sorry," she says, trying to pull back her hair, but her hands are full: beer in one and a cigarette idly burning between two fingers in the other. "My hair is too fucking long." She sighs in frustration, still combatting the strands. She ends up using her shoulder and neck to try to push her hair off her chest, looking like a spaz in the process.

I've noticed that Daisy curses more when she's irritated. Which is fine. But I'm sure our mother would need to spend an extra three hours meditating to forget about Daisy's foul mouth.

And that's precisely why I don't care if she swears a lot or not at all. Do what she wants to do, I say. Daisy needs to be Daisy for a change, and I'm actually excited to see her away from our mother's neurotic, maternal claws.

She settles down and sets her elbow on my shoulder for support. I *am* short enough to be her armrest. "Lil," Daisy says, "I know Lo isn't here, but I *promise* that I'm going to take your mind off of him tonight. No rehab talk. No mention of comics or anything that'll remind you of him. Nada, okay? It's just me and you and a bunch of friends."

"You mean a bunch of *attractive people*." I use the correct terminology. I am surrounded by pretty people who could sprint along a beach, *Baywatch*-style, and cause a wave of boners. Or they could walk down a runway and you'd probably be staring at their face more than their clothes.

At least I would.

Does that make me the ugliest person here? I'm probably the only un-model-ish girl. I nod. Okay. I'm cool with that. Surrounded by tens and I'm probably a six. I'll take it.

She blows out smoke from her lips and smiles. "They're all not that good-looking. Mark looks like a gerbil in bad lighting. His eyes are too close together."

"And he gets booked for jobs?"

She nods with a goofy smile. "Some fashion lines like the quirky thing. You know, the bushy brows, gap-tooth sorta look."

"Huh." I try to find Mark and his gerbil-ness, but he's nowhere to be found.

"I kinda wish I had a cooler signature trait."

Signature trait? Sounds like getting a badass patronus in the Wizarding World. Though I'm sure mine would be lame too. Like a squirrel.

I try to deduce her signature trait, scanning her black leggings, long gray shirt and army-green, military-style jacket. She doesn't wear a single stroke of makeup, her complexion smooth, fresh and peachy perfect. "You do have great skin." I nod, thinking I've solved the riddle. I'm so good. I nearly pat myself on the back.

Her eyebrows rise and she playfully bumps my hip with hers. "All models have good skin."

"Oh." I realize I'm going to have to come out and ask. "What's your signature trait?"

She puts her cigarette in her lips and then grabs a wad of her hair shaking it towards me. "This baby," she mumbles. She drops the strands on her shoulder and tucks the cig back between her fingers. "Long, long, long Disney princess hair. That's what my agency calls it." She shrugs. "It's not even that special. With wigs and stuff, anyone can have my hair."

I would tell her to chop it off, but that'll just rub in the fact that she *can't* do a damn thing about it. Not when the agency controls her look. Not when our mother would go into cardiac arrest. "You do have better hair than me," I tell her. Mine is greasy half the time.

I should probably wash it more.

"Rose has the best hair," Daisy says. "It's the perfect length and super shiny."

"Yeah, but I think she combs it a hundred times a day. Like the mean girl from *The Little Princess*."

Daisy's lips twitch with a smile. "Did you just compare our sister to a villain?"

"Hey, a villain with good hair," I defend. "She would appreciate that." At least, I hope so.

Daisy finishes off her cigarette and snubs it in a crystal ashtray on the fireplace mantel. "I'm glad you're here."

"You keep saying that."

"Well I am. You're always so busy. I feel like we really haven't talked much since you left for college."

I feel even worse. Being so much younger than Poppy, Rose and me must have been isolating and lonely. Me being an addict and shunning my entire family hasn't helped. "I'm glad I'm here too," I tell her with a large, honest smile. Even if this may be my biggest test since Lo's absence, at least I know I did something right. Coming here, spending time with Daisy, it *is* progress. Just a different kind.

All of a sudden, her eyes light up. "I have an idea." She grabs my hand before I can protest. We exit the apartment and head for the hallway. She sprints towards the stairwell, tugging me along in tow.

I'm just getting used to this new, impulsive Daisy. Who, Rose informed me, has apparently been around for the past two years. When we moved into our new house, we invited Daisy to help decorate. On her tour through the four-bedroom villa, she spotted the pool in the backyard. No mind that it's still winter. A mischievous smile warped her face, and she climbed out of Rose's bedroom window, onto the roof and prepared to jump in the water from three stories high.

I didn't think she would do it. I told Rose, "Don't worry. It's probably just an attention thing."

But she stripped into her underwear, took a running start, and splashed into the pool. When her head popped up, she wore the biggest, goofiest "Daisy" grin. Rose almost killed her. My jaw permanently unhinged.

And she floated on her back, barely even shivering.

Rose said when our mother isn't around, Daisy tends to go crazy. And not the *I'm going to drink my sorrows away and snort some coke* rebellion. She just does things that our mother would condemn, and Daisy probably knows we're more forgiving.

When Rose saw that Daisy survived the jump without a bruise, she simply called her stupid and then let the issue drop. Our mother would have ranted for a solid hour, flipping out over any injuries that could have ruined her modeling career.

More than anything, I think Daisy just wants to be free.

I guess I was lucky enough to escape my mother's strict scrutiny. But maybe not. I didn't turn out perfect. One could even say that I am royally fucked up.

We climb the stairs to the highest floor, and Daisy turns the doorknob, the biting cold prickling my bare arms. The roof. She took me to the roof.

"You're not planning on jumping are you?" I immediately ask with wide eyes. "There are no pools for you to land in this time."

She snorts. "No duh." She lets go of my hand and sets her beer on the gravel ground. "Do you see this view?"

Skyscrapers light up the city, and people even explode fireworks off other buildings, the colors crackling in the sky for tonight's celebration. Cars honk below, kind of drowning out the majestic atmosphere of the night.

Daisy extends her arms and inhales deeply. And then she screams at the top of her lungs. "HAPPY NEW YEAR, NEW YORK CITY!" It's only ten thirty, so technically it's still New Year's *Eve*. Her head turns to me. "Scream, Lil."

I rub my hot neck, anxious. Maybe it's the lack of sex. Or maybe sex is the one thing that'll help me feel better. So . . . is sex the cause or is it the solution? I don't even know anymore. "I'm not a screamer." *Lo would disagree.* My cheeks flush.

Daisy faces me and says, "Come on, it'll make you feel better." Doubtful.

"Open your mouth wide," she teases. "Come on, big sis."

Am I the only one who thinks that sounded perverted? I look over my shoulder. Oh yeah, we're alone.

"Scream it with me." She bounces on her toes, preparing to say "Happy" but she stops when I don't share her enthusiasm for the holiday. "You've got to loosen up, Lily. Rose is supposed to be the uptight one." She grabs my hand. "Come on." She leads me closer to the ledge.

I take a glance down. Oh God. We're super high up. "I'm afraid of heights," I tell her, shrinking back.

"Since when?" she asks.

"Since I was seven years old and Harry Cheesewater pushed me off a jungle gym."

"Oh yeah, you broke your arm, didn't you?" She smiles. "And wasn't his name *Chess*water?"

"Lo made up his nickname." Good times.

She snaps her fingers in remembrance. "That's right. Lo put a firecracker in his backpack in retaliation." Her smile fades. "I wish I had a friend like that." She shrugs, as though that time has passed for her, but she's still young. She can always grow closer to someone, but then again, with our mother dragging her every which way, she probably has less time for friends than any of us did. "Okay, enough Lo talk. He was supposed to be banned from the conversation tonight, remember?"

"Forgot," I mumble. Most of my childhood stories involve him. I can count very few where he isn't present. Family trips, he was there. Reunions, he was there. Calloway dinners, he was there. My parents might as well have adopted him. Hell, my grandmother bakes him her special fruitcake for no reason at all. She'll mail it to him every so often. He charmed her somehow. I still think he gave her a foot massage or something nasty.

I squirm. Ew.

"Let's play a game," Daisy suggests with a giddy smile. "We'll ask each other questions, and if we get them wrong, then the other person has to take a step towards the ledge."

"Uhh . . . that doesn't sound fun." My fate will rest in her ability to answer a question.

"It's a trust game," she says, eyes twinkling. "Plus, I want to get to know you better. Is that so bad?" Now I can't say no.

She's testing me, I think.

"Fine." I'll make the questions easy so she'll know the answer and I won't have to feel my heart pop out of my chest.

She positions us so we stand maybe four feet from the ledge. Shit. This isn't going to be fun. "What's my birthday?" she asks me.

My arms suddenly heat. I know this. I do. "February . . ." *Think Lily, think. Use those brain cells.* ". . . twentieth."

Her lips twitch into a smile. "Good, your turn."

"When's my birthday?"

"August first," she says. She doesn't even wait for me to tell her that she's right. She knows she is. "How many serious boyfriends have I had?"

"Define serious." I don't know this one. I truly do not. I wasn't even aware she started dating until I heard Josh's name thrown around while we were shopping for Charity Gala dresses.

"I brought them home to meet Mom and Dad."

"One," I tell her with a less-than-confident nod.

"I had two. Don't you remember Patrick?"

I frown and scratch my arm. "Patrick who?"

"Redhead, skinny. Kind of immature. He used to pinch my butt, so I broke up with him. I was fourteen." She takes a step closer to the ledge since I'm clearly the worst sister ever.

I sigh heavily, realizing it's my turn. "Uhh . . ." I try to think of a good question, but they all contain Lo somehow. Finally I land on something semi-good. "What part did I play in the *Wizard of Oz* production?" I was only seven, and upon Lo's request, his father pulled strings and took his son out of the performance so he didn't have to play the Tin Man. Lo was so happy that he never had to rehearse with the class. He slept in the back of the room, his mouth hanging open, taking an extra nap time while we tried to memorize condensed, age-appropriate lines.

I miss him.

"You were a tree," Daisy says with a nod. "Rose said you threw an apple at Dorothy and gave her a black eye."

I point at her. "That was an accident. Don't let Rose spread lies . . ." That story is in her arsenal to use against me, I swear.

Daisy tries to smile, but it's a weak one. I can tell my relationship with Rose is something that upsets her, so I let my words taper off. She asks, "What do I want to be when I grow up?"

I should know this. Shouldn't I? But I have absolutely no clue. "An astronaut," I throw out.

"Nice try." She takes a step forward. "I'm not sure what I want to be."

I gawk. "That was a trick question. No fair."

She shrugs. "Wish you thought of it first?"

I look at my distance from the wall and then hers. Two more steps and she's on the ledge. "No thank you." I'm ecstatic she's answering my questions correctly, but I feel a little guilty I'm sucking at hers. I think she knew I'd fail at this game.

Maybe she wants to lose, and this way, I can't tell her to jump down. Not if it's all part of the game. Jesus, I hope that's not the case. But my stomach sinks at the thought. It seems more and more likely that it is.

"What's my middle name?" I try an easy one.

"Martha," she says with a laugh. "Lily Martha Calloway. Doesn't it suck to be named after our grandmother?"

"Look who's talking, Petunia." She was saddled with a *second* flower name.

"You know what boys always ask me?"

"What?"

"Have you been deflowered?"

I've heard that one before.

Her eyes meet mine briefly. "Have I?"

The cold nips my neck. "Is that my next question?"

She nods.

"You're a virgin," I say, hesitant. Right? The last we talked about this, we played a game on our family's yacht, and both Daisy and Rose said their V-cards were still intact.

She takes a step forward, her boots hitting the ledge.

Whaaa... "You're lying," I say with huge, round eyes. When the hell did she lose her virginity? To whom?!

She shakes her head and her hair flaps in the wind. She tucks a strand behind her ear.

"Was it Josh?"

"No," she says lightly, as if it's not a big deal. Maybe not for me, it wasn't. I've actually tried to suppress the memory of my first time. It was awkward, and it hurt a little. Whenever I think about it, I start to blush. So I've buried it deep, deep in the recesses of my mind.

"Who? When? Are you okay?"

"A couple months ago. I don't know . . . girls had been talking about sex in class, how they've had it and stuff. I just wanted to see what it would be like. It was okay, I guess. Definitely not as fun as doing this." She wags her eyebrows playfully.

"But who . . . ?" My eyes may literally pop out of my face. *Please don't be like me*, is all I can think.

"A model. We did a shoot together, and he moved back to Sweden, so don't worry, you won't run into him here."

I am learning so much about Daisy in one night. It's hard to digest. I feel like I've just gorged myself on Five Guys burgers and fries, close to puking a little.

"How old is he?" *Please don't be statutory rape.* I don't know if I can hold in that secret.

"Seventeen."

I relax. "Does Rose know?"

Daisy shakes her head. "No, I haven't told anyone that I lost it. You're the first. You won't say anything, right? Mom would kill me."

"No, but . . . if you start having sex, you should be careful."

"I know." She nods a lot. "Do you think . . . do you think you can take me to the clinic? I kinda want to be on birth control."

"Yeah, I'll take you." Another secret I'll have to keep from the family, but this one I'll gladly take. Unplanned pregnancy can be avoided, and girls shouldn't feel ashamed to be on the pill. "Just promise you won't go crazy and have sex with a bunch of random guys." Because I would and look how awesome I turned out.

"Ew, I wouldn't do that." She scrunches her nose, and the bottom of my stomach drops. And this is why I can't tell anyone else in my family about my addiction. Rose was right. They just wouldn't understand. "Will I go to college?" she asks another question for our game. I can't even remember if it's her turn or mine.

"I can't predict the future."

"Do I *want* to go to college then?"

"That . . . is a very good question . . . that I do not have the answer to. Do you?"

She shakes her head. "No. Not yet anyway. I'm ready to be eighteen and do shoots without Mom there. I'll be able to go to France alone and see the city without Mom scheduling my whole itinerary. You know, this year she wouldn't even let me see the Louvre."

"That sucks."

Daisy nods. "Yeah, it blows." Then her boot sets on the cement ledge. My heart lurches into my throat.

"Okay, game over!" I throw up my hands. "Let's go back inside."

Daisy grins from ear to ear and stands, perched on the fucking ledge with a twenty-story drop-off. She straightens up and outstretches her arms. "I AM A GOLDEN GOD!"

Oh jeez. Quoting *Almost Famous* does not alleviate my panic.

Instead, she screams at the top of her lungs, which turns into a full-bellied laugh.

This bonding time has gone a little too far. "All right, game over. You win. Seriously, I'm going to break out in chicken pox." Or at least a rash that looks like it. I start pacing, too afraid to move closer and pull her down myself. What if I tug and she falls backwards like on television? That's how people die.

Daisy begins walking across like it's a tightrope. "It's not that scary. Honestly, it's like . . ." She laughs into a smile. "It's like the world is at your fingertips, you know?"

I shake my head repeatedly, so much my neck hurts. "No, no. I have no idea what you're talking about. Did someone drop you on your head?" That seems kind of likely right now.

And then she hops off.

Onto the gravel.

I breathe. She picks up her Solo cup on her way to me and wraps an arm around my shoulders. "It's possible that one of the nannies did. Maybe that explains why I'm not as smart as Rose."

"No one is as smart as Rose." Except maybe Connor Cobalt.

"True," she says with a laugh and turns to the door. "Now let's see if we can find you a hot guy."

Yeah, this isn't going to be good.

Two

Daisy tries to leave me with a scarily attractive blond model. Can a face like his really exist without Photoshop? Perfect bone structure, the prettiest blue eyes I've ever seen. Dear God, I'm in trouble.

"I'm going to go get some punch. You two stay here and chat," Daisy says. I try to grab her elbow before she disappears from me.

"Daisy . . ." I'm going to kill her.

She spins around and mouths, *mingle*, and tops it with another smile.

I look back. He towers over me and sips from a Solo cup. He bends to my ear, his hand sinking to my waist. And lowering. I swallow.

"You're like a little hidden gem," he tells me with a small laugh. I avoid those intense blue eyes that begin to rake my body, heating up places that should not, in any way, be made hot by anyone except Loren Hale.

I brush off his hands so frantically that I end up looking like I'm swatting flies. And then I mutter something unintelligent that sounds like *I have to pee* or maybe *there's a bee*. Either way, I disentangle myself from him and the mobs of models in the dance area. I find a safe spot on the couch by the floor-to-ceiling window, the glittery city lit up and awake with cabs and pedestrians.

Daisy is in a discussion with a guy who seems to be around her age. It's hard to tell in this group. He has black hair and European features, skinny like he could front an indie rock band. She's unaware that I've ditched her handsy friend.

Next to me sits a half-conscious, drug-induced boy, staring up at the ceiling. I follow his gaze, not finding what looks so damn interesting besides white plaster.

I take an impulsive glance at the oak table by the wall—decorated with a spread of cheap liquor. People serve themselves, and I subconsciously look for Lo behind a curly brunette. After she plops a couple ice cubes in her drink and passes to the kitchen, I see him.

Leaning against the beige wall, cupping a Riedel glass with amber liquid.

His cheeks cut sharply, and his expression flickers between slightly annoyed and amused. He takes a small sip and meets my gaze, *knowing* I'm watching—as though we share a secret beyond every person here. The corner of his lip rises as he takes another swig, and I pin myself to my seat.

He brings the glass down and puts his head to the wall, his chin raised a little. He stares. I stare back. And my whole chest inflates with helium.

I want him.

I need him.

To hold me. To wrap my arms around his body. For him to whisper in my ear that everything will be okay. That we'll be better for each other. Will we? Will we still love each other if he's sober and I'm wading through the things that torment me? Will he fit into my life if I'm struggling with my addiction while he's healthy and absolved from his?

I want to fit into his life. I just hope when he returns, he'll want me too.

And I blink. He's gone. Somewhere. No one will tell me what rehab he checked into, and so I'm left with these distressing fantasies, wishing for him to return. At least I managed to claw a few answers from Ryke. He said that for the first month of rehab, Lo isn't supposed to have any sort of outside communication. I'm not sure if that pertains to *only* me, but I have a feeling Ryke has been in touch with Lo since he dropped him off.

So maybe I'm the only one who's being shunned and kicked out of Lo's life like dirty garbage.

Still, I wait in anticipation for February. Email privileges will be restored. And then in March, he'll upgrade to the telephone. If I can just make it through January, I'll be okay. Or at least, that's what I keep reminding myself.

My phone buzzes, and I retrieve it from my pocket, wiping my eyes with my wrist while I read the text.

> I left my wallet at your place. I need you to open the gates—Ryke

I freeze and reread the text four more times. *Open the gates.* As in the gated house I'm supposed to be at right now—the one Rose bought in a secluded little town. Can I pretend that I didn't read it?

> Lily, I know you're there.

What? How?!

> I won't fuck you. Just let me in. I'm supposed to be in Times Square right now.

My fingers hover over the screen. If I refuse to answer, I can act like I never received the texts. Simple. And then I can just lie tomorrow about losing my phone. It'd be better than dealing with Ryke now.

> We both have iPhones. I can tell when you've read my texts, so stop ignoring me and open the fucking gates.

Uhh . . .

My phone rings, and I jump. RYKE MEADOWS fills the screen.

I'm in trouble. We haven't established a talking-on-the-phone type of relationship yet. As of late, we're strictly text-only. Even if he is Lo's half brother, he has *just* entered our lives. And while Lo may forgive all of Ryke's past transgressions—like spending seven years with the knowledge of his little brother's whereabouts and not doing anything about it (like saying "hi" at least)—I have kept Ryke at a lengthy distance. It has nothing to do with his boy-parts and sex but more to do with his annoying qualities. Like inserting himself into other people's business. Like being an alpha male when the situation does not call for one.

My finger continues to float above the big green button, and I make a rash decision and bolt for the patio to avoid music and loud chatter. Even outside, the wild streets make up for the lack of pumping bass as people gather down below for tonight's festivities. My phone vibrates angrily in my hand. Quickly, I press the speaker to my ear and wait for Ryke to speak first. I'm so not about to initiate *this* conversation.

"Open the fucking gate," he snaps.

"I can't."

"What do you mean, you can't? Get your ass off your bed and

come down here." I hear him jiggle the iron entry, as though trying to physically open it by pure brute force.

"Are you trying to break in?"

"I'm considering it." He sighs, agitated. "It's been seven days since he left, not *five* fucking years. You're acting pathetic."

I purse my lips. *This* is why I dislike him. His blunt honesty is so rude sometimes. Ryke takes the meaning of "tough love" to a whole new level. "I realize that. And I'll have you know, I changed out of sweats on day four, and on day five, I washed my hair." I am not *pathetic*. I'm trying to live without my best friend. It's hard. My whole reason for waking up in the morning and putting on a smile was taken from me.

"Congratulations. Now open the gate."

And then, my luck goes in the crapper. "HAPPY NEW YEAR MOTHERFUCKERS!" a guy screams five stories below. I am one hundred percent positive that Ryke heard the drunken exclamation through the receiver.

"Before you say anything," I speak rapidly, feeling the heated fury brew from Ryke through the phone. "Daisy *begged* me to come to this house party. She gave me these big green doe eyes. You have not been inflicted by Daisy's doe eyes, so you can't judge. And then I thought—hey, it can't be that big of a deal. She's fifteen. It has to be some small girly slumber party in the city. Nothing to fret about." I moronically point at my chest even though he's nowhere near me. "It's not my fault that my little sister has friends twice her age. I didn't even know she drank outside of our family until tonight! So *this* is not my fault. You hear me, Ryke? Not. My. Fault." I finish my rant with a heavy breath.

After a short pause, all he says is, "Where the fuck are you?"

"I'll probably head home after the ball drops." I dodge the answer in case he intends to find me.

"Do you trust yourself?"

I go quiet and glance at a well-built model who leans over the railing to grab the attention of a girl on the street.

He's shirtless.

And hot. But I guess that's self-explanatory considering his job.

Do I trust myself? *Not completely.* But I can't stay reclusive forever and wallow in my sheets like a dying hyena. I have to be brave. I have to try to be normal. Even if my mind screams *no.*

Ryke takes my silence as an answer. "If you can't even say yes, then you shouldn't be at any parties. Find Daisy and stay with her until I get there."

What? No, no, no. "You don't need to babysit me, Ryke."

He exhales loudly. "Look, I promised Lo that I'd make sure you didn't jump off a fucking cliff when he left. If helping you helps him, then I'll do whatever it takes. I'll see you." He hangs up and I realize I never told him the address of the apartment. Maybe he's bluffing and trying to instill fear so I'll avoid doing something rash and stupid. Like hooking up with a male model. Like kissing a random guy. I'm frightened by the place in my mind that says *go*—the trigger that forgets about the love of my life for a brief, horrifying moment. And then when it's over, I'll be filled with shame and disgust so deep that I won't know how to crawl back out.

I breathe in and shake off my trembling hands. I shuffle into the apartment and spot Daisy by the silver refrigerator with a dizzying array of letter magnets attached. Someone spelled *cum with me.* Clever.

Daisy sips from a red Solo cup, now filled with punch, and chats with a tall Italian model, his chocolate hair thick and his smile insanely bright. As I approach, she says a quick goodbye and hesitantly flips her phone over in her palm.

"What is it?" I ask.

"Something weird just happened. I don't know . . ." She takes another swig of punch and licks her lips. "Ryke texted me."

Oh shit.

"I mean, I didn't even think he noticed me."

As far as I remember, Ryke has met Daisy once at my family house in Villanova, a ritzy suburb outside of Philly, and it was more of a wave from afar than a true greeting. "What'd he want?"

"To know what party I was at. I gave him the address." She shrugs. "You think he likes me or something?"

". . . I don't know, Dais. He's twenty-two, and he's not the kind of guy that would hit on a fifteen-year-old." Because those guys are perverts.

Her lips downturn into a deep frown. "Yeah, I guess. But why would he ask me where I was? I mean, I do look older, Lily. And I make my own money . . ."

"You're still fifteen," I tell her. "He's still twenty-two." This needs to be squashed right now before he gets here. I cannot have her thinking she has a chance with him. No, no, no. I itch my neck. Maybe I am getting chicken pox.

She groans. "It's so fucking frustrating. I feel older than I am half the time. Some people treat me like I'm in my twenties, and then I go back to school, and I'm babied again. I'm given respect, and then it's taken away from me. Over and over and over." She downs the rest of her drink.

"I'm sorry," I say, not knowing what else to tell her to make her feel any better. "You're close to being sixteen, and then you'll only have two more years." I lamely shake my hands like faux pom-poms.

She lets out a weak laugh. "You're so corny."

I shrug. "It made you laugh."

"It did." She nods.

"How did Ryke get your number anyway?"

"I didn't give it to him. Maybe he called Rose and asked her for it." She pauses. "So . . . why do you think he's coming over?"

I inhale a strained breath, my muscles tightening. "I'm not sure," I lie.

"I guess we'll see." She stares at her empty cup. "I'm going to get a refill. How about you go hang out with Bret?" She tilts her head to the scarily pretty blond guy that I dodged.

"Getting rid of me?" I joke. "Am I not that fun?"

She smiles. "I just don't want to leave you here alone. I'm the one who asked you to come, after all. And it may take me a while to escape the punch bowl." She nods to the big tub full of red liquid and sliced pineapples. "See Jack over there." I spot the black-haired European guy that I noticed before.

"Yeah?"

"He's a talker. I can't ever get away from him, and I feel guilty when I try. It'll take me probably ten minutes."

"I can come save you," I suggest.

She shakes her head and tucks her hair behind her ear. "No, no. I have it handled. Have fun. *Mingle*," she tells me again. As if mingling is the solution. It is not.

My palms sweat and my nerves jostle as she disappears. I really want to go follow her, but she basically said, *do not follow me, Lily*. Didn't she? I swallow down my anxiety and accidentally lock eyes with a dark-skinned model, his biceps bulging as he sets two palms on the alcohol table.

I bite my fingernails, losing control. Maybe I should try to calm myself. Go off and do my own thing. Find someone . . . Bret . . .

No.

My body thrums with the usual cravings that I've denied myself for seven whole days. The only thing that will satiate the nerves, the fear, and everything that balloons my dizzy head is sex.

Sex is the solution.

But instead of picking a male model to throw myself at, I focus on the bathroom. *Go there and you'll feel better*, I think. Over and over. I don't need a boy. I can help myself.

So I head to the bathroom in the little hallway. After waiting in a semi-long line, I lock the door and settle on the toilet seat. I try to remind myself that I accomplished this ritual in far grosser places. I wiggle my shorts and panties to my ankles.

I take a small breath and relax and find the throbbing spot with my fingers. Closing my eyes, I drift into my mind, transporting myself from this party to other, steamier places.

I picture Lo. I re-create a not-too-distant memory where we were together for real.

The lights had dimmed; the movie trailers had ended, and the opening credits were rolling. In the blackness, I tried not to concentrate on Lo's heavy breath, the way his arm and leg pressed firmly into mine. His eyes fixed to the screen, not acknowledging the aching tension with a look towards me. Instead, his right hand skillfully roamed my leg, silently telling me to focus on the film. Even if the theater was empty, being secluded in the back row did not help ease my desires.

His hand rubbed the bareness of my knee, edging closer to my thigh with each passing minute. I squeezed them tight, the tension mounting with unbearable slowness. I inhaled shallow, sharp breaths, waiting for the inevitable plunge of his fingers, wanting so much more.

He was such a tease. That has never changed.

His hand drifted up and up. Under my skirt, touching the soft fabric of my panties. My mouth fell open as his finger brushed the pulsing spot. So light. Not enough force or pressure. I squirmed and ached and resisted the urge to cry out for more.

Silence. Darkness. The fear of being caught. That was the

tantalizing atmosphere we were playing with. I swallowed hard, keeping my head towards the screen, but the images flashed blankly at me. I was lost in these deep, deep feelings.

My heart quickened in fear at the thought of someone walking in. Ushers randomly checked the theater, and I didn't want to be banned or arrested. But I lost the strength to say *no* the moment his palm caressed my knee and slid upwards.

I sunk low in my seat and covered my eyes with my hand. My head naturally started tipping backwards as his fingers stroked my wet, sensitive mound.

"Lo," I cried in a soft breath, a little choked.

His parted lips brushed my ear so slowly I nearly came right there. And then he whispered, "Stay still. Don't moan."

I needed him to fill me. And as if on cue, his fingers dove inside, his thumb making circles on my clit. A breath caught in my throat. *Don't moan. Ohhh . . .*

The comedy in the background wasn't loud enough to drown out future noises that I knew would come. No way could I inhale these sounds. One already escaped, sharp and unrestrained.

He no longer focused on the film. His lips skimmed the nape of my neck, but the darkened theater masked his movements. I just *felt* him. The fullness of his lips, the way his arm brushed against my breast, pulsing his fingers in a toxic rhythm.

I felt the climax coming like riding up the hill on a roller coaster. *Take me*, I wanted to scream. I held it in. I swallowed my moans and gripped the armrest to my left. My mouth opened as he hit the right spot. I bucked a little, my toes curling and a layer of sweat gathering.

Oh no.

Instinctively, I clenched my legs tight together, putting his hand in an uncomfortable vice, anything to subdue the sounds that were about to leak from my lips and get us caught.

He kissed my temple and then whispered, "I need my hand, love."

My eyes were shut tight, and I shook my head repeatedly. *No, no, no.* If I was supposed to come without screaming then he couldn't do *that* right now. I had to . . . compose myself first. An insane part of me thought about removing his hand altogether and straddling his waist, getting something more substantial to feed this *need.*

His free hand gently skimmed my neck, and then his lips met mine, kissing so deeply and so hard that the insane part of me won out. I wanted his cock inside of me, completely, and I didn't give a damn about where I was. Hurriedly, I reached over to undo his zipper, fumbling in the dark for the entry.

His lips detached from mine, and he snatched my wrist to stop me. He leaned into my ear once more, his breath tickling my sensitive skin. "I want my other hand first."

I hesitated for a brief second before I relaxed my thighs and relieved the pressure from his hand. I went back to searching for his zipper, but then Lo pushed his fingers faster and harder inside of me.

My eyes fluttered, my back arched, and the cry I had been avoiding came out like I had reached the pinnacle of all pinnacles. *Tricky bastard.*

I thought that was it, but he kept his fingers in place, and my whole body skyrocketed again. And again. I leaned forward from the sudden waves and clutched his hard bicep and cotton shirt, his arm still pressed strongly against my chest, gliding down below, disappearing between my legs. Just thinking about the way he was inside of me sent me spiraling.

He slid his free hand over my mouth, blocking out the noises that persisted and rocked through me. One after the other. My body shuddered and wouldn't let up. Not when he would shift a little, touching a place that put me into a new tailspin.

Any fear of an onlooker was drowned by the ecstasy that filled my head. Clinging to him in desperation. In vital, palpable *need*.

I no longer craved something more. He was enough.

"Lily!" *Yes.*

"LILY!" The door bangs with an angry sound. *No.*

My eyes snap open back to the present moment. The house party. I'm in the bathroom, my forehead sweaty. My eyes had been halfway rolled in the back of my head, *almost* about to climax with the memory.

I have yet to hit my sweet spot. The tension burns, but Ryke's voice scares me enough to jump off the toilet like it zapped me. I hurry and dress. "Coming!" I tell him and cringe almost immediately. *Really?* I couldn't choose *any* other word?

"I hope not," Ryke says, his voice so close that I picture him leaning a shoulder against the doorframe.

My cheeks welt in an ugly red. I wash my hands with plenty of soap and peek at the mirror. Besides my flushed face, I look presentable. So far, I've been trying to eliminate porn from my life, not fantasies. I shouldn't be ashamed, but my stomach knots anyway.

That memory I focused on, I love. Because I later found out that Lo had paid the manager for a private screening of the movie, buying each and every ticket that would have filled the theater. He planned to arouse me. He planned to satiate my needs in a new way. Maybe Rose would call that enabling, but right now, it's one of the sweeter memories in my spank bank.

As soon as I open the door, a girl with jet-black hair mumbles, "bitch," and barrels ahead, shoving me into the nearby wall. Okay, that was *not* necessary. She slams the door, and then I glance up to see the aggravated, curving line of guys and girls— hands on their hips, eyes in tight glares.

My rash-like flush burgeons across my arms. Hopefully they believe I was puking up the punch, not fingering myself.

And when I turn slightly, I find Ryke, leaning on the wall just as I pictured. His arms are crossed and he scrutinizes me with hard, piercing eyes. His brown hair is styled nicely, giving these models a run for their money. He's also slightly unshaven, which makes him appear older and tougher. He gives me a long once-over, as if trying to spot the stain of debauchery.

I ignore him and head towards the living room, knowing he'll follow. I'm not surprised when I feel his presence like an annoying, *unwanted* shadow. When I reach the kitchen, he puts his hand on my shoulder, spinning me around to meet his accusatory eyes, as though I've already fucked up.

Maybe I have. I don't know anything anymore. I wish someone could give me a guide on what exactly I'm supposed to do, but no one seems to know. My addiction isn't fucking normal. That's the problem.

"You look like shit," he starts off.

"Thank you," I say dryly. "If that's what you scurried all across the city for, then mission accomplished. You can leave me alone now."

"Why do you do that?" he snaps.

"Do what?" I do a lot of things. As does he.

"Act like I'm a fucking rat, *scurrying*."

I shrug my shoulders. "I don't know. Maybe because you *lied* to me for months." He could have told me that he was Lo's brother. *I* feel just as duped as my boyfriend, but the difference is I don't let things go as easily. Not when Ryke is a rash I can't medicate.

He rolls his eyes and says, "Get over it."

I hate him. "Okay." I flash an irritated half-smile. "I'm over it." I try to pass him to go find my sister.

He sighs exasperatedly and grabs my arm to stop me. "Wait. I'm sorry, okay? I didn't know your relationship with Lo. I couldn't trust you with that information. Would you have told him?"

I pause, hesitating. I'm not sure. Maybe. I look up at him with furrowed brows, understanding his reservations. "I still don't like you," I always remind him.

"You're not growing on me either." His eyes flit around the room. "I couldn't find Daisy. I looked for like ten fucking minutes." He runs a hand through his hair, antsy.

I inhale a sharp breath. "Do you even remember what she looks like?"

"I've seen enough pictures," he tells me. "Tall. Really fucking tall. Your green eyes. The Calloway brown hair. Too skinny and no boobs. About right?"

I glare even though it's almost all accurate. Per her modeling agency's request, she dyed her hair a light brown-blonde last week. "She's fifteen," I say roughly.

He shrugs. "Maybe she'll get boobs then."

I stare at him blankly, trying to find words that represent my emotions right now. I blink.

Nope, there are none.

So I land on my usual phrase. "You're such an asshole."

He never denies it. "Let's just find your sister and go. We can watch the ball drop at your house." He doesn't rub it in my face that I ruined his plans for tonight. Who knows what type of woman he planned to meet up with and screw afterwards. I have avoided seeing Ryke in his natural habitat. It's a part of him that I plan to keep very, very far away. Because that would mean we're friends. And we are *not* friends. We're just two people who happen to coexist on occasion and see each other around. That's it.

I scan the area, pushing through the kitchen and towards the crowded dance floor. I don't see her anywhere. Not even by the punch bowl that's littered with picturesque male models. I trace their biceps with my gaze, their muscles spindling underneath their tight shirts. Jesus. This party is not for me. I feel my forehead heat with a layer of sweat in anxiety. *Get me out of here.*

"I don't see her," I mutter.

"How could you when you've been eye-fucking half the guys in here?"

I gape. I've had enough of his evil comments. I turn on him with clenched fists and fiery eyes. "What did I do to you?"

His jaw hardens to stone, and the muscles twitch in his face, holding back, restraining. *Let it on out, buddy.* My mental command must work because he says, "Do you look at other guys when Lo is in the room?"

That's what this is about? My stomach drops and aches. A punch to the gut would probably be more pleasant. Of course Lo would care that I'm staring. *I* would care. And I haven't truly fantasized about any other guy but him since he's been away. But that doesn't matter. Not when I know I'm one small step away from picturing a nameless, faceless body with all the right moves and all the right words.

But I don't know how to stop once I've started. And I'm trying to put the brakes on. I'm desperate and needy right now, and everything I really, really don't want to be.

I need a therapist, I think. I need to find someone who knows how to help me. *I'll try harder.*

"It's not cheating to look," I say in a small voice. "And he's not here, Ryke. Give me some slack."

He lets out a long breath and rubs the back of his neck. "I hate that he's dating an addict. You have no idea . . ." He pinches his eyes. "It makes this twice as hard, you know that?"

"Yeah," I whisper. "I know."

He exhales again, tension finally leaving his muscles. "Look, I know you love each other. I know you'll try to be together even if it fucking kills you. I may seem like a huge dick, and I'm riding you hard . . ."

Uhhh . . . I cringe and flush, a horrid combination.

"Dammit. Not like *that*, Lily." He shakes his head, his face contorting in slight disgust, and he points at me. "You think more perverted things than any fucking guy I know."

Guilty.

"And I don't know how to do this the nice way. I'm not like that, never have been. So sometimes that means being a pain in the ass." He jabs his finger harder. "*Don't* take that sexually." *Too late.* He drops his hand and says, "I'll choose him over you, every time, but you're a huge part of his life, so that means you're going to be a part of mine—whether you like it or not."

"Okay," I mutter. What else is there to say?

The party starts to liven as a famous pop star takes the stage on television. Everyone begins to sloppily mimic the dance moves, stumbling and knocking into each other. I don't spot Daisy in the dance mob.

"Should we split up to look for her? Cover more ground?" I ask, biting my fingernails.

"No." He grabs my hand, forcing my nails from my mouth. His eyes land on a group of guys snorting lines of coke, passing a glass dish between them by the window. "Should a fifteen-year-old be at this kind of party?"

Probably not. "They're models."

His brows furrow like *do I fucking care?* "So?"

I guess that's not an excuse, but it's so hard to talk to him. I feel like I'm constantly fighting with a Rock 'Em Sock 'Em robot. And I suck at board games.

I walk towards the punch bowl where I last saw Daisy and feel him trailing me again. He slips into the paths that I weave.

Six people surround a bong and pass it to one another, smoke pluming around their glazed eyes. Daisy's thankfully not in the circle, and I peek around a few arms before seeing someone hugging an armrest to a couch. Next to her sits Jack, the black-haired "talker" who edges closer while she sips her drink and flashes a weak smile. I must have missed her with all the people dancing in the center.

When she sees me, she says something to him and stands quickly. She wobbles a little and then sets a hand on my wrist. "Oh, good. I thought I was going to have to talk to him all night."

Ryke inspects her with his usual fierce look, eyes flitting from her face to her Solo cup. "Aren't you underage?" Technically, I am too, but I don't mention that, especially since I haven't been drinking, so the point is moot.

Daisy's eyes narrow at him. "Are you my father?" she asks with the quirk of her head, her casual tone subtly biting. "I don't think you are."

"Why ask me a question that you're going to fucking answer?" he snaps at her, not backing down even though she's my sister and a teenager. Why does he have to be so confrontational? Lo would have ignored her. I think.

"It was rhetorical. Do you know what that means?" she asks. "It's a question that's said in order to make a point. A figure of speech."

My eyes bug. Wow, she's hostile. Must have something to do with our conversation about being treated older and then younger. Why else would she go off on him?

"I didn't know," he says with the tilt of *his* head. "Do you know what that is? Sarcasm." He edges in her face a little. Taller than her by about four or five inches.

She raises her chin, holding her own. "You're hilarious," she deadpans.

His eyebrow arches. "I guess you do know what sarcasm is then." He pries the cup out of her hand, his muscles relaxing in his broad shoulders. "What is this shit anyway?" He sniffs it and cringes. "That's fucking foul."

"Hunch punch," she tells him. "It's kind of strong. I've only had a glass and a half." Her eyes droop a little though, but she seems coherent. Not yet drunk. Maybe buzzed. I decided not to drink because alcohol loosens inhibitions, and mine need to be padlocked.

Suddenly, two guys start yelling in the middle of the dance floor. Their girlfriends try to pull them back, grabbing on to their thick muscles, but they can't restrain them as they begin to barrel forward.

"Really?" Daisy shakes her head at the scene. And before I digest the abrupt fight, her boots clap against the hardwood and she slides between bodies to reach the two furious guys.

She's crazy. My sister is flat-out nuts. Dear God.

Tattooed Guy pushes Tan Guy.

"What the fuck is your sister doing?" Ryke asks, and when we see Daisy physically inject herself between the two guys, Ryke curses under his breath and dashes in her path between the bodies. I follow close behind, grabbing on to his shirt so I don't lose him.

Daisy throws her hands out between both guys.

"Get out of my fucking way!" Tattooed Guy shouts at her.

"Bryan. Come on, what are you going to do? Punch him?" She's not even a little scared of being hit in the crossfire. And then I wonder: *what if she wants to be?* This is so messed up.

"Stay out of it, Daisy!" he shouts. "That fucker, he slept with Heidi." A redhead tries to touch his shoulder, but he swats her away. A circle opens around them while people on the outskirts stare—like the two guys are Danny Zuko and Sandy Olsson, about to perform an epic dance.

Only this one will include fists and kicks and probably blood.

"She's a fucking liar!" Tan Guy yells, veins pulsing in his large neck.

I stay a safe distance away, too afraid of Tan Guy, who looks ready to beat the living shit out of Bryan for even suggesting he fucked some other girl.

Daisy keeps her hands up between them, separating their bodies, but her eyelids continue to sag. She wobbles a little, but she stands upright. Is she drunk? But she barely drank anything, and this seems to be hitting her really hard all of a sudden.

Ryke edges forward into the "fighting area" and places a hand on Daisy's shoulder. "Go."

"They're not punching each other here," she tells him. "This is stupid."

His lips find her ear, and I hear him say, "This isn't your fucking fight, Daisy. Let it go."

She weakly pushes him off, swaying too much, and then points at Bryan. "You think you're a man?" She snorts. "You hit him and then what? The other guy hits you back and you'll feel better?"

"Shut the fuck up," Bryan tells her.

Ryke shoots him the worst possible glare, one that could seriously shift mountains. Then his eyes drop back to Daisy. "Move."

She stares at Bryan in challenge. "You want to hit him? Get through me."

"Daisy!" I shout. Yep, she wants to be hit. To feel something, maybe. I don't know, but she's scaring me.

And that's when Tan Guy charges from behind. Ryke shoves her out of the way, and she falls on her knees while he takes a punch to the jaw. I shimmy around the crowd, people cheering and grimacing as Bryan knees Tan Guy and Ryke tries to fight his way out of their feud.

Daisy has already picked herself up off the floor, wiping her hands on her green army jacket. "Lily?" she stumbles into my chest. We push our way out towards the kitchen area, able to breathe in the open air.

"Are you crazy?" I yell at her. "You don't provoke guys to hit you."

She loops a weak arm around my shoulder. "You think Mom would have been mad if I ruined my pretty face?" She laughs lightly and it quickly dies off. She blinks repeatedly, as though she sees stars or black spots. "Lily?"

"What's wrong?" I ask her in a high-pitched voice. I shake her shoulder.

"I don't know . . . something's . . . not right . . ."

"Are you drunk?" What a stupid question to ask.

Ryke breaks through the crowd, a red welt blooming on his cheekbone. "That was the dumbest fucking thing I've seen in a long time."

She turns around very, very slowly. "Who's stupid? Them or me?" She keeps blinking, and he stares at her for a long moment, seeing the oddness in her movements.

"You okay?"

"Perfect," she says. "Are you okay?" Her eyes slowly move to his welt.

"Perfect," he murmurs, still inspecting her state. "You know, you have pretty huge balls."

"The biggest." Her lips pull into a dry smile, but it falls with her eyelids.

"Daisy?" His worried voice drives knives into my stomach.

Her knees give out. And he grabs underneath her arms before she hits the floor.

"What the fuck?" I say, my heart hammering.

He lifts her up, and her head lolls back, her arms hanging lifelessly by her side.

"Daisy." Ryke's hard eyes narrow, and he taps her face lightly. "Daisy, look at me." Nothing. He pinches her cheeks together and shakes her head a little. She's out of it.

I put two fingers to her neck and feel a weak pulse. "I don't understand. She had a beer and one glass of punch." Well, one and *a half* but I doubt that half mattered in the grand scheme of things. Right?

Ryke rests his ear to her chest, feeling for the rise and fall of her ribs. "She's breathing, but it's slow."

Okay. I bite my nails, trying to figure what could have happened. This isn't drunk. I know what *drunk* looks like, and this . . . this is not it.

Ryke adjusts Daisy in his arms so he has a better hold on her, and then he pulls one of her eyelids up. "Her pupils are dilated." His jaw hardens to stone. "Who poured her punch?"

My mouth slowly falls. "You think someone drugged her?"

"I *know* someone fucking drugged her."

Jack. I scan the room and land on the black-haired guy in the kitchen. He leans against the refrigerator, pushing the magnets around with his buddy to spell *lick my prick*.

Ryke follows my gaze, clenching his teeth. "That him?"

"Yeah."

"Support her for me," Ryke says, setting my sister's limp feet on the ground. He rests her chest against my body, and I wrap my arms around her waist, keeping her somewhat upright so she won't thud to the floor.

"What are you going to go do?" I ask. *Beat the shit out of him? Have a civil conversation? Throttle him for answers?* There are so many choices.

"Stay here."

That wasn't much of a reply.

Before I can ask again, Ryke enters the kitchen with a dark scowl. The first thing he does: shove a muscular arm at Jack, pinning him against the refrigerator with his bicep cutting at his windpipe. The colorful magnets slide off the fridge and clatter to the floor.

"What the fuck?!" Jack curses with an English lilt. He tries to escape Ryke's strong hold, but Ryke presses his weight against him, looking about ready to rip out Jack's throat.

"What'd you put in her drink?"

"I don't know what you're talking about," he says, glancing at his buddy nearby. The kid tries to cut in and put a hand on Ryke's shoulder, but Ryke flashes him a deadly glare.

"You fucking touch me, and I'll break his neck."

My eyes widen, partly believing the threat. His friend throws up his hands, backing away.

Ryke turns on Jack again. "My friend's sister, Daisy, has been drugged. You poured her drink. So I want you to tell me what the fuck you put in it."

Realization starts to process in his features. "Oh shit, mate. She's smashed?" He tries to look over Ryke's shoulder to see Daisy, but Ryke smacks the side of his face. "Jesus! Okay, okay, you don't have to hit me. I'll tell you what you want to know." He grimaces a little, guilty. "We put GHB in the punch, but it's only enough to get high . . . that's it. I honestly didn't think anyone would pass out from it."

"Yeah?" Ryke sneers. "Everyone's body reacts differently to

drugs. She weighs, what, one twenty? Don't you think it would hit her harder than you? Use your fucking brain."

"Okay." He swallows. "Okay, you're right, mate. I will next time. Brain power on."

Ryke eases off him. "And warn the girls at your party what's in the punch, especially if you're going to put a date rape drug in it."

"Got it." He nods stiffly.

Ryke rolls his eyes, still pissed. He walks back to me and effortlessly lifts Daisy's limp body in his arms. He gathers her hands and sets them on her chest so she doesn't look like a dead person. I'm stuck in a state of shock. The series of events tonight have electrocuted my mind. I feel dumb. Just dumb. Not even silly dumb.

Ryke stops outside the kitchen and yells at the crowd, "For anyone who doesn't fucking know, there are drugs in the punch! Have a happy *fucking* New Year!"

I slam the door on our way out, adding to the dramatic exit. Hopefully Ryke's statement helped someone tonight. Maybe it won't, but there's not much more we can do without ruining everyone's time and being complete buzzkills.

We head down the elevator and out of the apartment complex. "How far away is your car?" I ask as we walk along the sidewalk. The roads are crammed with vehicles and cabs. Brave souls dressed in night clothes walk in between the stopped traffic, going places but never getting there fast enough.

"Not too far. I paid to park in a deck," he explains, picking up his brisk stride. I try to keep up.

"How is she?"

His eyes flicker down to her and back up. "Can you do me a favor?"

"Yeah?"

"Google GHB symptoms for me."

Fear pricks me, and I scroll on my cell, typing quickly. "Uhh . . . unconsciousness." Duh. ". . . Slow breathing, weak heart rate . . ." My eyes begin to bug at the series of words: *lowered body temperature, vomiting, nausea, seizures, coma, death.* Death. "We need to get to a hospital now!" I begin to frantically type in 9-1-1. I end up dialing 8-2-2. Dammit!

"Hey, slow down for a second. Put the phone away, and tell me the other symptoms, Lily."

"Um, seizure, coma, death . . ." I think I might vomit.

"Well, she's not having a seizure. She's not in a coma, and she sure as hell isn't dead. So stop freaking out." He adjusts Daisy in his arms. "She's really fucking cold."

I snap my fingers and spring on the balls of my feet. "That was one. Lowered body temperature is a symptom."

His eyes darken. "Anything else you're keeping from me?"

Think. "Uhh . . . vomiting and nausea. That's it."

He nods. "I'll drive her to the hospital. She'll be fine. Just, don't have a panic attack in the street. Think you can do that?"

I glare. "Yes."

Thankfully we reach the dimly lit parking deck and approach his Infiniti that's squeezed in between a Mini Cooper and a BMW. "My keys are in my pocket," he tells me.

I glance at his pants pocket. Near his crotch.

He rolls his eyes. "Now's not the time to be perverted, Calloway."

"Right," I say, reaching in, my cheeks flaming. He doesn't look happy about me digging near his penis either. I pull out his set of keys and press the unlock button. The car honks and blinks to life, the taillights flashing.

"Get in the passenger seat, and I'll put Daisy on your lap," he tells me. I do as he says, and he sets my gangly sister on the seat with me. I drape her long legs to the side and put my hand to her head, clammy and cold. I rest her cheek to my chest. In this moment, I feel solely responsible for her.

"To the hospital," I remind him.

"I know." He turns the key into the ignition and pulls onto the street. Only five minutes in, and we're stuck in bumper-to-bumper traffic. So many people wander on the roads that they thud into Ryke's car and throw confetti at the windshield.

I keep my fingers pressed to Daisy's wrist, checking her pulse every few seconds.

As we sit in silence, I watch girls on the side streets, swaying as they walk in heels, their guys keeping an arm underneath them so they don't face-plant on the cement. The couples remind me of Lo—only I would have been the one holding him upright. Not the other way around.

Last year, I wore this sparkly silver dress and decided to be pantyless the entire night. I thought it'd be easier for a quickie in the bathroom with Mr. Random. In retrospect, it was a bad, bad idea. I danced all night at a fancy club and was too inebriated to realize that I flashed the crowds with every hop.

Lo ended up dancing beside me, keeping a hand on my shoulder to ease my kangaroo springs. He even tugged down the back of my dress for me. Near midnight, he offered to give me *his* underwear, which I promptly declined. I love the whole memory—even if it's a royally fucked-up one. The only thing I try to forget is the end of that night. Where he booked a room at the Ritz to pass out in, and I slinked into a bedroom one floor below to screw some guy.

"Do you think he'll still want to be with me when he gets back?" I ask softly. Even if I wait for him, I wonder if he'll still wait for me.

Ryke clenches the steering wheel tightly. "I don't know."

"What do you know?" I wonder, pulling Daisy's sweaty hair out of her face.

Ryke gives me a solid glare. "You masturbate too much."

My eyes widen, and I instinctively glance down at Daisy who is in another dimension. She may not have even heard. Hopefully.

"She probably won't remember anything," Ryke tells me.

That doesn't stop the mortification from swallowing my face. Of course he couldn't restrain himself from commenting about what I was doing in the bathroom.

Before I find the courage to reply back, Daisy groans and her lids flutter. I see the whites of her eyes until they roll back to show the green.

"Dais." I shake her arm.

She turns her head a little, sluggish and weak. Her eyes rise to meet Ryke's. He keeps one hand firmly on the steering wheel, his fingers clenched around it as he stares down at her. After a long moment of the two of them just fucking *staring* at each other, Ryke asks, "You going to puke?"

She blinks heavily and says, "No."

Ryke clicks off his seat belt and puts the car in park. He opens his car door.

"What are you doing?" I gape at him.

"She was being sarcastic," he tells me.

I frown. That did *not* sound like sarcasm.

He walks around the Infiniti to our side, able to leave the driver's seat. He yanks my door open, and she slowly spins her body to face the outside, her feet on the edge of the car. She leans a hand on the doorframe and breathes heavily, her color peaked.

I rub her back while her head begins to droop. She nearly falls forward into the street. I grab her shoulders to keep her on my lap, and Ryke kneels in front of her. He lifts her chin up with two fingers.

"Daisy, look at me." He snaps his fingers near her eyes.

I can't tell if she's meeting his gaze or not.

"Some . . . fucking party, huh?" Her whole body shakes.

"Yeah." Ryke nods, his eyes flitting over her arms and legs, noticing her trembles. "Some fucking party."

"That . . . was . . . rhetorical." Her body lurches, gagging. Ryke quickly moves out of the way and she vomits onto the pavement. He grimaces, and people start chanting outside.

"Ten . . . nine . . ."

We're too far away to see the glittering ball drop, but the crowds scream in unison, filling the world in a jubilant chorus.

This has to be one of the worst and scariest New Year's ever. Right behind the time I kissed a frog as a dare. Though that wasn't so much scary as it was gross.

"Seven . . ."

And this will be the first time I don't have a New Year's kiss.

"Five . . ."

Even when I was a kid, Lo would put his hands on my cheeks and kiss me really quickly, and we'd burst into laughter afterwards. He'd end up chasing me through the fancy parties that our parents brought us to, trying to steal another.

I'd always let him catch me.

"Two . . . one."

"HAPPY NEW YEAR!!"

January

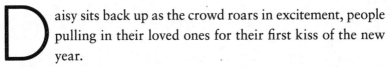

Daisy sits back up as the crowd roars in excitement, people pulling in their loved ones for their first kiss of the new year.

Ryke scrutinizes her for a long second. "You okay?"

"Amazing." She wipes the side of her mouth with her hand. "Can . . . you just take me home?"

He shakes his head. "You're going to the hospital."

She closes her eyes for a long time, and when she opens them, I can see her glare. "No."

"Yes," he states. "This isn't a fucking democracy. My car, my rules."

"My body, my decisions," she snaps back. ". . . Honestly, I'm just nauseous now." And as she says it, she shakes like she has the chills.

He puts his hand to her forehead, and she slaps it down. "Don't touch me."

He glowers. "You're an ice cube. You've been drugged, Daisy. If you go to sleep and fall into a coma, that's on us."

"He's right," I tell her. Wow those words taste gross in my mouth. "You're going to the hospital. Rose would have flown in a helicopter by now, so you're lucky we're just driving you and not making a bigger scene."

Daisy inhales a slow breath. She pulls her limbs back into the car and settles against my chest. Ryke slams the door closed and walks around to the driver's side.

"I'm sorry," Daisy whispers to me. "Tonight . . . was supposed to be fun . . ." She trembles. "I . . . was supposed to take your mind off Lo . . ."

I smile and nudge her hip. "You did. And you know what? Despite what happened at the end, I had a really good time." That's not a lie. I think I learned more about my sister today than I have in the past seven years.

"Really?" She closes her eyes, sinking back into a better place. I still check her pulse. Just to be safe.

"Really, really."

Ryke climbs in and shuts the door. He stares out the front windshield for a long time. "I just have to ask you one question, Lily." He glances at me. "Are all you Calloway girls this crazy?"

I choke on a laugh, about to deny it but I really can't. "Poppy's pretty normal."

He nods repeatedly, letting this sink in.

The traffic begins to break up, and we're finally able to drive. I take a deep breath, happy to be heading in a good direction.

Three

The hospital was a fiasco. Even a week later, I cringe at how Daisy lied to the nurse. She asked for her name, and Daisy blurted out, "Lily Calloway."

I didn't correct her because I understood her motives. She didn't want the hospital to call our mother and have her involved in the situation. So I handed the white-scrubbed nurse my ID, which could pass for Daisy because my sixteen-year-old picture is nearly obscured. I was even surprised the DMV didn't force me to retake it. In the photo, my hair nearly shields my whole face, and I tilted my head down, trying to end the photo-taking process as quickly as possible. Afterwards, Lo made fun of me for the picture, but his wasn't much better. He smiled sarcastically, looking like a supreme sixteen-year-old asshole.

Thinking about Lo does not help my mind tonight. I roll in my bed, clenching the sheets and pressing my face to my pillow. Some nights are worse than others. This one has been brutal.

My body heats with a layer of sticky sweat. I just want him. My eyes tighten closed, and I imagine his hands raking the bareness of my back, spindling up my hips towards my shoulders . . .

I need someone to take me in their arms, to rub their palms over all the aching parts, to knead my breasts and suck my neck, to make this tension explode into a high. I crave it so badly that I end up biting my fingernails to the beds, turning on my side and staring at the wall, wondering if I should go find something to ease this into a nice, blissful release.

No.

I lick my lips and shudder, my body shaking as I prolong what it wants. Or maybe, it's just my brain playing tricks on me. Maybe it's all in my mind.

I inhale a deep breath and rise against my oak headboard. I find the remote on the end table and click on the flat-screen television above my dresser. It swamps the wall, looking futuristic among my white, canopied, king-sized bed and red velveteen chaise. Rose decorated my room, and I have to admit, she did a pretty good job with the pop art and the black checkered pillows. I could do without the canopy. One night, I rolled into it like a tortilla and started moronically swatting at it.

I click through the On Demand channels and peruse the nightly specials, landing on an X-rated film where a professor seduces a student. So cliché, but it'll most definitely make me hot and bothered. I just hope that it helps me find the release I'm looking for.

I fast-forward the beginning where the girl usually just gives head. Normally, blow jobs in porn don't turn me on . . . unless the guy does something sweet like hold her hair back and tell her she's beautiful giving it. But I've seen too many scenes where the guy jackhammers the thing down her throat. Being choked by cock does nothing for me.

I reach the middle of the film, and the professor spreads the girl across his desk. He wears vintage framed glasses and a white button-down. His pants are already off and he quickly charges into her without any other foreplay. She lets out a frighteningly loud scream and then her moans start. "Mmmmmmmyeah. Like that . . . yeaaahhh." She massages her own large breast while he thrusts hard. I can tell she's faking it, and maybe horny guys don't care—but I do. Her noises heighten and I realize that her orgasms are making me cringe. Not all porn is created equal.

I exit out and order another film.

Wanting to be surprised, I skim the description and barely glance at the title. This time I fast-forward again and quickly discern what type of category the film falls into.

The girl is draped over a bench in a locker room while the guy spanks her bare ass. It's either submission or bondage or maybe a bit of both. I sink into my bed, silently hoping this girl doesn't scream like a hyena.

She lets out a small yelp when the guy pushes inside of her. His thrusts are hard and rough and she clutches to the lockers for support. He grabs at her body and lets out a series of carnal grunts. After only a couple minutes she says, "Please make me come, sir. Please."

Usually this does it for me. But I feel nothing. Not even turned *off*. I'm just . . . empty.

I mute the video and debate purchasing another, but I'm not even sure a film with my favorite porn stars will help. This seems silly when all I want is Loren Hale. Visual stimulation doesn't cure the craving for my boyfriend.

Tonight's miserable experience suddenly triggers a recent memory with Lo—when he was sober for a very short period of time. I pause the film and wipe my eyes.

Lo plopped onto my bed in our Philly apartment while I fired up my porn. I'd asked him if he wanted to watch a video with me, thinking it might be different now that he was sober. He had looked at me with crinkled eyebrows and a crooked grin before shrugging and following me into my room.

On the screen, a girl-next-door blonde rested in the jail cell, and a young, sexy cop entered, scanning her body with a lustful gaze.

"Why is she even there?" Lo asked, wrapping an arm around my shoulder. I rested my head on his hard chest, my heart beating wildly at the thought of what might happen next between us. I wanted him to take me just as the cop would take the girl.

"I think she was mistakenly jailed for soliciting or something, and this cop is going to question her about it. But really she's going to have sex so he'll let her go."

Lo's brow arched. "I see."

I swallowed hard, wondering if he was analyzing what I wanted. He sometimes watched porn with me. Whenever I put one on, I usually made it a private event, but with Lo there, the anticipation was enough to prick my nerves and tighten my insides.

The blonde girl fidgeted a little as the cop started to frisk her. His fingers moved down to the hem of her shorts. "Shouldn't he have done that before he put her in jail?" Lo asked with a smile.

"It's porn. It doesn't have to make sense."

Her back arched as the cop's fingers dipped into her panties and out of sight. "Are you hiding anything that I need to know about?"

She shook her head. "No . . . sir . . ." Her breath caught, and then she let out a long, pleased moan, practically convulsing from his touch. And my breathing went shallow.

That was until I looked back at Lo. He wore a deep frown, as though trying to understand me through the porn. I sat up and disentangled from him. "This is a bad idea," I said, about to shut it off. I scrounged around for the remote, but he grabbed my wrist lightly.

"No, wait, I'm watching this here." He stayed transfixed to the porn.

The cop unzipped the girl's shorts and tugged them to her

ankles and then completely off. "You've been a very bad girl. Leaving here will be very, very simple if you cooperate. Just take this right here . . ." He motioned to his dick, and she grabbed it, her eyes big and innocent. "Put it in your mouth and fuck it. Can you do that for me?"

The girl nodded rapidly. She leaned forward while he dropped his navy pants—no underwear on. She gathered his cock in her hands and filled her mouth.

"Fuck, yeah." He groaned deeply and pulled her hair off her face. "Take your punishment, baby." I actually thought this blow job scene wasn't a complete turn off. Of course, it probably helped that Lo was sitting next to me. She licked him up like a popsicle and then popped her mouth off it with a refreshing "ah-hhh."

Lo let out a long laugh, breaking the mood instantly. My whole body heated with embarrassment, *not* the type of "hot" I wanted.

"What's so funny?" I asked.

"Shhh," he said, a big goofy smile on his face. I tried to speak again, but he put his hand to my lips, covering my mouth while he watched the film, mesmerized and amused.

"You like that?" the cop asked. The girl responded with a deep, throaty moan, and she rocked her head back and forth again. Then she took his cock out of her mouth and smacked it against her cheek. "Fuuuuuck," he groaned. "Fuck, yeah."

The cop yanked the girl to her feet and pulled down her top, kneading her breasts. "These are very nice."

Lo laughed louder and looked to me, his hand still firmly planted on my mouth. "This really turns you on?"

Finally, he loosened his grip to let me reply.

"I usually skip the beginning," I confessed. "Unless . . ." Nope, not telling him.

His eyes lit up. "Unless what?"

I blushed as I said, "Unless the guy holds her hair back."

Lo's smile engulfed his face. "That's adorable." He took the remote though and sped ahead to the actual sex where the couple talks less and usually just moans and grunts.

"Watching this is better than having sex with another person?" Lo asked, narrowing his eyes at the screen.

"No . . . Maybe . . . Sometimes," I stammered. "It's convenient."

He looked back to me, eyebrows raised. "Better than me?"

I shook my head. "No way."

"So you've had sex that was *worse* than watching porn? Who the hell were you fucking?" he asked.

I shrugged, not really having a way to answer that question. My eyes slowly left his for the movie where the cop had the girl spread-eagle on the floor. It was hard to look away, especially since I anticipated some steamy action ahead.

"Hey," Lo breathed, brushing his fingers against my chin. He gently tilted my head towards him, and his parted lips looked ready to kiss me. I waited for him to close the gap between us, but instead of taking me in his arms and mimicking the film, he spoke. "In a competition between me and *this* . . ." He jabbed his finger towards the movie. "I'll win. Every time."

He licked his lips, his eyes skimming my breasts and my abdomen and the place that thrummed for pressure between my legs. He was about to prove that he was better than porn—even though I already told him so. He reached over and turned up the volume a little, right when the cop rolled off her to switch positions. I tried not to look at the screen, but the cop *was* big. Then the girl skillfully climbed right on top of him, arching her back so her enormous breasts became the focus of his attention.

Lo straightened up and grabbed my legs, yanking me so hard

that my breath rushed out of my lungs. My back thudded flat on the mattress, successfully distracting me. He hovered over my body and leaned close. His mouth found my ear, and his tongue slipped inside, my limbs quivering.

As he pulled away, he whispered huskily, "Can a film do this?" He grabbed my wrists, bringing them above my head as he did so often. He trapped them with one hand, and using the other, he lifted up my shirt and my bra. His lips sucked lines from my breast to the hem of my pants, teasing and drawing out intolerable sensations. I wanted him to push inside. To come with every thrust. And I knew he would give it to me. When it came to sex, he offered me everything.

A film could not touch me the way Lo could.

I'd almost give anything to hear him finish with, "I love you." As he always did.

Instead, I now stare at my paused television, wishing Lo was here to fill my needs instead of meaningless porn. I can't even try to reach my climax from it. All I do is think of Lo, and how he basically said—in his own sly way—that I should quit watching porn and find my fix with him.

The film seems corny and cheesy and so fucking stupid in comparison. So I shut it off.

I stand up and gather all of my videos, and I stuff them in the little trash bin under my desk. They don't all fit, so I pick up the aluminum bin and open my door, about to find a larger trash can that'll hold all my dirty secrets.

This seems right.

But ditching porn won't lessen any tension spun inside me.

Not yet at least.

As I head down the stairs to the kitchen, I hear distant voices. It's near midnight, but I'm not surprised by the conversation. Connor Cobalt and Rose schedule time together like one would a business meeting. She let me know that he may be over late in January since nights are the only time they can see each other this month.

"Why are you reading that?" Rose asks him. I inch forward and creep towards the living room. I edge closer and peek behind the curved archway. Their backs face me as they share the cream couch, draped with a purple throw blanket. From here, I smell the fresh cut flowers that fill the vase on the glass coffee table. Connor brings a new bouquet every time they wilt. This time, he picked out yellow and pink daises that remind me of my youngest sister.

Rose's arm presses against Connor as they sit close, each with their own laptop. Both are wearing insensible clothes to be hanging around the house. Connor sports a charcoal gray suit—worth thousands no doubt—while she wears a Calloway Couture piece: a black minidress with a see-through maxi skirt on top. Classy, as always.

Connor doesn't look up from his screen. "Because it's useful."

"Freud is not useful. He's infuriating and sexist and *wrong* half the time." She tries to shut his laptop, and he clasps her hand, bringing her knuckles up to his lips.

He gives her a light kiss before saying, "Just because you don't like his theories doesn't make him wrong. There's good stuff in here."

"Like what? 'Penis envy'?" she snaps.

I frown. What the hell is *penis envy*? And more than that, are they really talking about my sexual needs *again*? I caught Rose with a stack of books the other day, all about sex addiction, and they were not only highlighted and bookmarked, but there were *Post-it* notes stuck inside. And these notes, let me tell you, did not have Rose's handwriting. Since Connor Cobalt was *my* tutor first, I can spot his cursive, calligraphy-like penmanship.

I can deal with my sister in my business, but her boyfriend who thinks he's always right . . . well, that was a little hard to swallow.

I'm adjusting to it. Even if it's incredibly weird. For years, Lo was the only one who knew my secrets, and now I have three more people keeping the news quiet. It's a lot to handle.

And definitely too much to process.

"Yeah," Connor says, "penis envy and psychosexual development."

"You're so off base. My sister doesn't have penis envy—that implies that she could possibly have the Electra complex."

I cringe, knowing what *that* is. I have no craving to hook up with my father. No thank you.

"I never said she had it," he says easily, not defensive like most men with Rose, a girl who attacks full force, eyes icy and hard, ready to combat with claws and power. I love her for it. And whenever they bicker, I'm inwardly waving Rose Calloway flags, cheering for my closest sister to come out on top. "But your sister is a sex addict. Whose theories are you going to start with? Aristotle? The Hamburglar? Or how about Erik Erikson? Lily has a thing about names."

Rose gives him a sharp look. "The Hamburglar, really?"

"Freud pioneered psychoanalysis. You discredit him and that's when the McDonald's references start flying."

She slaps his laptop closed, and he rests an arm on the back of the couch, turning towards her a little. I have to edge back behind the wall, concealing more of my body from view.

Connor has rosy pink lips, thick wavy brown hair, and a smile worth the millions in his trust fund. "Yes?" he says, eyeing her lips, which pinch tightly.

Rose wears her brown hair in a slicked-back ponytail. Her yellowish-green, cat-colored eyes pierce him. "The psychosexual theory has a way of picturing women as broken, inefficient toys that need to be fixed."

"I know," Connor says. "A lot of it is misogynistic, but it's interesting, don't you think?"

"No. I find it infuriating."

His lips quirk in a smile. "Just like me?"

She rolls her eyes, but she sort of lingers there as she refuses to lose contact completely. I can tell she wants to kiss him, maybe just as much as he wants to kiss her. But then she turns her head, breaking the moment. Just like Rose to push a guy away. Sometimes I think she fears a lack of power that comes in a relationship, as though she may lose some sort of advantage if she lets Connor in.

He doesn't look defeated. In fact, his eyes pulse with the exact opposite. Determined. Challenged.

A hair falls from its hold in her pony, and Rose tucks it behind her ear. "I think I'm onto something here. This psychologist suggests that sexual addiction can be closely related to obsessive-compulsive disorder. If I look into OCD, then maybe I'll have a better understanding of what Lily is going through."

"*We*," he says.

Rose's brows furrow. "What?"

"You said 'if *I* look into OCD.' I told you I want to help, so I'm going to help. Lily is my friend too." He shifts so their bodies press a little closer, and Rose's laptop sits on each of their legs. They seem to be having a "moment" so I decide to make a quiet exit and head into the kitchen, but as I turn, one of the DVDs on the top of my bin slides off and clatters to the wooden floor.

I freeze, my eyes widening as their necks turn. I'm a deer caught in their headlights. *Please don't say anything. Let me drift away and pretend we didn't meet gazes.*

No such luck.

Rose shuts her laptop so I can't see her screen, and she rises from the couch, smoothing down her dress with her hands. "What are you doing up? I thought you took a sleeping pill." And then her eyes wander to the DVDs in the trash bin.

"I haven't taken one yet," I say, avoiding Connor. His presence has increased the volume of my embarrassment. And yet, both of them act completely innocent, as if this isn't out of the ordinary. Why am I always the one to roast a new shade of red?

"What's that?" Rose wanders over to my frozen state by the archway, straddling the space between the granite kitchen and the living room. Connor stands and puts his hands in the pockets of his slacks, casual. Having your girlfriend's sister carry an overflowing bin of porn is *so* normal.

"I was tossing it," I tell her as she inspects the DVDs with a quick glance.

"What brought this on?" Rose asks, but something hopeful flickers in her eyes. She can see that I'm trying, and my chest floats, feeling a little better by her reaction.

"I just thought it was time to get rid of it all."

"That's the rest?" Connor asks, sidling to Rose. His presence drives knots in my stomach—the way he stands a good four inches taller than Rose, more than that for me. His strong, muscular build reminds me of what I'm missing.

Uncomfortable, I take a step backwards and shun their gazes. "I'm going to trash this and then head back upstairs."

Rose must read me too well because she uses her arm to push Connor back. "You need to go."

"Rose, she's fine. She can't be afraid of men forever. And anyway, she attended a party with male models. How am I any different than one of them?" I catch him flashing his impeccable smile.

"You did not just compare yourself to a high fashion model."

"I did."

Rose stares at the ceiling like, *oh my God.* "You want to know how many times a day I question why I'm with you?"

"Five times."

"A hundred."

"If you told me you were going to exaggerate, I would have picked that, but I thought we were being realistic here, hun."

I snort. "Smooth."

Connor gestures to me. "See, she's fine."

Rose sets her hands on her hips and looks to me for a final verdict. If I said no, she'd toss out Connor. And Connor is kind of right, as much as I hate to admit that. I shouldn't be scared of the opposite sex being so close. Even if I have been a bit jumpy after New Year's.

"He can stay," I tell her.

Her eyes narrow at me like I chose the wrong answer.

I mouth, *what?*

She makes a small motion with her head to Connor. Did *she* not want him over here anymore? But then I see Connor and he's—no lie—grinning from ear to ear, as though he won the Academic Bowl tournament against Princeton, Rose's college (and now mine).

She lost that tiff, I see.

"I'll help you with your porn," Connor says. He goes into the kitchen to find a trash bag while I try to wipe that line clean from memory. I set the bin on the floor and wait for Rose to explode. Her face scrunches like she's ready to give birth.

When Connor disappears into the pantry, Rose lets loose. "I can't stand him," she says. "Honestly, he drives me nuts, Lily."

I try really hard not to laugh. Rose and Connor broke up five times in December. I'm suspecting that number will double in

January. They both call it quits and then they'll reunite in a couple days. It's as cute as it is exhausting.

"I think you drive him crazy too," I tell her. "And I mean this in the Britney Spearsian sense." I hum the nineties tune and sing the chorus. Her face darkens, not amused. I can't help but laugh. That's Rose for you.

Her shoulders relax as she takes in the DVDs again. "Are you sure you want to do this?"

"Yeah," I say quickly, not wanting to think too much about the giant leap. I'd rather race towards the finish line than slow crawl right now. Which is why I nervously tap my foot, waiting for Connor to hurry back with the bag that'll seal my fate. Hopefully I'll trample the urge to buy new films in the future or click into dirty sites on the internet. I think I can do it. I *hope*. That's all I really have at the moment.

"So . . ." I say, nervously twiddling my fingers. ". . . You think I have OCD?" It would make sense, sort of. I do relate my sexual needs to compulsions. The *need* to obtain that natural high. Kind of like an obsessive-compulsive's *need* to follow their systematic routine. I just never related the two.

"Some psychologists believe that addictions correlate with OCD, but I can't diagnose you," Rose says truthfully. "You really need to visit the therapist—"

"I know," I cut her off. "I know, I just . . . I haven't decided which one I want to go to." Who knew there were so many sex addiction therapists in the area? And I already searched for a Sex Addicts Anonymous group and came up completely blank. Since most groups consist of men trying to thwart their sexual cravings, they have a strict no-female policy. It makes sense, but it has also made it nearly impossible to find an SAA that accepts women. I've given up the hunt for now and plan to do one-on-one therapy.

There are also in-treatment facilities for sex addiction. Rehab, like Lo. But Rose squashed those as an option pretty quickly. She really wouldn't give me a definite answer, and after beating around the bush, she blurted out that I have social anxiety. That I shouldn't be in large groups trying to fix my problem.

Yesterday, I rebutted, "I don't have social anxiety." And in the same instance, I was nervously pacing my room.

She tilted her head with raised eyebrows. "When's the last time you were in a group setting?"

"Lots of times," I told her. "I go to clubs, Rose. People are *everywhere*."

"But are you forced to talk to them? Do you talk to *anyone* other than Lo? Really, Lily, think about it. Do you even bring up a conversation with your one-night stands or do you just give them a look and screw them?"

She was right. Maybe I do have social anxiety. And according to Rose, I should concentrate on one thing at a time. I also think she'd rather look after me than send me away. She'd go crazy not knowing what exactly the rehab's program would be or what they would do. So right now, therapy is the best solution.

"I'm working on that for you," Rose tells me. "I have meetings with two tomorrow." Literally, she has been setting up appointments just to quiz the therapists. I love her more than she knows. "The last guy was a complete idiot. I asked him about cognitive behavioral therapy and he gave me a blank stare. I'm not lying."

Connor approaches with the trash bag. "She's not," he adds. "I was there."

My cheeks redden, but they hardly notice. Or maybe they just don't care. Yeah, that has to be it.

Before I can put the DVDs in the bag myself, Connor picks up the bin from the floor and dumps it into the garbage. The fact that he's in close contact to my porn has seriously knotted my stomach and heated my entire chest.

Connor says to Rose, "That last man was a complete asshat."

She hesitates to agree with him, though I can tell she does.

"What'd he do?"

Connor ties the bag and sets it by the wall. He casts a furtive glance in Rose's direction, all secrets, something that I had with Lo. My heart sinks, but I push the thoughts away quickly.

"Well, we showed up to the therapist's office, and Rose introduced herself and told him her sexual problems—"

"Wait . . ." I hold up my hands, my eyes bugging. I look between the two of them, and they stand as though nothing is out of the ordinary. As though this story is fucking normal! I blink at Rose. "You did not pretend to be me, did you?"

She shakes her head. "Of course not, Lily."

I exhale. *Good.* That would be embarrassing.

"I told him that I was a sex addict, but I gave him my personal information. You're fine."

Oh my God. "Why would you want to do that?"

She shrugs. "It was the only way this man would see me. I had to be a patient first."

I cringe, refusing to look at Connor. I'm more shamed for her than I should be. I realize this may be what I feel soon. Maybe even tenfold. "And what happened?"

Rose scrutinizes my reaction and immediately closes a short gap between our bodies. She puts her hand on my shoulder. "You don't need to hear this. Not every therapist is like him, and I promise you, Lily, that I would never send you to one that I didn't think was absolutely perfect."

Right, but a glimmer of fear still strikes me cold. "Still, I want to know."

Connor puts a couple fingers to his lips, inspecting me the same way my sister had, wondering if I can handle the truth.

"Please," I add.

My pout must win them over—or at least Rose because she breaks first. "He asked me what my sexual preferences were, and I told him that I gravitate towards porn and one-night stands but nothing too kinky." The weekend Lo left for rehab, I actually professed to Rose most of my secrets. I explained my habit of ditching family events (and even told her which ones) for a quickie in the bathroom or hookup at a club. Nothing earth-shattering. Get in. Get high. Get out. That's how I liked it with everyone but Loren Hale.

"And what happened?" I almost go to bite my fingernails, but I decide to cross my arms instead, keeping my palms buried beneath.

"He went through a list of things, asking me if they turned me on," Rose says, unabashed.

Connor looks equally unaffected. God, they ooze confidence. He chimes in, "Fingering, dildos, vibrators, head, anal, doggy style—"

"She gets it," Rose snaps.

He grins back, and I swear they have another "moment"— Rose looking like she wants to rip his face off, and Connor looking like he wants to kiss her for it. So weird.

I rub my hot neck. "Have you guys *ever* been embarrassed?" If this is a smart-person superpower, I totally want it.

Connor stares at the ceiling in thought. "Well, there was that one time . . . actually, no . . ." He shakes his head. "No, that wasn't me." His deep blue eyes meet mine. "I'm embarrassment free."

"Me too," Rose says.

I squint at her. "Really?" There has to have been a time . . . oh yeah. "What about when you were in sixth grade on a school field trip to D.C.?" I wasn't with her, but her classmates rehashed the story with such theatrics that only a robot would go without feeling. My mom said she cried angry, *embarrassed* tears all the way home.

Rose's eyes widen in alarm. "Do you want to know what the therapist said or not?"

"Are you blushing?" Connor asks Rose with a laugh. Connor: 2. Rose: 0. She's going to kill me.

"Let's get back to the subject at hand," I say, trying to cover for her, but the damage is done.

Connor nudges her hip with his elbow. "What is it? Did you fall into the Reflecting Pool?"

"No," she deadpans, glaring at the wall.

"Did you misquote Abraham Lincoln's speech?"

"That wouldn't happen, and that's not the least bit embarrassing."

"I would be embarrassed," he says with raised eyebrows.

"Yeah? Well you're like a green rooster. If your kind exists, there's only one of you."

He grins. "Say that again."

"I'd rather embowel your cat."

I laugh. "Ooh, burn." Bringing Sadie into the arguments always livens things up. Rose has threatened to mutilate his pet about twenty different ways. It's her main weapon against her boyfriend, but he finds each one as amusing as the next. Apparently, Rose has yet to enter his apartment on account of Connor's tabby cat that hates women. Since the cat is also full-fledged female, Rose finds the creature as close to a demon as an animal can be.

Connor tries hard not to break into an even wider smile and

show defeat. He cocks his head to the side. "Some idiot boy gave you a wedgie, didn't he? Give me his name; I want to talk to him."

"It was the sixth grade," she says with furrowed brows. "You don't need to go through my history book and attack all the people who have wronged me."

I chime in, "Yeah, because she's already castrated most of them."

Connor lets out a laugh, and I swear, he's about ready to drop on one knee and propose. He licks his lips to hide his growing pleasure. "So I'm right then? Wedgie?"

"What? No." Rose jerks back, offended. "I don't even find it that embarrassing anymore. It actually just chaps my ass, which is why I think we should *move on*."

"I don't want to move on from this, hun. Just let it out. Breathe and release." He inhales strongly and blows out of his mouth, teasing her a little, and her cat-eyes burn holes in him.

"Fine, Richard." Oh, she even used his real name. Things are getting serious now. I can't deny—their tiffs do take my mind off missing Lo and my habits. Sometimes I think that being around Rose and Connor helps take the edge off. Other times, I just feel like they stand in the way of me and my desires. "I was walking through one of the Smithsonian museums, and I stopped in front of a model of the solar system. While I was reading the labels, a group of boys in my class gathered behind me and pointed and snickered before saying, 'I can see Uranus.'"

Connor doesn't laugh. "That's not even clever."

It gets worse, is all I think.

Rose's lips twitch, trying to smile, but anger flits in her eyes at the memory. "I ignored them, and then they said, 'Hey, your anus is bleeding.'"

Connor frowns.

"I started my period that day."

I grimace at her pained memory. Those things stay with some-one forever. Even if they seem small and insignificant, childhood stories like Rose's are the ones that last a lifetime.

"Give me their names." Connor motions to her with two fin-gers as he takes out his phone and opens the Notes app.

Rose actually lets out a weak smile. "I yelled at them," she tells Connor, "that day—I turned around and told them to shut up, and I ran into the bathroom and cried and called my mother." Her face turns serious. "I never want to have children."

My stomach drops at the bomb she just exploded in the room. I knew this about Rose, but talking about kids in front of a pretty new boyfriend would be a trigger for them to scamper away.

Clearly, this is a Rose Calloway test.

Connor inhales deeply, as though digesting the sudden procla-mation. His face stays blank, accepting Rose's challenge. She's practically asking him to run the other way. "After that, I wouldn't either. Boys should be more respectful about the female reproduc-tive system. It's what brought those fuckers into the world."

Rose laughs at this, almost cackling. I can't help but smile too. "Fuckers?" she repeats.

He shrugs. "It's better than dipshits."

"I actually think dipshit is more appropriate."

My eyes scrunch. "Are you two seriously discussing curse words?"

"Yes," they say in unison, turning their attention back to me. Rose picks up where she left off on the story involving the thera-pist. "Anyway, he went through a list and asked me what I pre-ferred, I told him, and he asked how often. Then, he asked me if I tried to stop, but he said it in a way that was completely unpro-fessional."

Connor elaborates. "He told her that most women come into his office seeking attention, especially from him since he's good-looking and fit, and that in order to verify her problem, she would need to—and I quote—'suck cock until her mouth bled.'"

My jaw unhinges. "What?" I say in a small voice.

Rose punches him in the side, and he feigns wincing, incensing her more. "I was trying to be brief about it," she says. "You didn't need to tell her word for word."

"I hate paraphrasing. To use your vocabulary, it *chaps my ass.*"

Rose holds up a hand to his face, ignoring him and telling him to shut up in one swift motion. Her eyes meet mine and they soften considerably. "I learned *later* that he had never treated a female sex addict before. I'm trying to find a woman who understands your condition. And I *promise*, she will not only be respectful but she'll be intelligent and know more than Connor and me put together."

"That's impossible," Connor tells her. "We're the two smartest people in the entire world. You put us together, and you get a superhuman."

Rose rolls her eyes dramatically, but she's actually smiling. "You're an idiot." She nods to me. "Okay?"

I believe Rose. I trust her more than anyone else in the whole world, maybe even more than Lo. He would be so offended if he heard me say that, but in this moment, I think it's true. He's not here. But I have her.

There's something beyond comforting about that. "Thanks, Rose." I give her a hug and hope that no matter how horrible I am, no matter how much I bitch and regress, she'll forgive me.

My wedges dangle in my hand. My bare feet touch the dirty sidewalk. I'm running. Well, more like *chasing*. As I try to catch up with Lo, a freshman dormitory looms in the background, cop cars swarming the brick building. Underage drinkers cuffed or given a not-so-pleasant citation.

Lo spins around, slowing *and* shuffling backwards at the same time. He's so good at running away from things. At eighteen, I still struggle to keep up with him.

"Faster, Lil," he tells me, but he has a goofy smile on his face. As if this could be considered a new adventure. Racing from the cops during our first week of college. Me, chasing after him.

"We're . . . going . . . up a . . . hill," I huff, my pace between a walk and a jog. Something sticky glues to the bottom of my foot, and I cringe with a downturned frown. I hope that was just gum.

"I'm going to leave you," he threatens, but I hardly believe him. Especially with the way he nearly laughs at me. And then he picks up speed again, sprinting forward, hoping that I'll gain the strength to finally reach him.

I never do. But it's a nice thought.

My knees bend beneath me, and I use the last ounce of my energy to dart towards him up the steep hill, traffic on the left side of us as cars return from the clubs and bars. The dorm party we attended wasn't even that fun. The beer sucked, as Lo put it. There was no room to move, and the halls were so crammed with people that a weird smell permeated the air. Like weed and sweat mixed together. Gross.

But I don't regret it. Because Lo was there, and we'll have something to laugh about later.

His black shirt begins to mold to his taut back and chest and arms, outlining the shape of his lean muscles, giving me an idea of what lies beneath. When he runs, he looks beautiful. As though no one can touch him, as though he's leaving behind a burning world and heading towards a peaceful one. His cheeks will sharpen; his eyes will narrow in determination. Of course I can't see any of that.

I just have a nice view of his ass.

That's not too bad to look at either.

And then I begin to fall. Pain shoots up my ankle, so excruciating that I let out a cry. *Fuck, fuck, fuck.* I sit on my butt and inspect the bone. It's not protruding from my skin, but the muscle feels tight and strained.

"Lil?" Lo rushes back to me, nearly skidding down the hill with a face full of worry. He bends to my ankle and inspects the bone just as I did. His fingers lightly touch my skin. "How bad does it hurt?"

"Bad." I grimace.

"As bad as when you broke your arm?" he asks, reminding me of the bully on the playground when we were little. Harry *Cheese-*water.

I shake my head, and he puts his hands underneath my armpits, hoisting me up like I'm a little doll. I try to put some pressure on my foot to test it, but the pain intensifies like a thousand sharp needles. My eyes begin to water, and I wipe them with a furious hand. Pissed that I fell. Especially with police sirens blaring in the distance.

Lo does not need to be thrown in jail. The last time he was in there, his father threatened to ship him off to a military academy. The only thing that changed his father's mind was my promise to help "fix" Lo, which was solidified with our fake relationship. Even if I wanted to help him, I can't. He glared at me tonight just for suggesting he should switch to beer. I still wonder if he would have left me alone at the party if I told him to stop altogether. The best I can do is try to convince him *not* to drink an extra bottle. That's in my power, and I use it as often as I can. But the only way he'll truly get better is if he wants to first.

And clearly, he's nowhere near that point. I'm not even sure what it will take.

He drank so much that his eyes glaze over. He's still present— he's still *here*—but I see the hunger to drink more, to lie down and just sleep with the drift and ease that liquor offers him.

"You probably sprained it," Lo says, his gaze falling to my foot again.

"I can limp there," I tell him. We should call Nola to pick us up. We hate cabs enough to risk being seen by a cop, but we still have my family's driver. And Lo's. But Anderson would be a last resort. For some reason, neither of us suggests our drivers as an option. It's late, and I really don't want to wake Nola to save us.

"That sounds like a stupid idea," he says.

I look over my shoulder, the red and blue lights flashing in the distance. "Just go without me. I'll catch up."

And then his cheeks sharpen as they always do. "That sounds even shittier."

"I haven't had any alcohol," I tell him. "If the cops catch me, then I'll be fine. They catch you, and you'll be in trouble with your dad."

"Thanks for reminding me." He lets out a deep sigh, and then spins around—back facing me. Just when I think he's going to take off running, actually listening to my request, he does something quite different. He bends down, lifts up my legs and hoists me on his back. "Grab tight, love."

My hands wrap around his neck, and he speeds off.

The wind whips my brown hair, and I listen to his easy breath as he carries me away from the chaos and towards the city where we live. I've ridden on his back before. When we were kids. When I couldn't make it up the Great Sand Dunes in Colorado. When I forgot to wear closed-toed shoes in the Costa Rican rain forest. When I just needed a lift. He was always there.

Minutes pass and then those turn into hours, and Lo has slowed to a walk, the Philadelphia streets alive and glittering in the middle of the night. We head to the Drake—to our new apartment that we share together.

Lo has spun me around, and he holds me in a front-piggyback while I rest my head on the crook of his neck and shoulder, my eyes fluttering closed.

My desires have already been satiated for the night. The only person who crosses my mind is the man carrying me. "If you were an X-Men, I think you would be Quicksilver," I say with a small yawn. He has superhuman speed, able to run as fast as lightening. He's also the son of Magneto, who expects too much of him at times, their father-son relationship one of the rockiest among mutant kind.

He mulls this over and then whispers, "I'd rather be Hellion."

I know. I'd rather be Veil most of the time and escape my most embarrassing moments by whisking into nothingness, but the truth is, I'm probably not even worthy of being compared to an X-Men. At least Lo is like someone. At least he can relate.

He glances down at me as I begin to fall asleep. "How's your ankle?"

"Wonderful," I whisper, "because I'm not standing on it."

"I think we have an ice pack in the fridge."

My eyes shut fully. "Mmm, sounds nice."

He kisses the top of my head and then whispers, "I love you, Lil."

We say the words all the time, but the power has not been lost. They mean more to me than he'll know. Because at the end of the day, this type of love is different than a first-sight encounter with a man at a bar, a crush in prep school or a bubbling, new romance. Our *I love you*s encompass years of heartache, of hurt, of laughter and pain.

And every time we say the words, I feel the rush of our childhood. I couldn't imagine ever losing that.

After a full night of icing the muscle, I'm so chilly in the morning that I crave warmth. At 10 a.m., I fill up a bubble bath and lie in the soapy suds, letting my injury soak in the soothing waters. Bliss doesn't even define this feeling. That is . . . until Lo opens the bathroom door and sluggishly walks in. I sink farther down into the water and gather some foamy bubbles to hide my naked body.

"You have your own bathroom," I remind him as he runs water over his toothbrush. A blue Spider-Man one that he carried in here.

He turns around, supporting himself against the edge of my counter. Only drawstring pants on that leave absolutely *nothing* to the imagination. But I keep my eyes firmly planted on his.

"I wanted to see how your ankle was doing," he admits before putting his toothbrush in his mouth. One week into college, and I still haven't fully adjusted to living with him. We were comfortable before, but sharing space has blurred even more lines that really didn't need any more blurring.

"I'm warming it," I explain and lift my foot up from the water, leaving out the part about wanting the heat a lot more than my ankle needing it.

I didn't expect him to walk over, toothbrush still hanging out of his mouth, and press his fingers to the swollen area. I try not to let the pain cross my face too much.

Lo pops the toothbrush from his mouth and points to me. "Bed rest for you," he orders before turning and spitting into the sink. He rinses and swishes with water.

"You feel okay?" I ask, watching him wipe his lips on the towel.

When he returns his attention to me, his eyes land on the bath. "I could use a bubble bath," he says, a smile playing at his lips. Another moment where I should say no and not submit to his teasing and playfulness.

But the words just don't come, and he's already shedding his pants down to his black boxer briefs and hopping right into the water. The Jacuzzi is large enough for seven people, so it's not *that* awkward.

He lets out a loud moan as he sinks into the waters. I can't help but smile.

"Just don't come any closer," I warn. "I'm naked." I flush at the words.

It's his turn to smile, a mischievous one that I do not like.

"Lo," I warn him again.

He raises his hands from the water, coming in peace. "I'm

staying right here." Good. "It's you that we both should be worried about."

I frown. He may be right about that. I scoot a little farther back, avoiding his silly smile. I press my body firmly to the porcelain tub.

After a moment, Lo clears his throat and plays with the bubbles, running them between his fingers. "So . . . last night, did he use a condom?"

"Yeah." I nod, giving into his question even though I have no desire to talk about last night.

"You know, because college guys are different," Lo says, still fixated on the bubbles.

"They're hornier," I agree. It's my very own sexual playground. Maybe that's why Lo looks so concerned.

"They drink more," he adds, "and may forget to use one. You can't let that happen, okay?"

For the past week, I've been so neurotic about Lo being in college, surrounded by parties every night where the liquor never runs out (most of the time). I never thought he'd have fears about me.

Against my better judgment, I scoot forward a little and nudge his foot with mine. At least, I hope it's his foot. I can't really tell through all the bubbles. "I'll be fine," I say confidently, "I'm always the one in control during sex. I call the shots." It helps that I don't drink since I usually need to drive Lo home afterwards. Last night we had Nola drop us off with the intention of going home at a reasonable hour without the cop lights flashing in the background. Oops.

"Do you even realize how small you are?" Lo asks in disbelief. "Honestly, Lil."

I splash some bubbles in his face. "I'm big enough."

"You're ridiculously skinny and five-foot-five. *I'm* big."

My eyes drift down. Unintentional. At least I hope so. He's already smiling again and my cheeks burn. "Can we move on?" I ask, partly whining. "I just don't know what you want me to say." He won't tell me to stop, so there's no use in revolving around this topic like some vomit-inducing carousel.

"No, I don't want to move on," he says roughly. "And I want you to convince me that I shouldn't be nervous whenever you run off with a guy who looks like he could snap you in half."

"If I can convince you, you'll drop this subject for at least the rest of the year?" I ask, already thinking of what I could say . . . or do.

"Deal."

"Fine," I reply. "Then you act like the horny college guy—"

"Not difficult."

I roll my eyes. "And I'll show you just how in control I am."

He stares me down. "You do realize you're naked."

Oh . . . shit. I forgot.

"Which makes this even better," he tells me. "More realistic, right?"

Right. But my heart has started to thud in my chest, also reminding me that this is real, but maybe it's not. We are still kind of pretending. Good God. Alice in Wonderland had an easier fucking time discerning reality than me.

I give him a nod, and before I can process anything else, Lo reaches into the water and grabs my hurt foot. I don't know where this is going. Maybe he's worried about my ankle again. He gently takes it in his hands and then kisses the heel sweetly.

I'm so confused. How am I supposed to convince him I'm in control if he's just kissing my foot?

His eyes meet mine, and they don't break away, not as he leans in and puts his mouth around my toe. Holy shit. I can feel his tongue swirling around it, and then he starts sucking. I feel like someone lit me on fire. The bath does not help smother the flames.

When he licks the arch of my foot, I pull it right out of his hands.

His eyes rise accusingly. "You didn't like that?" he asks, knowing full well I did.

"I don't let them suck my toes," I say.

"Let's see what you do then," he challenges me.

I take the bait and edge closer, glad that the bubbles hide my body from view. He relaxes against the porcelain tub now, leaning back while I straddle his waist. He tries to sit up and take charge again, and I slam my hands against his chest. My mouth finds his neck and I start leaving a trail of kisses while my hips move back and forth over him. The hardness in his pants grows beneath me. I'm thankful he still wears his boxer briefs even if I don't have any clothes on. I just need to remember this is to prove a point. *Nothing more.*

Before he can make another move on me, my hand lowers to his cock and I grip it firmly but not too hard. He groans and leans back into the tub. I smile into my next kiss and start to massage outside his underwear. I've got this.

But then he grabs me by the waist and in a swift motion, I'm suddenly on the bottom. I try and jerk away but his fingers find my wrist and his other hand sinks beneath the waters and touches the spot in between my legs. I shudder in *need.* My body just so damn confused at this point.

He leans in, his lips brushing my earlobe. "You're in control?" he asks huskily. "*Fight me.*"

I try to push him off again, but he just pushes back, pinning me to the slippery tub. My slick, naked chest touches his and my mind can't process anything but the words *more* and *need.*

I know I'm losing.

"I can't."

He doesn't back away. Just shakes his head in slight distress. "Why not?"

"You're too big." *And I think I want it.*

He breaks into a smile, but it quickly disappears when he realizes what this means. "So you're going to . . ." he trails off, not able to say the words.

"I'm going to . . . not fuck any linebackers or burly guys. And I have pepper spray, and like I said—I can take care of myself as long as the guy doesn't get too aggressive." *Or isn't Loren Hale.*

"You didn't say that."

"I'm saying it now." He's about to move away and I quickly blurt out, "Can you put them in me?" No. No. No. I did not . . .

His hand still lingers on my pussy, cupping it. I don't look at his eyes but I can feel him staring at me with amusement.

"You have rules," he reminds me. "I can't make you come, remember?" Right. I initiated that rule after Lo and I went a little too far one day. We didn't have sex, but I climaxed and it was too much. Even if we were in a fake relationship. But we still fool around. He still touches me. I still touch him. And right now, I'm so eager that I just want to feel him inside of me. Somehow.

"Make up your mind, Lil," he says softly.

I know he'll do it if I ask. He'd do anything for me, but I don't know if it's fair to him.

"I'll just . . . get something else." Like a toy.

"You sure?"

I give him a weak nod and he finally pulls away from me. Even in the warm water, I feel kind of cold by the absence of a body.

By the absence of him.

Four

slide into the limo where Poppy, Rose and Daisy sit on the leather seats, my two older sisters filling glasses of champagne. We each wear a cocktail dress, and the different styles reflect our personalities a little too well. Poppy wears a bohemian maroon silk dress with draping sleeves and a plunging V-neck, a brown belt tight around her waist. Rose sports a tailored, dark blue beauty, the neckline straight at her collarbone and a simple diamond necklace against her breast. She looks ready for a political commencement speech, not the grand reveal of Fizzle's brand-new soda.

And then my youngest sister wears a green gown, the back nothing but strings crisscrossed in a wild array of patterns. I, on the other hand, rushed out of my parents' house in a strapless, black, plain number. Nothing special about it. Not too flashy. Not exceptionally cute. But it's comfortable *and* makes my boobs look a little bigger.

"Hi," I say, running my fingers through my brown hair, which reaches my shoulders. Poppy tries to pass me a glass, and I shake my head, lightly pushing her hand away. "I'm not drinking." I tried to get out of this event at least twenty times in the past week, but my mother wouldn't hear of it. I'd rather not find a reason to ditch my sisters and dance with an eager guy.

"I'll take it," Daisy says with a coy smile. She wags her eyebrows.

"No," the three of us tell her in unison. Even though I withheld the knowledge about the New Year's debacle from our parents, I had to spill to Rose and Poppy. I expected Daisy to rampage and hate me afterwards for sharing the details of the night, but she acted mature about it. In retrospect, I think keeping the birth control secret has nullified blabbing about being slipped GHB.

"You shouldn't want to drink ever again after what happened," Rose tells her.

"Why? Are you going to drug me, Rose?" She gasps, mocking. "My very own sister. The betrayal. The scandal!"

Rose gives her a sharp glare. "I wish you'd be serious about what happened."

Daisy sighs and slouches, crossing her arms. "I'm never going to drink hunch punch at a party again. Lesson learned."

"Thank you." Rose puts the rim of her glass to her red lips.

"You're so much like Mom, it's scary."

Shit. Rose's solidifies to stone. I see hurt coursing through her, even if no one else can. I don't think Daisy realizes how much Rose is trying to avoid being like our mother. She fears that path more than any of us.

"So . . ." I say to break the tension, ". . . this is fun." *Way to spark a conversation, Lily.*

The car bumps along the road towards the Ritz where the event will take place. Fizzle hasn't created a new soda in five years, so the unveiling is a big deal. My father has even kept the new flavor pretty hush-hush from the media and *us*. It could be Dragon Fruit Fizz for all I know—which sounds incredibly disgusting.

I make a face.

"What?" Poppy says with a short laugh. My oldest sister looks like a California native with a golden tan year-round. A fishtail braid lies against her shoulder. "You look like Maria when I try to dress her in pants." Her three-year-old daughter is a mini-fashionista. It's kind of frightening.

I share her smile—about to tell her my thought.

"No, no, no!" Rose shouts, typing furiously in her phone. "I cannot believe this."

My stomach knots, hoping, praying that her outburst has nothing to do with me.

Daisy pops a piece of gum in her mouth and offers some to the rest of us, as though Rose did not just have a sudden outburst. I suppose she's overly dramatic a lot. We kinda all are. I take a piece, but Poppy shakes her head.

"What is it?" Poppy asks.

Rose puts her hand to her forehead and then glares at the window. "Our mother has taken it upon herself to wrangle us dates for the evening."

I choke on my gum and start coughing.

Daisy groans. "Not really."

Poppy pats my back, but I seriously think I inhaled the gum straight into my lungs.

"She does this every time we go out. It shouldn't be that surprising," Poppy exclaims, putting the rim of her champagne glass beneath my lips, "mothering" me. Gratefully, I take a small sip, the bubbles tingling my throat.

"I specifically told her that Lily doesn't want to be seen with another man while Lo is in rehab."

I slump in my seat and put my hand to my forehead, shielding my eyes. This is not good. This is not good *at all*. "Who did she call?" I ask Rose. This has happened before. Only, I wasn't in a relationship with Lo. I would actually fuck whoever my mother picked for me at the end of the night. What if she called someone I've already slept with? The bottom of my stomach drops.

"I don't know," Rose says, pounding her fingers on her phone's screen, texting our mother rapidly. "She won't tell me."

Daisy blows a bubble and it pops against her face. "I don't see what the big deal is," she says, using her tongue to bring the gum back in her mouth. "I mean, it sucks, yeah, but Lo isn't here, and it's just for appearances. Plus, you can always ditch him. Mom set me up with Adam Colefinger last year." She grimaces. "He smelled like he showered in Axe. I was about to hurl the whole night, so I took Mom's perfume and doused myself in it to give him a taste of his own medicine." She nods proudly.

Rose kicks Daisy's leg. "You're forgetting the part where he threw up on your heels."

"That's the price you have to pay for retribution."

Poppy holds up her hands before the tension rips all of us in half and explodes. Rose is seething enough to cause a category five tornado. I just want to disintegrate and flutter away.

"There's nothing to worry about," Poppy tells all of us.

I exchange a hesitant glance with Rose. *Nothing to worry about?* There is a huge possibility that this guy is one I've met— that he's back for round two. What if he's expecting Lily 1.0: the girl who dragged guys into the bathroom and drowned them in pleasure? What then?

I put my head between my knees, trying to breathe normally. *Wait for me*, Lo said.

I'm trying! God, I'm trying. I wish everyone could see that.

It's not so easy when my whole family believes my only problem surrounds Lo's absence. They only understand his addiction, and I know—deep in my heart—that they'll never understand mine.

Rose dials a number and rests the phone to her ear "Mother—"

My mother's high-pitched voice cuts through the receiver. "Don't you dare argue with me, Rose!" I raise my head and see

Rose holding the receiver away from her ear. "I have done so much for you in the past week. And I ask you to do one thing, *one thing*, and you put up a fight! Can't you do something for me without disagreeing? Is that at all possible?!"

Her screaming rakes my insides like nails bloodying my back. Rose inhales deeply through her nose, taking a calculated, measured breath. A perk to being completely off my mother's radar—I never have to deal with her coarse personality. She can be in your corner one second and then completely victimize herself the next just to guilt you.

"Let us pick our own dates then," Rose says. "I can call Ryke to come escort Lily. He'll be happy to be there." *Happy?* That is a very strong adjective.

Daisy crawls over the seat to pick up a remote. "Don't torture the guy."

I kinda agree. Even though I'd love for him to bail me out, he's done enough for me, and I'm not sure I can ever repay him.

Rose shoots her a loathing glare and mouths, *shut up*.

Daisy cocks an eyebrow and presses a button on her remote. The sunroof starts sliding open. The mechanical noise bleeds into the silence like the awkward chorus to our tension.

Our mother snaps, "I'm not calling her date and canceling on him. He's doing me a favor."

"Then I'll call him. Give me his number."

"He's already *here*, Rose."

Rose's fingers tighten around her silver clutch. And Daisy stands up in between us, sticking out of the sunroof.

"Not helping," I tell her.

I barely hear her voice that's lost to the wind. "I don't . . . like . . . trapped . . ."

I sigh heavily, feeling Rose's panic and mine mix together in a toxic mess.

Rose nods to me like, *I'll handle this*. I nod back. I have faith in her, but there is one person not even Rose Calloway can destroy with her words. "Okay," Rose says, "I'll be with Lily's date, and she can go stag since I don't have a date either—"

What? I thought she invited Connor. Or . . . maybe I assumed she was going to bring him.

"I know," my mother tells her, "I called Connor this morning and asked him if he was planning on riding with the four of you. I don't know what was more embarrassing, being informed by your daughter's boyfriend that *you* broke up with him or calling him and being made a complete and utter fool of."

Rose touches her forehead. "I highly doubt Connor made you look like a fool."

"He didn't have to. Just being on the outside of my own daughter's life was embarrassing enough. I should have known what was going on. You should have told me."

"Did he tell you that I broke up with him?" Rose asks now.

"Did you hear me?!" my mother shrieks, about to have a nervous breakdown. "I should have known."

"I didn't even tell Lily!" Rose screams, hair coming loose from its slicked back position in her pony. She holds the phone to her lips, putting it on speaker, not that we couldn't hear it before . . . "Did he tell you that I broke up with him?!"

"Oh, let it go, Rose. The longer you control a man, the more likely they'll leave you. Is that what you want? To be alone and miserable for the rest of your life?"

"I don't know. You're pretty miserable, Mother, and you're married."

My eyes widen so big that they may very well fall out of my face. Our mother inhales a sharp breath. After a very long pause, she says in a controlled, scarily calm tone, "I called a date for you, Rose. I'll see you girls at the event." She hangs up, and Rose collapses back against the seat, as though she just finished a UFC match.

I don't think either of them won.

Poppy slides over to her and squeezes her shoulder. "She probably invited Sebastian to be your date." Before there was a "Connor and Rose," my sister took Sebastian as her arm candy to appease our mother.

Rose shakes her head and begins smoothing her hair back into place. "No, Sebastian went on a trip to the Cayman Islands with his boyfriend this week. She knew that."

I can't even imagine who she set Rose up with, probably someone she hoped Rose would marry down the line. That's how Samantha Calloway operates.

Jitters run through my body on high speed. Rose, my rock, has eyes as wide as a Kit-Cat clock. It's like my mother has zapped her cold. When she wakes from her stupor, she reaches into the ice bucket and pulls out the expensive champagne. She chugs straight from the bottle. I jerk back in surprise. Considering Rose usually wipes the rim of her soda cans, I think it's safe to say she's upset.

Daisy remains oblivious outside, her long hair whipping behind her. I guess we all handle our mother in different ways. Rose yells. Daisy finds fresh air. I sink into a corner. Poppy remains calm.

Rose offers the drink to Poppy. She declines. "I'm safe from her. I have a husband." Yeah, our mother has lost interest in Poppy's relationships.

"She should know who I am by now," Rose mutters. "I tell her all the time, you know? *I'm never getting married, Mother.* And it goes in one ear and out the other. I thought dating Connor would make things better. My first actual boyfriend. She'd be off my case. Instead, she's whispering in my ear about what to say to him, how I should be, worrying over whether he'll end things before I do." Rose curses under her breath and stares up at the ceiling of the car. "How can you love your parents so much one minute, but then absolutely hate them the next?" She inhales a deep breath. "I need to go back to therapy."

I break into a smile, trying to lighten her downtrodden mood. "You know Connor goes to therapy compulsively too? I asked him where he was going last week, and he said to his daily therapist for just a regular session to let off some steam. Funny that you two have that in common, huh?"

Rose glares. "His therapist is also his 'best friend.' So no, we do not have that in common. I actually have people close to me that I love. Like you and Poppy and Daisy . . ." Her eyes trail up to the torso that stands in the center of the car. "Does she realize we're on a highway?"

"I think she prefers it that way." My eyes widen in mock horror. "The danger!" I mimic Daisy's voice.

Rose and Poppy laugh, although Rose's dies out rather quickly. She rubs her eyes and groans.

Normally, I'd be excited right now, wondering what face will greet me once we arrive at the event. But I've been trying to forget what it feels like to climax, the tingling of my body—the sensation of masculine, hard hands sliding along my skin. And I'm afraid once I see a guy, willing and wanting, I'll take the opportunity and jump. Without thinking. Without breathing. I'll just do it and ruin the one good thing in my life.

Rose lets out another long groan.

I have to ask. "What happened with Connor?"

"I thought everything was fine," Poppy says.

Rose wedges the bottle between her bony knees. "When I'm

with him, I roll my eyes so much I feel like they're going to fall out of my face." She talks with her hands—so unlike Rose that I scoot forward on my seat to be closer to her. Rose gestures to her body, trying to express herself, but she looks like she's swatting the air instead. I reach out and hold her hand. Rose calms a little. "I can't believe she's doing this after I asked her not to."

"It'll be okay," I say, but the words coming from me only worsen the look on her face.

"Did Connor want to break up?" Poppy wonders.

"I don't know. When we fight, we both talk about it all the time . . ."

I interject. "Yeah, but you two break up in strange ways. Last month, I heard Connor say something like, 'Sadie never disagrees with me.' And you said, 'If you want a doormat for a girlfriend, then your cat is perfect. Have a happy life together.' Then you slammed the door to your bedroom, and he stormed out of the house, *smiling*."

It was all really weird, and Rose ended up walking back into his arms the next day, not admitting defeat exactly, but I think Connor would count it as a success.

"Is this time different?" Poppy wonders.

Rose blinks in confusion, wracking her brain. "I don't know. I guess not. He told me that I was being inane about something. I can't even remember what, but we both split at the restaurant. We rode in separate cabs home, and we haven't talked since." Realization hits her, and she collapses back against the seat. "*God*, what am I doing? I feel like I'm in prep school when I'm with him sometimes. It drives me crazy."

I open my mouth, so tempted to sing the Britney Spears song again.

Rose shoots me a look. "Don't. You. Dare."

I laugh instead, and it takes a long moment for Rose to join in. She puts the bottle to her lips, swigging one last time just as the limo rolls to a stop.

Here we go.

Five

ssigned seating. I curse you.

Fifty tables fill the grand ballroom, and my mother wedged us near the front under the brightest lamp. Not only do we have to endure our dates, but we have to do so under the scalding heat of a spotlight. While we wait for the guys to find us, I play with the glittery napkin ring on my plate and try not to anxiously scratch my arms.

My mother's party planner had too much fun with the black and gold decorations. A black sparkler centerpiece fits in the center of every gold-clothed table. Photos of gold Fizz cans with black carbonation bubbles are framed along the walls. Diet Fizz is the reverse color scheme with black cans and gold bubbles.

At least Fizzle's logo isn't lime green and puke pink—two colors that would induce an instant migraine. Still, you'd think she could have branched out a little bit. Maybe added a splash of blue or red. But no, those are Coca-Cola and Pepsi's colors. No Fizzle-loving person would dare touch them.

I'm going stir-crazy waiting for our dates, but at least Rose and Daisy sit next to me, not allowing any room for a guy to settle near me. I also choose not to glance around for them like Rose, who scans the floor trying to speculate who the hell our mother invited to be our arm candy. Anyway, too many people mill about the ballroom for me to play that guessing game. They congregate by the open bar or eat fancy hors d'oeuvres as servers pass.

I feel like I'm at a million-dollar wedding reception.

Daisy leans back on the legs of her chair and folds her cloth napkin into a flower, clearly bored. "How convenient that Maria suddenly came down with a stomach bug." Poppy never even made it out of the limo. The nanny called her as soon as Maria threw up, and she turned around to take her to the doctor. "I need to have a baby so I can use it as a way to bail."

Rose clenches a champagne glass firmly in her hand. Her eyes shoot to our youngest sister. "Let's not talk about children."

"Yeah," I say with a small smile. "The word *baby* gives Rose hives."

Rose sips her drink, not disagreeing.

And that's when I feel a hand plant on my shoulder. And by the force and the size, I know it's *male*.

"Lily Calloway," he says with added pleasure. I know that voice. I just can't place it. I rarely can.

I slowly crane my neck over my shoulder, and my eyes widen in horror. I recognize the all-American build, blue eyes, and swept back brown-blond hair. Even outside of prep school, he looks like a star quarterback—even if his sport of choice was lacrosse.

I didn't sleep with Aaron Wells. I didn't *touch* a hair on his head, and I never would. Because this douchebag tried to stuff Lo into a locker in ninth grade. Lo spun out of his grasp and sprinted down the hall, away from Aaron and a pack of restless bullies. Aaron wasn't fast enough to catch him.

Lo fights indirectly with people. So I knew he wouldn't retaliate with a baseball bat, swinging at Aaron's head in angry retribution. There are some things that hurt worse than a punch. I think his father taught him that. Lo paid a guy to break into the school and alter Aaron's exam grades, and his GPA fell. For guys like Aaron, reputation is everything and being on the bottom of the graduating class can ruin status. He must have realized Lo was the cause, so one day after school Aaron tried to confront him with fists bared. He clocked him. Lo escaped. As he always did. Four years passed and their feud escalated.

I became a target.

Aaron would try to trap me in the bathrooms, and I vehemently dodged him. I stayed glued to Lo's side during every hour of the day. In those couple months, I remember being really scared to go to school. I didn't know what Aaron wanted to do to me, but since their rivalry already became physical, I didn't necessarily want to find out. I remember skipping often and fearing moments in between class. I'd jump even when it was just Lo who approached, and when he could tell I was becoming psychologically fucked from Aaron's threats, he decided to do something more drastic to protect me.

He threatened Aaron's future. Not just a little drop in his GPA. He would contact the colleges that planned to scout Aaron and pay them off so they'd reject him on the spot.

And it happened. Aaron's dream university denied his application because Lo reached them first. And with the Hale name and a hefty donation, they couldn't refuse Lo's offer.

So Aaron shut up. He got accepted to his safety school, and he left us alone.

Until now.

I don't greet him. I turn back to give him the biggest cold shoulder. I don't care if I'm rude. Because if my suspicions are correct, he's only here to make my life hell.

"Not going to say hi?" Aaron wonders. I watch him circle the table and sit across from me. He actually takes the centerpiece and puts it on the floor so I have a direct view of his smarmy face.

I hear Rose beside me. "How old are you?"

I glance at her and nearly laugh at her date. He's a twig, and his suit is two sizes too big.

"Nineteen," he tells her, fixing his bowtie, but he makes it even more lopsided.

Rose raises her glass with a bitter smile. "Wonderful." Our mother set her up with a guy three years younger than she is.

He takes the open seat to her left. "My father is your father's lawyer." He scratches the back of his longish brown hair, his skin golden tan. "I'm Matthew Collins."

"Nice to meet you, Matthew," Rose says, motioning for the server to bring her another glass of champagne.

Daisy's date sits to her right. I don't catch his name, but he's too distracted by his phone to even acknowledge my sister. She doesn't look like she cares either, refolding her napkin into a rose.

The food starts parading around the room, sea bass and winter squash making rounds on each circular table.

My appetite is gone. Especially as Aaron leans his forearms on the table, practically hunched over to force my attention to him.

"What have you been up to, Lily?"

I shrug and then spit out, "Why would you want to even come here?" It's almost been three whole years since I've seen him. *Why now?*

"I heard your boy was out of town. I thought I'd check up on you, make sure you were safe and doing okay."

I glare. "I'm fine."

He nods, his eyes skimming the length of me. Thank God, my body stops at the edge of the table.

"Did my mother really call you?" I ask tensely.

"She called my friend first. She seemed a little desperate to get you hooked up, and I told her I was available." He flashes an ugly smile. "I have nothing better to do." And so the truth comes out.

"That's why you're here? You're bored?"

He shrugs. "Now that I'm almost graduated, Loren has nothing on me. And I think me and you—we have unfinished business."

I go cold and look to Rose for backup, but she's in a heated discussion with her younger date. Well . . . she seems to be educating him about the stock market, as though he said something inane and she has to correct him.

Daisy is watching me carefully, but I don't have the heart to explain my history to her. Not now anyway. Plates of sea bass slide onto our placemats, and I stiffly pick up my fork. I can't eat, not until I let some words loose.

"I'm not having sex with you," I immediately blurt.

His eyebrow quirks and I realize that might not have been the "unfinished business" he had in mind. And then he says, "We'll see." Okay, maybe it was. Or maybe he's just planning on cornering me, putting me in some provocative situation and then snapping a few pictures, taking a video, and then sending them to Lo.

Oh God.

Daisy butts in. "Hey, back off. She has a boyfriend."

Aaron snorts and says to Daisy, "Do I look like I give a shit?"

"I do," a new voice enters. And this time, I internally cheer at the sound of Ryke's deep, threatening tone. He slides into the seat between Daisy's date and Aaron, closing the circle. He wears a fitted charcoal suit with a skinny black tie. His brown hair is styled, but he's not clean-shaven. How did he get invited to a Fizzle event? Better yet, why would he accept it and come here?

I don't really care. I'm just glad he is.

"Who the fuck are you?" Aaron spits.

Ryke motions to a server and points to his placemat, silently asking for food. Then he faces Aaron with narrowed eyes. If Lo was here, I think he'd appreciate the backup. We've never had it before, and I have to say, it's kind of nice.

"Loren Hale's brother," Ryke tells him.

Aaron chokes on a laugh. "Bullshit. Lo's an only child."

"Then don't believe me. I don't really fucking care. But you start messing with his girlfriend, and then I will care." A server places his plate in front of him, and Ryke digs into the mashed potatoes, not giving Aaron any more attention.

Aaron looks back to me, and his eyebrows jump up, but he mouths, *later.* No, I don't like later. He even *winks.*

Shivers run down my arms.

Daisy squints at Ryke. "Why are you here?" she asks over her oblivious date, still texting. "Did my mom call you?"

Ryke cuts into his fish. "Nope. My father did."

I frown. "What?" That makes no sense. Jonathan Hale basically blamed Ryke for Lo's decision to go to rehab, leaving him with an empty house. Why would he want to invite him?

"Yep," Ryke says. "He called me up, spewing some shit about how we should put the past behind us. But he's an awful fucking liar." He swigs his water. "He wants information about Lo, but like hell I'm giving it to him."

I try not to acknowledge Aaron, but I don't like the way he's listening so intently, digesting our families' secrets and filing them for *later.* I sip my own water to clear my throat. "So why come?"

Ryke points at me with a knife. "Knew you'd be here. Knew Lo wouldn't."

Ah, yes, he doesn't trust me. "What confidence." I love Lo enough to restrain myself.

I glance at Aaron, who stares a little too forcefully.

But without Lo to hide behind, my only defense against Aaron is to run. And I'm not as fast as Loren Hale. Not even close.

Daisy keeps leaning on the legs of her chair. "I'm confused," she says, tossing her rose-shaped napkin on the table.

"Eat," I tell her.

She sighs and picks at the fish.

Thankfully, the lights begin to dim so we're not the main focus in the room. Aaron turns around, back facing me, so that helps ease the tension in my shoulders. The stage brightens, and I try to relax in my chair and concentrate on my father.

He walks onto the stage and mans the glass podium. The ballroom quiets, except for the sound of silverware hitting dishes. He looks rich. How else do you describe a man worth billions? Even in his fifties, any gray hairs are masked by brown dye. He always has a genial smile, the kind that makes him seem approachable, even if he's usually too busy to greet. I love him for what he's given me, and I think he'd buy us the world just for the chance to see us smile.

"Friends, family," he says, "I'm so glad to have you all here today to celebrate this special occasion. I founded Fizzle in 1979 with an extremely ambitious—and somewhat naïve—plan to create the next best soda that could rival the likes of Coke and subsequently Pepsi. With the help of angel investors and some faith, Fizzle became a household name in just three short years." Everyone claps. I join in, admiring my father for his drive and passion. I can't imagine coming out of high school or college and starting my own business with such fortitude and strength. I'm not him. Or Rose. Or my mother.

I'm just so very lost.

He holds up a hand to shush us, and the noise settles to silence. "Almost thirty-five years later, Fizzle products are sold in more than two hundred countries. Just in the United States, we've taken away the title of the northern soda of choice from Pepsi. By next year, we plan to steal Southern hearts with our brand-new soda. We believe the taste and contents of this drink are unlike any Coca-Cola product and we'll have diehards choosing . . . *Fizz Life.*"

He steps back from the podium and a screen behind him shows an animated graphic of a Fizzle commercial, a gold background with dark colored bubbles rising up. A silver can spins in the center with gold writing that reads FIZZ LIFE, white bubbles decaled at the bottom. No black on the can at all.

"Fizz Life is zero calories, aspartame-free. It's naturally sweetened with a recipe blended by our food scientists." Servers with gold-plated trays begin to walk around the room with cans of Fizz Life, passing them to the tables. Our waiter sets down a can in front of my plate. Hundreds of people begin popping the tabs, air expelling and carbonation bubbling, the noise so very true to the soda company's name. "This is not only the healthiest soda on the market, but it's also the drink of the future."

The tagline *Fizz Life, Better Life* flashes across the screen. Underneath sits my father's exact words: *the drink of the future.* Maybe it is.

Daisy holds out her drink to me. "Cheers." I clink her can with mine, and she turns to her date to do the same, but he's scrolling through his Facebook app. Ryke already has his open, sipping the new soda.

When he notices her date and her chagrin, he says, "He's a winner."

The guy doesn't even realize he's being talked about.

"First place, pure bred," Daisy agrees, raising her soda before throwing her head back, taking a very large swig.

I sip mine a little. The flavor tastes different than Diet Fizz and Fizz Lite. Not sweeter or bitter. Just . . . different. Good different, I think. I could most definitely grow to like this one more than Diet Fizz.

"Wow that tastes really good," Daisy says. "I totally had my doubts."

Ryke nods in agreement. "Not bad."

I glance at Rose to see how she likes it, but her can sits untouched by her uneaten plate of food. Her fingers pinch a full champagne glass. But I just looked over there and it was half full. Which means this is a new one.

Maybe I'm hyperaware of alcohol now, but I feel like she's drinking more than she normally does. I don't think I've ever seen her drunk or even "composed" drunk—which is what I imagine she would be, the kind where you can barely tell. Sort of like Lo. But not.

Her eyes sear holes into our mother's back, her table adjacent to ours. This is not good.

My father continues to talk about the soda and the company's history and each investor individually.

I don't think I can help Rose. Not because I don't have the strength to, but I'm almost a hundred percent positive she would never let me. She does not see me as her equal. I am the damaged, broken sister, the one who needs repair. If *I* act as though *she* needs help, then she'll freak out. I have to find someone that she'll actually listen to without becoming incredibly defensive.

I make a sudden decision, silently hoping it's the right one, and pull out my phone from a little pocket in my dress and start texting.

Where are you?

The reply only takes a few seconds. Not surprised. At my house. Everything okay?—Connor

I type quickly. No. I need you to come to the event. Rose isn't doing so well.

My phone begins to buzz repeatedly in my hand. Connor is calling me. Before I stand from the table, I glance at Aaron. He no longer watches the stage, his eyes set on me. If I leave the ballroom, will he follow?

I can't answer the phone at the table. So I have to take the chance. Just as I rise, Aaron begins to push his chair back, about to stand too.

But then Ryke points at him with his knife. "You follow her, and I'll slit your fucking throat," he deadpans. That was a little unnecessary, but the warning works because the longer Aaron looks at Ryke to see if it's a bluff, the longer Ryke digs into his food. I can't even tell where his head is at. Neither can Aaron. My enemy scoots closer to the table, leaving me alone for now.

And I thankfully weave around the tables and out the grand double doors.

I already missed his first call, but the phone still rings incessantly. I answer. "Hi."

"What's wrong?" Connor asks, his voice deep with worry that I'm not used to. He's always confident and poised and self-assured. "Are you okay?"

"I'm fine," I say with a nod. "It's Rose that I'm concerned about." I falter, trying to pick the right words. "I don't know if you realized, but my mother set her up with someone tonight. And she's more pissed than I've seen her in a while . . ." I wonder if I should mention the drinking.

"Wait . . . what? That doesn't make sense," Connor says. "Samantha told me that she would be going to the event alone."

I roll my eyes, not in the least surprised by my mother's betrayal or the fact that she got caught. "She lied. Mother has never let Rose go stag. I think Rose hoped that she could go alone if our mother believed you two were still together." But no one could have anticipated Samantha Calloway talking to Connor before tonight.

"Who's her date?"

"Matthew Collins, the son of—"

"Robert Collins, Fizzle's primary lawyer, I know. I've met him. I had brunch with him and your father." Oh . . . that's awkward.

"Are you on your way?"

"I jumped in a limo when I read your first text," he tells me. "Rose may not be pleased to see me, regardless of her mother's affairs."

I hesitate, wondering if he's right. Will she be resistant if he interferes? "She's not used to letting someone else help her."

"I don't think any of you Calloway girls are," he says. I take this in and realize he might be right about that. But I'm learning to relinquish my control to other people. I'm learning to accept help that's been offered. I hope Rose will do the same, even if she feels like she has everything taken care of.

"Promise me that you won't run away from her," I say in a sharp breath. "Even if she pushes you away—"

"I won't let her go," Connor says. "But is there something you're not telling me, Lily? Has something already happened?" I catch the strain in his voice, so subtle and brief but present.

She's drinking more than usual, I should say. But what if I'm just projecting my insecurities about alcohol onto her? With Lo in rehab, this is totally plausible. Still, I'm learning to say how I feel. I inhale a deep breath and let it out. "I'm afraid by the time you get here, she'll be drunk. And I've never seen Rose drunk, so I'm not entirely sure what she'll do or how she'll be . . . she just keeps glaring at our mother from across the room . . ."

"Okay," Connor says. "Okay, don't provoke Rose. Try not to set her off."

I internally laugh. Yeah, that's going to be a little hard. Most topics ignite fire in her eyes when she's in a mood. And I know, without a doubt, that our mother has put her in one. "When will you be here?" I shift anxiously and rub my arm.

"Soon. Will you be okay or do you need to stay on the phone with me?"

"I'll be fine. Ryke is here . . ." I trail off, knowing that Connor and Ryke have never really been friendly after Lo left for rehab. I think the only reason they endured each other's company was because of their mutual like for Lo, and when he's not here it becomes painfully obvious they'd rather be on separate continents.

"Well, I'm sure he'll fuck tonight up somehow," Connor says. I remember Connor describing Ryke as a "Rottweiler you keep on a chain in the yard, guarding your house, but something you'd rather not let inside."

I hesitate to agree. Ryke has helped more than hindered thus far, but that could always change. "I'll see you," I tell Connor. He says bye and we both hang up.

I sneak back into the ballroom, the lights still dim, but no one stands on the stage. Everyone is lively with chatter, and I smell chocolate ganache cake, my father's favorite. When I approach my table, I see Rose sitting on the edge of her seat, her nails rapping against her champagne glass. Her poor date looks like a wilted flower, beaten to death by Rose's intelligence. I'm sure she schooled him on another subject, and he has nothing left to do but pick at his dessert.

Speaking of dessert. I sit and find a beautiful slice of cake in front of me. Actually *two* beautiful slices. They almost make up for the fact that Aaron creepily stares at me on the other end. I ignore him. That seems like the best solution right now.

I glance at Daisy who teeters back on two legs of her chair again. "You don't want your cake?" I ask her. Of course I noticed that *she* was the one to push her plate into my area, offering me a second slice when I haven't even touched my first.

She shrugs. "I would eat it, but you know . . ." She rolls her eyes and glances at Ryke, as though they've already had this same conversation. I shouldn't have asked. I know she's not allowed to gain an obscene amount of weight because of modeling. So she watches what she eats, lest our mother criticize her waistline even more.

Ryke has his plate in his hand, and he leans back in his chair like Daisy. Her date hunches forward, now playing a game on his phone. Jeez, he really doesn't want to be here. Ryke has a good view of Daisy and vice versa. He scoops a large bite of gooey chocolate fudge on his spoon. "This looks so fucking good," he teases her. "So moist." Okay, I know he says that I always think sexual thoughts. But that was sexual. *Moist* is a gross word, and *I'm* a sex addict. He's definitely trying to ruffle her.

I don't approve of his methods.

But at least she refuses to glance at him.

I can tell he's trying to get her to eat, and I think he enjoys pushing people's buttons. The only problem: I think my youngest sister is made of armor—kind of like him.

He licks the rim of the spoon and then sucks the cake off it, letting out a deep, masculine moan.

My eyebrows scrunch at him and I mouth, *stop*. I know his plan won't work. Daisy won't eat if she feels like our mother's going to scold her for it.

Ryke keeps the spoon in his mouth and he glares back at me. Then he points at Daisy's plate. I sigh heavily and slide it in front of her.

"Oh no," she says to me, "you are not in on his stupid plan."

"You love chocolate," I remind her.

"I love a lot of things I can't have," she says pointedly.

True. I shrug at Ryke, giving up already. I'm not so resilient. Ryke, on the other hand . . .

"Daisy," he coos, waving his spoon around the air to try to get her to look at him. She barely stirs. He tries a different tactic. He dips two fingers into the gooey chocolate filling. *No*, I internally scream in my head. He's not going to . . .

My eyes widen and my mouth falls as his fingers rise to his lips. What the fuck is he doing?! Ryke . . . needs to stop pushing the line with her. He might find it amusing, but I'm afraid she'll take his teasing as a sign of something . . . more. This. Isn't. Good.

Daisy frowns at my expression, and she follows my gaze for the first time. Ryke puts his two (not-so-chaste) fingers in his mouth. I am screaming at him in my head. Even as he sucks the gooey ganache off, he shuts his eyes, faking a fucking chocolate orgasm just so she'll eat the damn cake.

Daisy snorts and tilts back a little farther in her chair to act all cool and composed. And then, the legs begin to slip underneath her. I gasp, picturing her smacking backwards on the ground. But Ryke is faster than my frozen joints. His eyes have already snapped open. He reaches out and grabs the top of her chair, setting both of them on four legs at the same time.

My sister puts her hands on the table, leaning forward as though a roller coaster just came to an abrupt stop. She looks winded and stunned all at the same time.

Ryke barely misses a beat. He pushes an extra spoon in front of her.

And to my surprise, she actually picks up the silverware and scoops a big bite of cake on it. She hesitates for a second.

"It's not arsenic," he says.

Her lips rise in a small smile. "Your hips also don't have to be measured in the morning."

"They can be," he tells her. "Will you eat the fucking cake if I measure my hips?"

"And your ass," she says.

"You want to know the size of my ass?" His brow rises.

"Yep."

"Eat the cake."

She hides her growing smile and takes a large bite. She closes her eyes and sinks back into her chair, relaxing more than before and melting into chocolate heaven. "I wish I could eat this every day."

"You can, but then you'd be 'fat.'" He uses air quotes.

"The tragedy," she says, pushing around the rest of her cake and smashing it until it's a mushy lump.

"Okay, enough abusing the fucking dessert."

"Do you always say *fuck*?" she asks. "I don't think I've ever been around you where you haven't said it at least once."

"What can I say? It's my favorite fucking word." He flashes a dry smile.

"You know what's scary," she says, pointing her spoon at him. "You're a journalism major, aren't you? Shouldn't you be a wordsmith?"

"Shouldn't you be a voiceless mannequin?" he retorts.

"Touché." With this, she takes another bite, but since her dessert is a pile of goo, she steals a piece of mine.

I can't concentrate on Daisy anymore, not when Rose springs from her chair, following my mother who suddenly stands and motions to her with an icy finger.

I scoot from my chair, tailing them as they head towards a lounge room for special guests, meaning family. A presence weaves behind me, keeping up with my pace. I glance over my shoulder and see the all-American build, the swept brown-blond hair, the ugly blue eyes—I hate him. I wish he'd leave me alone.

But Aaron Wells isn't going to stop me from being there for my sister. Not when she's been around for me. I shut the door behind me as I enter the lounge area, which is filled with buttoned couches, a minibar, and a couple queen-style chairs. Nothing too fancy except the chandelier in the center and the gold wallpaper.

Jonathan Hale and my father sit on one of the navy couches, whiskeys in hand. They only look up when I drift farther into the room and away from the door. Aaron should be here in a matter of minutes.

I try not to approach Lo's father. I don't want to talk to him without Loren present. Because he wouldn't want me to. My dad keeps him in a long discussion about stocks, but I feel Jonathan's hot gaze on my body, most likely glaring.

Rose stands still, fingers clenched around her champagne glass, full now. *A new one again?* She seems utterly poised, though. A string of pearls choke my mother's bony neck, and she has hair nearly identical to my sister's dark chocolate. Maybe Daisy's comment in the car has been stirring Rose too—about being so similar to our mother. No one in their right mind would want to be compared to her.

"What is your problem?" our mother snaps. "You've been incredibly rude to your date. Olivia Barnes heard you from across the room, scolding him like he was a child."

"He is a child," Rose retorts. "You set me up with a nineteen-year-old who has never switched on the goddamn news in his life."

My mother grabs hold of the nearest chair, as though Rose physically impaled her with that curse word. "Language, Rose."

"Grow up, Mother," she retorts. "I have."

I take a step towards them to ease the situation, but the door opens and Aaron slips through and begins to walk over to me. In order to dodge him, I glance at my father and decide to take a seat beside him.

"Hi, Dad," I say with a smile, scooting onto the same couch.

"Hey, sweetheart."

I sit on the edge of the cushion, anxious and timid, especially as Aaron waits by the bar, wondering if he should approach I guess. And all the while, I feel Jonathan staring between me, Aaron, my father and my sister, taking in everything with a scrutiny that I do not enjoy.

"Should you break them up?" I ask my father and scratch my arm.

"They always fight," he says. "Better to just let them work it out." He grabs my hand. "Have you been biting your nails? You haven't done that since you were a kid."

I shrug, keeping an eye on my mother and sister. "With Lo gone . . ." I trail off, not able to say the rest or tell him the whole truth. I shrug again, a go-to response right now.

My mother's voice escalates. "And what did he say that was so bad?! What could it have been, Rose?"

"He didn't know who David Cameron is!"

I frown. *I* have no idea who he is.

My mother looks equally lost.

Rose chokes on a laugh. "He's the Prime Minister of the United Kingdom, Mother."

"That doesn't make him unintelligent."

"It does to me," Rose tells her. "I don't want to share someone's company if they can't count to five. I'd rather hang myself."

So dramatic. And I'm assuming family gets a pass on Rose Calloway's incredibly high friendship standards.

I swear I hear my father mutter, "That's my girl." After a short moment, he nudges my arm. "How is Lo doing?"

Jonathan's muscles twitch at this question, and as I look over, his eyebrows rise, waiting for me to answer.

"I'm not sure," I say truthfully. "I haven't been in contact with him. I'm not supposed to until he gets further into the program."

My father nods. "I think what he's doing is admirable. Really admirable. Not many young kids realize that they have a problem when they do."

I glance to Jonathan. "Do you . . . feel the same?" I wonder, gaining a little confidence.

His lips upturn in that bitter, amused smile, so familiar that my breath knocks from my chest. It reminds me so much of Lo—that's the scary part. "I think he should have come to me first. We could have solved it together. That's why I'm so angry, Lily. I gave him the life he has, and he walked away from me."

"That's not entirely true . . ." I trail off, scared of his pulsing eyes. He took away Lo's trust fund. He refused to believe that Lo had a problem. He may have wanted Lo to stay in his life, and maybe he was frightened by the idea of admitting that he has the same addiction. Maybe he didn't want to confront his own demons. And in the end, he left Lo no choice but to leave and seek help elsewhere.

Before Jonathan responds, I feel Aaron sit by my side. His arm wraps around the back of the couch behind me, as though we're together. I stay stiff and wiggle closer to the edge of the cushion, not wanting to touch any part of him.

He introduces himself to Jonathan and my father, and they all act cordial. But I am utterly frozen inside. To make matters worse, Rose and my mother's fight has increased to new levels.

"I don't need a man to fulfill me," Rose sneers. She points at my mother with her champagne glass, the liquid sloshing onto the floor. She hardly notices.

My mother inhales, her collarbone jutting out and cheeks

caving in. "You're so naïve, Rose. You think this world is going to respect you? You're living in a fantasy," she nearly spits. "Women like us have a figment of power. In the end, we're all marionettes to men. Accept it now."

Rose's nose flares, her cat-colored eyes piercing. "Lily is with Lo," she says. "Why would you ever cause her such pain and make another man escort her?"

"This again?" she snaps.

"Yes," Rose retorts. "This *again*."

My mother sighs. "What if Lo never returns? What if he chooses to be single by the end of this? I am creating a backup plan for her. I'm giving her options."

Her words sting my chest, and I hardly notice Aaron laughing about something with my father, as if they're long-lost buddies. Lo will return. Won't he? He will come back to me. He'll want me . . . but the doubt festers in my soul. And I try to rid it with a confident nod, but I'm not feeling so assured right now. Not when my mother has zero faith in the man I love.

"Options?" Rose shrieks. "You've never given any of us an option. You know what option I would have liked? The option to disown my own mother."

"Stop it," she snaps. Her chin raises, but I can tell she holds in a breath, a sign that Rose's words have truly started to infiltrate and infect and seep and hurt. "I helped you grow your company."

"And you never let me forget it," Rose sneers. The door cracks open, but no one notices Connor Cobalt slipping in except me. He has on an expensive tux, but his equally expensive smile is locked away. He wears a dark frown and stands guard by the door, watching Rose with serious, calm eyes. I am so grateful he's here. Because I'm scared for Rose. I'm not sure how to calm her. I'm not sure what words will take away the pain of tonight.

I wish my mother could hear what Rose is saying. I feel like she's screaming to be heard, but no one can understand. No one *gets it*. I stand up, about to go to her, but Aaron grabs my hand and tugs me back down. He says something to Jonathan and wraps his arm around my shoulder.

I'm too fixated on my sister to push him off and start an argument over here. Connor crosses his arms over his chest and glances at me. He looks at Aaron, and he's about to come over but I shake my head and mouth, *her*.

He hesitates and nods to me in acceptance.

"What do you want from me?!" our mother yells. "I've been there for you your whole life!"

"I want you to say you're wrong! I want you to apologize for this evening and for putting me with Matthew Collins and for thinking I'm a tool that a man can use and dispose. I'm your *daughter*!" Rose screams, angry tears burning from the corners of her eyes. "You're supposed to love me by telling me that I'm beautiful and I'm smart and no man is good enough for me. You're *not* supposed to tell me that I'm worth less than I am."

My mother inches forward a little. "Can you listen to yourself, Rose? We're at an event for your father's company, and you're making it about you. You think you're a woman? You're acting like a child."

Rose stares directly at our mother. Unflinching, unwavering. And very coldly, she says, "Go to hell."

My mother's hand flies and connects with Rose's cheek, the slap heard like a gunshot in the lounge room. Jonathan, Aaron and my father go silent.

Rose drops her champagne glass, and it shatters on the marble floor. She stares in a trance at the ground, as though she felt nothing when the contact was made. My heart hammers so hard that the only thing I hear is the pulsing in my ears.

I have never seen my mother hit anyone. Maybe because I

spent most days with Lo. Maybe because I haven't been attuned to the happenings of my family. But the shock strikes me cold. I don't have the same relationship with our mother that Rose does. We're not hostile towards each other. In fact, we're . . . nothing really. I say hi, she asks me how Lo is, and we move on.

I don't wish for this. To be silently boiling, having to restrain myself from spewing hateful words and from feeling a hand sting my cheek. No one would ask for that. And I want to take Rose away from it, but she's twenty-two.

The damage is done.

I think we're all old enough to feel the scars of our upbringing. Now we just have to find a way to heal.

Our mother lets out a breath and says, "I'm sorry . . . We'll talk later. Clearly we've both had a lot to drink . . ." She shoots a quick glance to my father, and he stands and excuses himself too, following her out of the lounge room and back to the party.

Aaron keeps pulling me closer to his lap, and I swat him away, keeping track of Rose in case she needs me. I doubt she'd like to be reminded that she's losing control. My interference is like saying, "Your fucked-up little sister is going to rescue you. How screwed up does that make you, Rose Calloway?" Which is why I asked Connor here in the first place.

He approaches her like a man tiptoeing towards a sleeping lion. "Rose," he breathes. "Darling . . ."

She's shaking. Her arms tremble, and her eyes keep growing wider and wider. "She's wrong," Rose whispers. I can practically hear her chant in her head: *I'm not like her. I'm not like her.*

Connor closes the gap between them, and his hands touch her face, holding her cheeks, and gently soothing the reddened one with a soft stroke. "Look at me, hun."

Rose tries to push him off. "Why . . ." She keeps shaking her head, but he holds her tight, trying to make her focus.

"I'm right here," he tells her.

She weakly tries to push him off again, not really wanting to, and he grabs her hand. "I don't need you," she reminds him. But the silent tears start flowing. She's crying in front of him, actually letting Connor see her cracks. I wonder if the emotions are too hard to bottle since she drank so much. "I don't need you," she repeats, her voice breaking.

"You're right," he says softly. "You don't need a man, Rose." He pauses and I barely hear him whisper, "But you do need me."

She looks down and then back at him, her lashes wet and glistening, making her face look more porcelain and delicate than I ever remember. "What are you doing here?" she asks with a shake of her head. "You shouldn't be here." Her tears drip onto his hands, both rising back to her face. He tucks a flyaway piece of hair behind her ear, and his eyes graze the welt on her cheek.

"A little bird told me you were upset."

Rose lets out a choked cry. "Are you crazy?" She places her hands on his arms that hold her face but doesn't force him away anymore. "You're talking to birds now?"

His lips twitch into a weak smile. "I'd talk to any woodland creature if it gave me answers about you."

"Would you walk through fire for me?" she deadpans.

"Yes," he accepts the challenge.

"Brand my name on your ass?"

"Possibly."

"Drink cow's blood in my honor?"

"You're so fucking weird," he says with the biggest grin.

She breaks into a smile, but it's a pained one and then she starts sobbing. Like truly sobbing. He wraps his arms around her, and she falls into the hug. He guides her to the bathroom door to the right, and they disappear inside.

The room has almost cleared out, and I remember who I'm

actually sitting next to. Aaron leans close and whispers in my ear, "I will ruin you the way Loren ruined me."

I gape. A mixture of shock and fear prick me at the sudden proclamation. Bad timing can't even begin to describe tonight. I try to stand, but he grips my wrist so tight that when I jerk up, he brings me right back down.

Jonathan, frighteningly the only other person in the room, sets his whiskey on the glass end table "Is there a problem here?" he asks Aaron.

"Didn't Lily tell you?" he says with a false smile. "We're dating now."

I shake my head quickly. "No we aren't."

Jonathan stares between us, reading my closed body language and Aaron's aggressive movement. And then he says, "Get the fuck out of my sight, kid."

"Excuse me?" Aaron jerks back in shock.

Jonathan stands and straightens his tie. "Lily." He holds out his hand for me to take it, and I am momentarily struck by the change of events. Is Jonathan Hale really saving me from this douchebag right now?

I shouldn't take his hand. I should spit at it and walk away. Lo would. But he'd also kill me if I didn't leave Aaron when I had the chance. And I'm not an idiot. I want to be far, far away from him. So I stand, and this time, Aaron lets me disentangle from him. But I don't touch Jonathan. I walk right on past him and head for the door, my exit in view.

Before I leave, I hear Aaron say, "She's a slut, you know that, right?"

"And you think I don't know what my son did to you? I helped him ruin you, you piece of shit," he says.

Lo told his father about Aaron? About how he tormented him? I don't question this. Because Lo's relationship with his father was a taboo topic between us. It fluttered in and out of our conversations, and I was only allowed a glimmer. And I know, without a doubt, that Jonathan Hale would move mountains for Lo. He just needs to be in the right mood first.

"Like father, like son," Aaron says.

I have to leave, but I'm glued next to the door. I glance back one last time, and Jonathan's eyes briefly flicker to me. "That girl is practically my daughter-in-law." He sets a firm hand on Aaron's shoulder. "If I hear you did anything to her, you'll wish all you had to deal with was my son. Now get out of my fucking face."

I am so confused.

I don't know who to root for anymore.

I don't know what sides to take or who to praise or condemn.

All I know is that my family is royally fucked up. And no amount of money or luxury can fix these problems. Maybe they even helped cause them.

I enter the grand ballroom where people are wandering, standing up and chatting as though it's cocktail hour. Streamers and gold and black balloons lie on the carpet. I missed some sort of celebration. I kick them away and spot my mother by the stage.

What possesses me to approach her? I'm not quite sure. But as she talks to my father, I feel like I should just say something. Maybe help explain Rose's feelings but in a softer, gentler manner. *Maybe she'll listen to me*, I think. She never really has, but it's a nice thought anyway.

I approach, and my father excuses himself to go mingle with some older corporate men. She looks a little stricken, her lips pinched and her hand a bit shaky. "What is it?" she asks, on edge.

"Are you okay?" Why do I start with this? Of course she's not okay, and does she really deserve my sympathy after slapping

Rose? No, not one bit. But I can't take it back, and her domineering posture sucks my confidence dry.

"Fine," she says, turning her back on me almost immediately. She waves to her friend and acts like I'm a piece of furniture that chose to bump into her leg.

I try again. "I think she's just trying to express herself, but she doesn't know how to do it without yelling . . ."

My mother continues to wave at her friend in the distance. She puts her hand on my shoulder, patting me once. "Sure, I have to go talk to Barbara. Find Aaron. He'll keep you company." With this, she drifts into the pack and wears the fakest smile. I watch her hug a bejeweled woman in a red bandage dress.

I feel like she just punched me in the gut.

Ryke suddenly sidles next to me. "There you are." He hands me a glass of water, and I thankfully accept it with a smile. "You okay? Nothing happened did it . . . ?" His brows furrow, and he glances behind me, probably looking around for Aaron, who I'm sure has ceased and desisted. Jonathan Hale's warning was strong enough to listen to. And Aaron isn't that stupid.

"No," I say, "nothing like that." We both stare at the party that seems to relax—calm after the split tension. "Unchained Melody" by the Righteous Brothers begins playing. Couples grab their significant other, swaying to the lovely tune.

"Who was that guy anyway?"

"An old enemy," I tell him, watching an elderly woman put her cheek on her husband's shoulder.

Ryke stuffs a hand into his suit jacket and nods, as though fully understanding what it's like to have enemies. I have no doubt that he has his fair share.

"My mother slapped my sister," I say, completely detached from the words.

Ryke doesn't even flinch. He just stares off at the dancers. "Funny, my mother did the same thing to me when I told her I was coming here." He sips his own water.

"I think your father saved me tonight."

Ryke stays quiet, letting this sink in.

We're so fucked up. That's all I can think and process.

And another batch of balloons begins to fall at the end of the song. The ceiling flickers with soft-lit multicolored lights.

I made it.

No guy touched me. I didn't touch them. Sex was the last thing on my mind tonight.

Each day feels like an obstacle.

And a victory.

February

Six

Three different pints of ice cream squeeze in between my thighs, the chill seeping into my Ms. Marvel pajama pants. Valentine's Day sucks. Connor and Rose planned their date for the past week at some fancy restaurant, leaving me to gorge on Chunky Monkey, Half Baked and Cherry Garcia alone. I watch late-night cartoons on the high-def television, being transported back to my childhood years with *Looney Tunes*. With each "that's all, folks," my heart thuds and I turn my head, about to mention how much I liked or hated the episode to Lo.

Who's not here.

He hasn't emailed yet. Fourteen days into the month, and I haven't heard a peep from him, not even a mention that he's alive and well. The last couple days of January, he sent me a bouquet of red roses. I think he meant for them to arrive today. At least I hope so—that way I'd know he still thinks about *us* and hasn't planned to end our relationship for good.

My mother's comment at the Fizzle event hasn't calmed my worries either. If she thinks I need a "backup" plan, I wonder who else believes he'll ditch me when he returns home.

That paranoia—it festers like a sore. I glance at the glass

vase on my end table. The roses droop and wilt, but the card sits open. Remembering the words in Lo's messy scrawl eases me a little.

These are real.

My chest swells. These are real.

Reality TV blares through my flat-screen. Nothing beats faking sick on a school day and staying home in pajamas to watch trashy television. I lazily unwrap the individual chocolates from the heart-shaped Valentine's box on my lap when a knock bangs on my door.

For a moment, I debate on hiding the sweets, but I go against it. Too much work, and really, what's the probability that my mother is on the other side of the door? The last time she willfully entered my room was probably two years ago when our housekeeper accidentally hung one of Daisy's debutante dresses in my closet. I opened my door to find my mother hysterically screaming at the air—haphazardly flinging my clothes in wild distress and anger. When she found the maroon gown, she told me I should have realized the dress was misplaced. And then she stomped away.

Leaving me alone.

It's safe to say the knock did not come from her.

My door slowly swings open without an invitation, and I immediately relax. Lo fills the archway, wearing his Dalton Academy uniform: black slacks, white button-down and the skinny blue tie that has been loosened at his neck. It fits him well . . . maybe *too* well.

He scans me in a long once-over, and then his brows rise in accusation. "No runny nose, no clammy skin, cough or even a wad of tissues," he says. "I must say, Lil, you are the worst at faking sick."

"Good thing I'm not really trying."

"Why didn't you tell me you were going to skip?" he asks, still lingering by the doorframe. Odd, but I try not to question it.

"I didn't want you to feel obligated to skip with me." I straighten up and lean against my headboard. The truth: pretending to be in a relationship with Lo consists of PDA. Lots of it. Since it's Valentine's Day, I didn't want to be in class and have a candy gram delivered to me. Or be in the hallways trying to escalate the flirty looks and make-out sessions just to show off our fake romance. I'm exhausted just thinking about it.

His eyes land on my nightstand. Twenty-four red roses bloom in a crystal vase. The little card sticks out from the sea of petals. I already read it out loud this morning at Daisy's request. *Happy Valentine's Day. With all my love, Lo.*

"Nice touch," I tell him after the moment of silence. "Daisy nearly died when she saw them, and I think my mom was really pleased." We're definitely selling our fake relationship well. Six months in and no one has questioned it thus far.

"Do you like them?" he wonders, undoing the rest of his tie.

I break away to look at the roses again. No boy has ever sent me flowers. On my birthday, the house will be overflowing with lilies to commemorate the occasion, but they're usually from family or friends of my parents.

At first I thought these roses were another pretend gesture of our fake relationship. Now that Lo asks me if I like them, I'm not so sure anymore.

"They're pretty and much better than lilies," I admit.

"I'm the best fake boyfriend ever then," he says with an easy smile. And my suspicions sputter out. *Fake boyfriend.* Of course. He finally closes the distance between us and plops down next to me. He tilts my box of chocolates with his finger and grimaces. "You're nasty."

"I don't like the fillings." All the chocolates are bitten in half and some have been spit back out into the box. I have yet to find one that isn't revolting.

"Well, I can't look at this." He closes the box and sets it on the nightstand. He scoots nearer, leans a little closer and gently rests his palm on my forehead, successfully invading my space and causing my breath to whoosh from my lungs.

"You're not warm," he says softly and drops his hand to my neck and lightly presses. "Lymph nodes aren't swollen."

I narrow my eyes. "How do you know about lymph nodes?"

"I had the flu last year," he reminds me. "Shhh, and let me finish my diagnosis."

My cheeks grow hot.

"You're flushed." He nods and tries to suppress a growing smile. He puts his hands on my shoulders and leans my head back against the pillow, kneeling and towering over me. "I have to listen to your heart."

"No," I retort weakly, not in the mood to play with him. Not when it always has to end with me tense and aroused and needy. He loves to tease me, and I worry about the day where I won't have the strength to say *no*.

He ignores me and places his ear to the bareness of my collarbone, the place peeking from my V-neck shirt. I inhale a sharp breath, his face too near. After a long moment, he rises a little and says, "I knew it."

My eyes narrow. "Knew what?"

His hot gaze traces my lips, and then flits back up to my eyes. "You're suffering from a clear case of . . ." His mouth brushes my ear. ". . . *infatuation*."

I slap him on the arm and try to sit up, but he's ready for me. He leans in and tickles my waist and hips so quickly that I never see him coming. And I laugh and squirm beneath him until I cry out for him to stop, happy tears squeezing from my eyes.

We settle down with heavy breath. Both lying on our sides, our feet tangled together, we stare at each other in the easy silence.

"And what's the cure?" I ask, playing along this time, even though I know I shouldn't.

He wears a crooked grin that could melt a thousand girls.

Very softly, he says, "Me."

My eyes pin to his soft lips, begging me to press mine to them. He leans in a little, but doesn't close the gap, uncertainty still lingering. It feels like his body pulls me into it, a magnetic force too strong to fight. I scoot nearer, and my foot brushes his bare ankle. His breathing deepens.

I can't stop staring at his lips, imagining what they'd feel like against mine. Soft, forceful, hungry. My resilience sputters out and I bridge the distance, landing a quick kiss on his lips before pulling away. I think I hoped the chaste, PG-rated kiss would satisfy my desires. Nope. In fact, all I want to do is wipe that silly smile off his face with a deeper one.

"What was that?" he asks, amused. His lips skim mine and fall back teasingly.

"My cure," I say, playing along. It makes this less real. Right? Still on our sides, our bodies have moved closer and closer on their own mission, separating from our brains. His hand runs up and down my back, stopping at the dip above my waist.

"That was the wrong dose," he whispers.

"Oh."

It only takes him a moment before he leans in and our lips mesh together, mimicking the state of our bodies. His hand cups the back of my head and he sucks on the bottom of my lip, making them ache all over again. My lower half starts to move out of instinct, pressing harder into him as the kiss deepens. His tongue slips into my mouth and a moan escapes my lips.

I have to detach. "Lo," I whisper, trying to clear my mind and assess what the hell my body is doing. Literally, I'm gripping his shirt and my leg has somehow made it over his hip.

"It's Valentine's Day," he reminds me, breaking away from the game. "I want to give you something."

Something. Vague—and in my perverted mind, I'm thinking all types of nefarious things.

"You already gave me flowers." But I don't remove myself from this position—pressed so tightly against him that I can feel the slow rhythm of his heartbeat against my chest.

"Something better."

I want it. Even if I don't know what *it* is. But there are some lines I can't cross with Lo, no matter what he offers me, so I ask, "What?"

He pulls my head into his chest and brushes my hair back. I feel his warm breath as he leans into my ear and whispers, "I want to make you come."

Inside, I am cheering at the idea but my head starts shaking on another, different automatic setting. I move my head back while my body stays glued to him.

"No?" His eyes rise and he props himself up just a little by his elbow. "I thought it was the perfect Valentine's gift, especially since I planned to keep all your clothes on."

My heart begins to beat even quicker at the prospect. We've done things since we started "fake" dating. When we practice making out, it sometimes leads to touching and stuff, but I've managed to stop before it progressed to a climax. Sex isn't the same thing as fooling around. The latter of which has been a staple in our pretend relationship. It's been a couple weeks since my last lay, and I already made plans for this Saturday to get my next fix. I strike at any opportunity to attend a party thrown by a public school kid, and I don't know if doing something with Lo today would be right.

"I'm going to that bonfire party this Saturday," I end up saying.

I wait for him to pull away, but he doesn't. "Me too," he breathes and lightly kisses me on the lips.

"I'm going to have sex there."

"I'm going to get wasted." He presses his lips quickly to mine once more and then rubs his thumb over the sensitive skin on my ear. I practically shudder at the touch.

"Lo."

"Lily." His fingers drop to his button. I stare in fixation at the small movements.

Somehow I'm able to mutter, "I didn't get you anything."

His lips quirk but he doesn't say anything else. I can see the hem of his boxer briefs, and I realize I have to move away from him so he can slide his pants completely off. I detach myself, scooting back as the spot between my legs throbs.

My mind charges into convince-mode. *I can do this. I can stop myself from something worse happening. He said I get to keep my clothes on. That means no sex. That means we can do this and it'll still be okay.*

His flask slips out of his pants as he jerks them off. I pick it up easily, debating on taking a large swig. Maybe it'll ease my warring thoughts. Silencing either the part of me that says *stop* or the other that says *fuck yeah.*

Now in his boxer briefs, Lo turns and sees me with his alcohol. He takes it quickly from me, his eyes still light. He raises his drink. "Mine," he says. He takes my hand in his and places it over the bulge in his boxer briefs. "Yours."

Ohhhhh . . . shit. I'm doomed.

I think I should remove my hand, especially since normal people would probably jerk back at this point. But something keeps it right there. On him.

He doesn't seem surprised by this. In fact, he continues to strip in front of me, unbuttoning his shirt and tugging it off. It feels like my birthday or something, only I have to keep reminding myself that this is Lo and not some stripper in one of my fantasies.

Now nearly naked, I pull my hand away, and he playfully folds the hem of his boxer briefs. I gasp and he grins. "On or off, love? Your choice."

My brain zeros out into nothingness. It cannot compute his question. "I'll take that as a *you can't handle it*," he says huskily and leaves his underwear on. No. I definitely cannot handle seeing his dick right now. I can barely handle breathing at this point.

He climbs onto my body and leans in for another deep kiss. It's different feeling bare skin against my fully-clothed body. With my conquests, it's usually the other way around. I like this though. Running my hands over his bare back and down to his ass. My body pulses for something more, and I hear his words like a chorus in my head—*I want to make you come*. All protests and sensibility leave my mind completely.

His kisses suddenly turn feathery light again, teasing me a little. When he lands another PG-kiss on my lips, I let out a long groan. I can barely take this much longer. I am not a Disney princess. I do not swoon over kissing unless it involves tongue and force and leads to other lustful events.

Deciding to take matters into my own hands . . . or hips, I buck up a little so that our pelvises meet. The contact feels much better. I just . . . need to be closer.

Lo pushes my body down in response and presses into me, the hardness in his pants grinding against the ache in between my legs. His lips turn from light to determined, devouring mine with rapt attention. And as he rubs against me, the tension escalates, pushing my body into a hyperaware state. Every touch sets me off, and all I want right now is for my clothes to disappear. For me to feel him inside. For the ache to be taken away with a thrust and a blissful high.

My trembling hands try to grip the bottom of my shirt and yank it off. I get it halfway up before Lo stops moving and puts his hand on mine. "No. Your clothes stay on," he breathes. His lips are red and raw, and I can barely move my eyes off them.

I blink.

Lo pulls each finger off my shirt and then laces them with his. His lips find the nape of my neck and then glide to my earlobe, nibbling and kissing. My hips lift as he presses down, and I can feel him getting harder and harder, adding to my arousal. His lips move down to my chest, tracing their way even farther across my shirt, his hands tight against my hips.

He kisses me again, his tongue flicking into my mouth.

I'm dying inside. I want *more*.

I lift my hips and this time he grabs my ass and squeezes. Hard. I let out a long moan and my body shudders. He keeps me tight against him, as his hands move and knead my inner thighs all the way up. Slowly. Slowly. Slowly. Avoiding that one spot that demands attention.

I let out a whimper and he sets me back down. His breathing deepens, and he starts moving his body even faster, pushing and making sure to rub himself against me. It works. The tension starts to build and I rock with him as he finds my mouth again. And then all of a sudden, everything explodes. I have to break away from his lips, burying my face into his bicep as my orgasm bursts into waves.

He cups the back of my head and holds me as I shudder in euphoria and bliss and the high that turns me into a wild beast.

It only takes a couple minutes before it flits away, leaving me with a sinking feeling. Without the urges, my mind clears and the enormity of what I just did hits me cold. I break away from Lo, refusing to meet his eyes that follow me in utter concern.

I quickly grab my phone on the table.

"What are you doing?" he asks, insecurity bubbling in his voice.

A lump has taken residence in my throat, but I manage to mutter, "Nothing . . . just . . . clothes on." I motion to his pants on the floor. I can't look at him nearly naked. I don't trust myself anymore.

He fumbles around with his clothes while my heart beats wildly. And then . . . I find it.

"I think we just had sex," I say in horror, staring at the small screen on my phone.

"What?" He frowns and walks over, still shirtless but at least he has his pants on.

I hold up my phone. "*Non-penetrative sex,*" he reads and then licks his bottom lip in thought. His eyes meet mine. "That's not *real* sex, Lil."

"That's not what this says." I continue reading. "Outercourse. I think we had outercourse! Oh my God." My heart is going to detonate. I crossed a line. I let myself get caught up in all the mixed-up feelings and I crossed a fucking line.

"Whoa!" Lo puts his hands on my cheeks, forcing me to look at him. "Take some breaths." He waits for me and then says, "It's

Wikipedia. Not the fucking Holy Grail. You get to choose what you consider *real* sex for *you*. Okay?" His eyes look a little guilty, and I feel even worse for making him remorseful for something that I clearly wanted.

"Okay," I say with a nod. "Then that wasn't real. Outercourse doesn't count."

Relief fills him.

"But," I continue. "I don't think we should do it again." I don't trust myself.

He drops his hands from my cheeks. "That's fine," he says, sounding a little detached. "I just . . ." he shakes his head. "It's Valentine's Day."

"I know." I can't let him go with that. "And it was the best present I've ever gotten. Honest."

He smiles and kisses me lightly on the temple before picking his flask up on the desk.

I let out a deep breath. *Never again.* But as I remember the way he looked at me, commanding and determined and so very powerful, as though making me cry was his sole goal in life—well, I know I may never find that with someone else.

Never again is a very, very large price to pay.

But we're not really together, after all. We're just two friends playing make-believe.

Seven

couple months at Princeton and I stopped going to class again. Seeing people walk around campus with smiles and laughs puts knots in my stomach, so I've been doing all the coursework and attend only for the exams. I've been pulling C's, which is better than failing.

Rose scolds me when I sit at home, moping again. I guess I just feel like February has turned into Day 1 without Lo—all the pain that crushed me from the first moment he left swallows me back in its dark, black abyss. I kept hoping that he'd email me by now. And he hasn't.

But my vibrator keeps me company. My fantasies do too. But I rarely climax. It's like my sadness has eked out any possibility of feeling that high again.

To keep me busy and to lift my spirits, I decide to change my ways a little. For the past three days, I've consumed my time at Calloway Couture, making good on a bet that I lost with Connor. I promised him that I'd help Rose at her blossoming fashion company by being her assistant.

Which I've quickly found out just means being the errand bitch.

Although I do have my own desk that sits off to the side in a spacious city loft. The room is decked out with racks of dresses, blouses, coats, boots and handbags. Rose glances from her computer in her dictatorial office—a glass cubicle that literally overlooks the whole room. She has two other girls manning desks near me in the center. They're in charge of social media, websites and inventory.

While they're productive members of Rose's company, I'm more like a little hamster running along a stationary wheel. I fetch coffee and file notes. Busy work. But it beats masturbating for a whole two hours without any sort of release. I did that yesterday. Not fun.

After a short minute, Rose exits her office and struts over to my white desk. "Did you get the business card I left you?" She made me a whole box, as though solidifying my position as "Assistant of CEO" for the future.

"Yep, they're pretty." They're even "lily" scented. I asked her if her cards smelled like roses and she shot me a cold look. Apparently, Mom had the idea to scent the business cards, and Rose had to go along with it. Our mother has her claws in Rose's company in more ways than just one. Rose started the business at fifteen, too young to realize that our mother would deem herself co-founder. She acts like a silent partner, but Rose would rather she wasn't involved at all, considering the only contribution she makes is painful irritation. She's a nosy gnat, but she's also someone easy to love if she agrees with you.

"No, not those cards. The therapist."

"Oh . . . yeah, it was taped on the computer screen. Pretty hard to miss."

"Have you called?"

I lick my dry lips. "No, not yet. I thought you were still researching."

"No, I'm done. That's the one. I know she is, but if you don't like her, then I'll keep looking. But you should meet her at least. She's a lovely woman."

I inhale. "Okay, yeah. I'll meet her soon." Maybe she'll prescribe me some drugs and take these feelings away. That sounds nice.

As her heels clap back to her office, I Hulk-grip the mouse and click my way through Microsoft Excel with efficiency. Rose has detailed my tasks and their importance by numerical code. I realize that calling my therapist is number one. Checking shoe sizes for shipment to Macy's is number thirty-five.

Just as I reach for my phone to make an appointment, it buzzes on the desk, vibrating across the glass surface. I frown and check the screen, an unknown number popping up. *Could it be . . . ?* I frantically pick up the cell, my heart hammering. If it's him, what do I say? I hesitate, words coursing through my brain in overdrive. I don't know if there's any right way to start a conversation. Maybe it's not him. Maybe it's just hopeful thinking. He's not even supposed to be calling until March. Isn't that what Ryke said?

I drown my insecurities and put the receiver to my ear. I inhale a deep breath before saying, "Hello?"

"Hi."

He called me. *Lo* called me. I let the words sink in with the sound of his deep voice. I lean forward on the desk, putting a hand to my eyes to shield any tears that'll threaten to fall. I'd rather Rose *not* see me from her office and end the call before it even starts.

I've thought about all the things I would say to Lo in email and on the phone in March, but they've breezed out of my mind since the first ring. I'm left with a not-so-eloquent reply. "You called."

I hear him shifting, as though adjusting the phone and holding it up with a shoulder to his ear. I picture one hand on the wall and a long line of guys waiting behind him to use the black cord phone. Sort of like prison. I don't know why I relate them. He's not in jail. He's in rehab. The latter of which will *help* him. I'm sure my new therapist will psychoanalyze that comparison.

"I've been doing well, so they're letting me get in touch with my family." He pauses. "You're the first person I called." He lets out a weak laugh, and I imagine him rubbing his lips. "Hell, you're the only one I'll probably call."

"Not Ryke?" I wonder.

"I've seen Ryke," he explains quickly, brushing over the topic. "How have you been?"

"Why didn't you email before? Ryke said you'd be able to this month." Yes, I dodged the question about me. I need to hear him explain this before I can quantify anything going on in my life.

He pauses for a long time. "I planned to. I sat down at the computer and stared at the screen for a full hour."

I bite my thumbnail. "What happened?"

"I'd write a couple sentences, reread them, and delete. Everything sounded so fucking stupid. I mean, I'm not a writer. So by the end of the hour, all I had was 'hi' and I was so pissed that I just walked away."

Sounds like something he'd do. "I'm not a good writer either." I glance up at the glass office, and Rose busily talks on her own cellphone, back turned to me. Good. "I'm glad you called."

"Yeah?" His voice breaks a little, and my breathing deepens. I want things to go back to normal. I don't want our relationship to change, but I know it has to. I just hope it's better than before. Not worse.

"What have you been doing there?" I ask. "Are you going to come home early? What's it like? Have you met anyone else?

How's your counselor? Is the food any good?" All these questions tumble from my lips, and I stop for a second, wondering if I scared him away.

"It's been all right. I'm not done with the program, so I'll be here for a while still." He clears his throat. "So, how are you doing?"

"Have you met anyone?" I try again.

"Lil," he says, pained. "You're killing me. *How are you doing?* That's not such a hard question to answer, is it? Just give me something."

"I'm okay," I say. "What are you doing right now? Where are you?" I want to paint a picture of him, not have prison be the backdrop to our conversation.

"I'm sitting on this giant orange chair that looks like something from an Austin Powers movie. It's so fucking ugly. And then last week some guy drew a penis on it with a magic marker."

I smile. "You're sitting on a penis?"

I can almost sense a grin stretching his face. "You would find that amusing." He pauses. "I miss you, love."

"Yeah?" My stomach clenches.

"Yeah."

"Tell me more."

"I'm using the facility's phone in their rec room. There's a pool table, a couple Fizzle machines, beanbags and a huge television that's always on ESPN. Most people are eating lunch right now, so it's pretty quiet."

Lunch. I glance at my clock. It's noon here. His rehab is probably located somewhere with the same Eastern Time Zone. Maybe he's close . . . I shouldn't ask. Not when we agreed to keep the information a secret. I don't want to be tempted to drive out to him. I really will be the pathetic girlfriend then.

"I . . ." He pauses, trying to find the right words. "I tried to ask Ryke about you a few times. He won't tell me anything. It's so fucking annoying; you have no idea." The bitterness seeps from his tone.

I let out a weak laugh. "I think I do."

"Yeah?" Lo inhales, as though preparing himself for the next batch of questions. "What have you been up to?"

"I'm helping Rose," I tell him, nodding to myself. "It's not so bad. She's been keeping me busy . . . it's . . . it's worked out for the most part."

"That's . . . good, Lil. So you're really doing okay?"

My throat begins to close, swollen with a lump. I don't want him to spend his days worrying about me. Ryke has infiltrated my mind, and I hear him whispering, "You'll ruin his progress by saddling him with this large burden. You have to separate yourself from him, Lily. Let him go."

All I've ever wanted was for Lo to be happy. I just never thought his happiness would coincide with my depression. It seems stupid and moronic, but in order for him to become healthy, he needs to stop focusing on me so he can worry about his own problems. That's what Ryke keeps telling me, right?

So I give in to Ryke's constant pleas. I let Lo off the hook. He no longer needs to be my rock. I'll have to find another one or maybe I'll be able to stand up on my own.

"Yeah," I say, my heart constricting as I restrain a wave of emotion. "I've been doing *really* great. I have this new therapist, and I threw out all my porn." Silent tears begin to brew, and they slowly streak my cheek, but I keep my voice steady so he can't tell. "I even stopped using toys." He'll believe the lie, but I doubt he would if I added, *and I stopped masturbating.*

"Really?" His voice breaks, sounding on the verge of tears.

"Yeah, really. I've never felt better." I bring the speaker away from my mouth, the lie crushing my chest.

After a long moment, he says, "Good, good. I'm glad." He inhales another sharp breath. "I don't have much longer—"

"Lo," I interject. *Please don't leave me just yet.*

"Yeah?"

"I'm waiting for you." *I love you.*

I imagine a smile spreading across his face. Even if it's sad, it's still one that I'll hold on to in my dreams. "I knew you could." He pauses. "I have a meeting with my counselor in a couple minutes. I'll call again . . ."

I want to leave him with something better, something more satisfying. "You're officially in my spank bank." I fantasize about Lo every day. He's my number one, go-to image.

"You've always been in mine." *Ohhh . . .* "Talk to you later, love."

"I'll be waiting."

"Me too." With this, we hang up at the same time, and I stare at my phone, as though the conversation I just had was all constructed from my mind. I have to double-check my recent history to verify.

Yes, it was real.

And what's more than that—it's going to happen again.

Eight

I sit in the therapist's waiting room with Rose by my side. She skipped all of her classes for the day to be here with me. I've thanked her about a hundred times. My eyes dart between the exit and the door to the office. Fleeing sounds tempting, but with Rose here, I stay situated to the white couch cushion and refrain from biting my nails. A window overlooks the New York skyline, the interior just as modern with glass bookshelves and purple orchids.

When the door finally opens, I spring to my feet as though the couch electrocuted my butt. And the therapist greets me with a warm, sincere smile. Looking in her early forties, her chocolate brown hair bobs at her chin, and she wears a black skirt, fitted jacket, and a cream blouse. With her heels, she just barely reaches my height. She must be super short then.

"Hi, Lily, I'm Dr. Banning." She holds out her hand, and I shake it, momentarily embarrassed by my sweaty palm. When she lets go, I'm surprised she doesn't wipe her hand on her skirt like she caught something infectious.

She gestures to the office, opening the door wider for me.

I look back at Rose.

"I'll be right here," she assures me. I try to soak in some of her confidence, but unfortunately, it's never really been contagious.

I raise my chin, pretending to be strong, and enter Dr. Banning's office. A few glass bookshelves line the walls, and her cherry oak desk sits off in the corner. In the center lies a white fur rug and two pieces of furniture: a brown leather chair and an identical brown leather couch.

"Take a seat," she says, motioning to the couch.

I rest on the edge of it, my foot bouncing in anxiety. I glance out the large window, a park in direct view, the patch of green actually calming me a little.

Dr. Banning holds a notebook in her hands, and my eyes transfix to it for an extended second. My problems will be documented within the pages for (hopefully) only her to see.

"Are you going to tell me why I'm like this?" It's the very first thing I ask. Not even starting off with a cordial 'how's your day?' Nope. I begin by blurting out my biggest insecurity: *what the hell is wrong with me?*

"Maybe in time. Why don't we begin by getting to know each other first?"

I nod. Oh my God. I even do therapy wrong . . . I can't do anything *right*.

"I went to Yale for my PhD, and I've focused primarily on addiction, especially sex addiction. Now, tell me a little about yourself. It doesn't have to be related to sex."

This should be the easiest question she'll ask, but my tongue feels heavy in my mouth. "Can I have some water?"

"Of course." She stands and goes to her minifridge that sits beneath a Vincent van Gogh painting. When she returns with a bottle of water, I take a long minute to spin off the cap and sip.

"I . . . um, I grew up in a suburb outside of Philadelphia. I have three other sisters." My eyes flicker nervously to her. "You've met one."

Dr. Banning smiles encouragingly. "And your other sisters—are you as close to them as you are to Rose?"

"Not really," I say. "Poppy is married, and she has a little girl. She's much older than me, so I didn't really grow up with her. And Daisy's a lot younger, and when I entered high school, I kind of went my own way."

"What were you like in high school?"

I shrug. "I don't know. I was the quiet girl. No one bothered me unless I was pulled into Lo's fights. Normally, no one ever really acknowledged me, except when there was a group project. I was kind of . . . just there."

"Did you have any friends?"

"Yeah, Loren . . . my boyfriend. He, um, is in rehab." I scratch my neck.

"It's okay, Lily," she says easily. "Rose explained your situation. We're going to talk about him in time."

I'm suddenly afraid she's going to say that he's the root of all of my problems. What if she tells me to never see him again? What if *that's* the solution? My chest thrums with rapid anxiety that I end up blurting out, "I know that I have an unhealthy relationship with him, but there has to be a way that we can be together and work through our problems. Right?" *Please say yes. Please don't end this for me.*

Dr. Banning inspects me for a long moment and tucks a piece of her bob behind her ear, but it pops back out, so thick and so much volume that it won't stay in place. "For now, I want to concentrate on your addiction, Lily, and then we'll talk about how your boyfriend plays into it. You don't need to worry, okay? We're going to try to work through this together to find the answers you want."

I relax only a little and slide farther back on the cushions to refrain from bolting out of the office. "Okay."

"Okay." She nods and glances at her notebook. "Let's go back a little in time. I want you to tell me about your relationship with your parents. How did they fit into your life? And how do they fit into your life now?"

I squint, processing these relationships that I desperately tried not to quantify for the longest time. "When I was younger, my father was always busy. He still is. I've never hated him for it. His success has given me a lot of opportunities." Hell, I wouldn't have been accepted to Princeton or the University of Pennsylvania without my family's prestige.

"You've never been upset that he couldn't spend more time with you?"

I shrug. "Maybe when I was little and didn't understand how his hard work paid for our house and our nice things. But now, I only wish he'd retire so he could have more time to himself."

"And your mother? She doesn't have a job, does she?"

"No," I say. "My relationship with her is . . ." My brows furrow, trying to put to words how my mother used to treat me compared to the other girls. ". . . I'm not sure how it was. But now, she leaves me alone. We talk briefly here and there, but that's about it. It's probably mostly my fault. I just haven't been around much."

"Why is that?"

I take a moment to process her question. When I got to college, I started going to less and less of the weekly family luncheons. Then I just kind of stopped all together. It was really the only scheduled "family time" and I always found a way to bail. For sex.

I take a shallow breath before saying, "I didn't find them all that important. Not compared to my own stuff, I guess."

"Your own stuff being sex," Dr. Banning clarifies for me, her tone clinical.

I nod once. "It sounds awful, doesn't it?" I mutter, the shame slithering in like a virus.

"It sounds like you have a problem, and you're seeking help for it. That's a monumental step."

"I just want it to stop," I confess.

"Be more specific. What exactly do you want to stop? The sex?"

I shake my head. "Not all together. But my brain feels like it's going to explode sometimes. Even if I'm not doing it, I'm thinking about it almost every minute of the day. It's like I'm stuck on this loop and I don't know how to get off it. It's exhausting."

"It's normal for addicts to be consumed by their addiction, especially sex addicts where a large portion of the obsession is in terms of fantasizing. How have the fantasies changed since Lo left? Are they less frequent?"

I pause and think about this for a moment. "I think so," I say with an unsure nod. "I spend more time missing him. So maybe, yeah." Of course that might change if he returns to me. He'll be home and I'll have more energy to fantasize. God, I hope not. I just want my brain to *stop*.

I take another sip of water. "Are you going to ask me about sex?" So far, I feel like we've been beating around the topic. Aren't therapists supposed to be direct?

Dr. Banning tilts her head a little, and I'm lost to her pretty brown eyes, which remind me of Loren. Only, his have amber flecks that resemble his favorite alcohol. "Of course. Do you feel comfortable enough to talk about it? Rose says that the topic makes you nervous."

She told her that? I wonder how transparent I am in front of my sister. "What do you want to know?" I ask.

"What does sex mean to you, Lily?"

I've never been questioned about sex before. Lo even dodged

the topic in order to avoid the subject of alcohol in return. "It makes me feel good."

"In your questionnaire, you wrote down that you like having sex in public places. Why are you okay with this, but you're not comfortable with ménage or voyarism? Take your time to answer. I know you probably haven't thought about this before."

She's right. I haven't. And for some reason, my muscles begin to loosen at her words. I don't feel as though she's judging. She genuinely seems to want to help me. Kind of like Rose. "I like doing it in the bathroom or somewhere besides my apartment because it's easier to get away afterwards. The moment can start and end with the sex, and I don't have to wait to talk to the guy."

"And when you're with Lo?"

His name causes my cheeks to flush. "It adds to the excitement." I remember the gym locker room. Where he grabbed my wrists and forced them above my head. I had a leg hiked around his hip while the other struggled to stay on ground, but he lifted me off the floor with each thrust inside. He filled me until I nearly burst at the seams. All the while, some guy could come around the corner and catch us. The alarm bristled my nerves and heightened the tension. I was on fire, flying seven feet above the ground with a high so natural that I nearly collapsed at the end of it.

"And why not the other two?"

"Two guys at once . . ." I cringe, remembering that happening one time. "Lo . . . he looked at me funny when I *thought* I slept with two guys. I drank too much, so I can't recall the moment, but . . . I don't want him to ever see me like that." I bite my nails, catch myself, and bring my hand down quickly. "I can take the judgment from other guys, the 'slut' and 'whore' but I couldn't have my best friend looking at me like that. And maybe for another girl, it would have been okay to reach those points, but I knew for me, my addiction was progressing to new extremes. And I couldn't let it go there."

She nods. "That's good. So your boyfriend helped you realize what was considered safe for you personally and what was not?"

"I guess so."

"And you had the willpower to stop."

I shrug. I never thought I had much of anything other than *hope*. Willpower—that seems like a strong word.

"You don't think you have willpower?" She must see my hesitation and insecurities. My weak shrug must have given me away.

"I'm not any better, am I?" I tell her. "I let Lo sleep with me during Christmas Eve, and I knew he shouldn't have. I masturbate all the time, and I *just* threw out my porn. I'm not even sure how long that will last."

"Lily," she says, edging forward on her seat. She stares at me for a long moment. "You wrote on here that you've been monogamous the entire time you solidified your relationship with Lo. *That* is an achievement that you can claim. I have patients who've spent years with multiple partners, and they still struggle to stay faithful. You spent those same years with different men, and yet, you're here, telling me that your problem is *not* cheating but rather compulsive masturbation, pornography, and intercourse. That is a huge hurdle."

My chin quivers. No one has ever told me that I've done something good. This whole time, I thought I failed Lo in a huge way, I thought that my problem hindered my ability to help him. Maybe it still did, but Dr. Banning is telling me that I tried to be healthy for Lo. And I succeeded in a large way. "Oh," I mutter under my breath, not able to form any other words. I wipe my eyes before the tears come.

"You love him," she tells me. "But your situation is incredibly delicate. Rose tells me that he's enabled you your whole life, and in turn, you've enabled him."

I nod, pain weighing on my chest. "I'm going to change."

"Good. In order to become healthy, you're going to have to do the reverse. Instead of enabling each other, you'll need to help each other."

The only problem that stands in my way now—I'm not so sure Lo's willing to come back and help me. What if he's set on his own path that no longer involves me? I won't force him to be a part of my life if he chooses not to be in mine. Even if . . . even if it kills me a little, I'd do anything that Lo wanted.

Obviously that's been our problem so far.

This isn't going to be as easy as it seems, I realize.

"Was Lo your first sexual encounter?"

"What . . . what do you mean by that?"

"Was he the first person to touch you?"

I cringe a little, trying to draw my brain back to those early memories. "Yes . . . we, uh . . . were nine, I think." We played "doctor" and I sprawled on the leather couch in his game room. Naked, not knowing any better, I suppose. But maybe we did . . . we knew a little about sex by nine. He touched my breast. I touched him. And then I grabbed his hand and put it in between my legs. We separated after that and never played the game again. Buried the moment like it was some embarrassing story. I explain this to Dr. Banning. Briefly.

"It was consensual from both of you?"

"Yes. Is that weird?"

"It's a little old for children to be playing doctor," she informs me, "especially since, by that age, you have somewhat of an understanding of sex or at least sexuality. I would call it experimenting. Did anyone interrupt you?"

"No one ever came in. Lo's nanny was kind of a flake. She used to sit on the couch and watch soaps all day. So . . . it's not abnormal?"

"If something like this happens, it's best if the children get caught and then hopefully the parents can sit down with them and explain appropriate behavior. It's unfortunate that you didn't have that guidance, but I wouldn't fixate on it too much. Between nine and twelve sexual experimentation is a normal part of child development. You and Lo are roughly the same age, neither of you were coerced or forced into it, so I wouldn't consider it abnormal."

I try to take in her words before she asks another question.

"And after that, did anyone else touch you?"

I shake my head. "No, I touched myself a lot. And then, I had sex."

"With Lo?"

I sink in the seat. "No, not with Lo." I knew I was going to talk about the loss of my virginity—as though it solidified the rest of my nefarious acts for the future. The buried memory has already surfaced these past couple of days as I mentally tried to prepare for this discussion. "I was thirteen."

"Was he older?"

"Not much. He was a fifteen-year-old kid, the son of my mother's friend. I was at his house for his father's surprise birthday party. It was during the day, and everyone mostly stayed outside by the pool. Lo was supposed to be there."

"Why wasn't he?"

The memory hurts a little because if Lo's plans had changed, I know, without a doubt, that I wouldn't have lost my virginity that day. But I believe I still would have gone down this road. Even if my first wasn't mind-blowing, I still loved the sex. The way it exploded my nerves and rocked my body to an ultimate high. Once I felt a glimmer of it for the first time, I was sold.

"He didn't want to go to the party. He wanted to find booze and hang out by the lake. But Rose begged me to go. She didn't want our mother to be focused on her the whole evening, so I went to keep Rose company. And in the end, I left her to go hook up with some guy who paid me a little bit of attention. We went to his room, and what's done was done." My stomach hurts as I admit the rest. "Rose forgave me. She always does, but I can't really ever forgive myself, you know? I'm a horrible person, and I convinced myself that it was better if I wasn't involved in anyone's lives. If I just stayed away, then they wouldn't be hurt by me and I could do what I wanted." I nod to myself. "Yeah, so that's how it went afterwards. But Rose doesn't take lightly to being ignored. She never allowed me to push her away completely." I rub my eyes quickly.

"And Lo?" Dr. Banning asks, not missing a beat. "What happened to him that night?"

"I snuck from my house to his. We lived down the street from each other, so it wasn't so hard. And I climbed through his window. I found him passed out on his bed. So I shut away all of his bottles before his father found them, and I tucked him under the covers." I nod again, as though accepting the memory for what is. A painful reminder of our fucked-up relationship. "The next day, we just acted like nothing happened."

She stares at me with dark eyes, a sort of worry that I think therapists are not supposed to possess. It flickers away before she scares me more, but I realize that she's beginning to understand just how deep our tangled, messy, destructive relationship actually goes.

"After you lost your virginity, how did your relationship with Lo change?"

I squirm a little in my chair before I say, "I mean . . . we've always been friends." I'm about to say *nothing changed*. But I can't muster the lie. After I started having sex, everything changed.

"So take me through your sexual experiences between the day you became sexually active and now. How did things progress? Especially with Lo."

My mind spins as I think about eighth grade and feeling like utter trash for losing my virginity so young. I didn't tell anyone for months, and even though I was hooked to the feeling—I refused to do it again for a while. Too scared of the obliterating guilt that haunted me like a shadow. The second time happened at a graduation party. A public school kid threw it. Lo and I barely knew them, so it had the right requisites to attend. We both liked the anonymity. As years passed in prep school, people often grouped us together because of our friendship and status. We were Fizzle and Hale Co., and the more they wiped our identities away, the more we clung to each other.

The party was like any other, except for bedrooms upstairs. They were open and available, and so was the fifteen-year-old soccer player I met. It felt better than the first time, and I devised this theory that it would just keep getting better and better the more I tried.

I remember leaving the party with Lo braced on my shoulder. We couldn't hide the fact that he'd been drinking from Nola, but she kept her opinions to herself and dropped me off at the Hale house. It was that night, with Lo sprawled half-asleep in his bed, that I asked him if he was a virgin.

I wanted him to tell me *no*. To ease my shame.

"I'm waiting," he mumbled sleepily.

My eyebrows furrowed. "For marriage?" He fell asleep before he could answer, but I think I knew it anyway.

He was waiting for me.

I began having sex every few months, nothing serious. Mostly

I spent my time with porn and self-love. The day Lo found out I lost my virginity wasn't even a monumental one. We were reading comics together during a rainy afternoon, and I complained that Havok and Polaris needed to just fuck and get it over with. Their sexual tension was killing me.

Lo looked up at me, and out of nowhere asked, "Have you had sex?"

It was like someone vacuumed the air right from my lungs. "What?" I squeaked.

He pulled his knees up and shrugged, like it was nothing. Maybe he was just trying to make me comfortable. "When we go to parties, you disappear. And when we leave, you're always a little different."

I didn't know how he'd react. If he'd call me a slut, kick me out for being dirty. But I had never lied to him before, and I couldn't bear the thought of starting. So I spilled everything in the briefest way possible. I didn't want him to think I had been taken advantage of, so I made sure to emphasize that I've been seeking out most of the guys lately. That I liked sex.

His first question was, "Does Rose know?"

I shook my head, told him that I didn't want to tell anyone else.

"I can keep a secret," he said, but his words didn't ease the panic in my chest.

He knows, I kept thinking over and over.

He sensed my alarm and gave me a reassuring nudge in the side. His warm amber eyes met mine, a little concerned but more understanding. I let out a small breath of relief.

"Just . . . can you let me know if you're going to do it at the parties? If someone hurts you—"

"I'm careful."

His eyes darkened. "Still. We look out for each other. Okay?"

"Okay."

So I did. We reveled in our acts and hid our secrets from other people. To everyone else we were Fizzle and Hale Co. To each other, we were safety, love, and free from judgment and scorn. At fourteen, Lo finally lost his virginity.

To me.

One sloppy night that we buried with our hedonism.

We moved on like always, and by sixteen I was having sex at least once a month. Senior year, we became a fake couple and everything changed yet again. He kissed me. I kissed back. And I believed all along that we were pretending. But there were times where I questioned it. Where our "practicing" and the teasing turned to sinful touching. More than we probably should have.

When I left for college, I couldn't last more than a week without some kind of release, and I wasted hours to porn. Having a place away from my parents became my bane. Everything escalated; my rituals began at dawn and ended at dusk. An obsession that cut into my sleep, my dreams, my *everything*. It consumed me whole like some sort of rabid beast.

Lo and I may have enabled each other for years, but I know for certain I'd be on a street corner or worse if Lo hadn't been there. Whenever I felt like I was spiraling, I turned to him. To talk. About anything really. His companionship was my saving grace.

My mouth dries as I finish spilling my life story. I feel cut up and drained and really can't believe I let it all out like some sort of emotional flood. Dr. Banning stares at me with an expression I can't gauge, but she must think that I'm fucked up beyond help. Our co-dependent relationship began as children, and even though we've hurt each other, we've also been the only real support system for so many years. How do you fix that without damaging it as well?

"Have you changed your mind?" I ask her. "Are you thinking we shouldn't be together after all?"

Dr. Banning taps her pen to the notebook. "No. I just think you both have a lot you need to work out. And hopefully we'll reach that point. I want you to uncover the source of this addiction, Lily, and maybe I'll be able to help you get there in time."

She's telling me there may be an answer, but I'm not going to have it anytime soon. I can wait. "I just . . . want to know what I should expect. Are you going to give me medicine? Am I going to need to go through the twelve steps or something?"

Dr. Banning shakes her head. "No medication. Drugs aren't going to solve your problem."

"But . . . I can't sleep . . ." Nights are horrible. All I want is to orgasm, to feel this release, this high and if I don't take a sleeping pill, then how will I rest?

"Right now, there's an imbalance in your oxytocin levels. With compulsive orgasms, you've offset chemicals in your body. That's why you're going through withdrawal. It's important that the chemicals readjust to a normal balance. You'll be able to cope better and fight sexual compulsions. Drugs will only mask the problem."

I try to process her words, and my head begins to float away. "What about when I'm sad?" With Lo absent, I feel such a strong pressure on my chest. I've always heard about depression, but I never understood how debilitating it can be. Some days, I just want to go to sleep and never wake up.

"I can give you a prescription," she tells me. "But I'd rather you didn't take any antidepressants. Like I said, the chemicals in your body need to readjust. They've been out of flux for probably a long time. Now, will you be going through the twelve-step program? No."

I frown. "But Lo . . ."

"You're not an alcoholic," she tells me. "The goal of the twelve-step program is to completely eliminate the addiction from the addict's life. For sex addicts, that is unfeasible. Sex is a part of nature. Alcohol is not. Your sister knew this, which was why she didn't want you to go to an in-treatment facility that promoted the twelve-step program for sex addiction. Permanent celibacy is not going to be the answer. Intimacy with your partner is what we're going to strive for."

Intimacy with your partner. "So Lo . . ."

She nods as though she can read my thoughts. "When he returns from rehab, he'll be an important part in your recovery. I'd love for him to accompany you to some of the meetings."

I blush. "I'm not sure he'll want to do that . . ."

"From what Rose has told me, it sounds like he'd be willing to do just about anything for you." She glances at her clock. "That's it for today. Did I scare you off?"

I shake my head. "No . . . actually, for the first time, I feel like I'm headed somewhere."

And I know that place is somewhere good.

Nine

fter more days filled with class, therapy and loneliness, winter break arrives. And every year with winter break comes Daisy's birthday. Our mother asked her what kind of Sweet Sixteen party she wanted, and she chose to take the yacht around Acapulco and Puerto Vallarta, Mexico. Samantha Calloway put her foot down almost immediately at the idea. Not because it's too lavish but because she has a special brunch with her tennis ladies on Wednesday that she won't miss. Daisy was asking for a week-long birthday, not just one night.

Our father has a business meeting, so he wouldn't be able to make the trip either. But I stepped in and told my mother that I would chaperone. Since Lo's call, I've been feeling better, and I kind of want to test myself—to see if I can hold myself back from doing something with a steward. I know I can, and I'm ready to experience that personal victory. Dr. Banning even thought it'd be a good idea.

My mother was more than happy with these terms, but Rose wasn't. She has an Academic Bowl competition all weekend. So does Connor. Her solution? The dark-haired, know-it-all track star.

Ryke.

He even went as far to *personally* ask Daisy if he could join her party because I would need some help. I was there when she told him that if he could handle a boat full of estrogen, she wouldn't be the one to stop him.

He choked on a dry laugh and said, "I think I'll be okay."

She flashed an equally tight smile. "Just warning you now."

Daisy invited twenty of her closest girlfriends from prep school who look like they're used to getting what they want. He should be scared.

After a flight to the port, I wait by the dock while stewards collect our luggage to bring on the yacht. The sixteen-year-old girls pool out of two limos, adjusting their Chanel sunglasses and reapplying a sheen of lip gloss to combat the daylight. I feel a little underdressed in my jean shorts and halter top. These girls look like they took a pit stop in L.A. and went shopping: long billowing skirts and tight bandeau tops with designer bags on the crook of their arms.

They bring me back to my prep school days. I spent most of my time avoiding these girls, too scared about what I would be labeled if my secret was exposed. Lo was my only friend, and as a result I'm a bit socially inept when it comes to girls. This trip is going to be *awesome*. I just need to remind myself that I'm four years older. And even if they make me feel like a small shellfish . . . I am a shining sea star. Uh . . . I seriously need to come up with better confidence boosters.

Daisy sticks out among her friends at five-foot-eleven. When she spots me, she waves and her eyes flicker over to the handsome twenty-two-year-old beside me. Ryke wears black Wayfarers and leans an arm on the dock's post with such confident nonchalance that the rest of the girls begin to look over, eyeing the cut muscles of his biceps and the ridges visible through his green tank. It's like a herd of lionesses stalking their prey.

I smack his stomach, my knuckles hitting the hardness of his abs.

His eyebrow quirks like I've gone mental. "What the fuck?"

I shake my hand off. "Stop doing that."

"I'm just standing here."

This is going to be a long trip. "Don't stand like *that*."

"Like what? Seriously, how the fuck am I supposed to stand?" He throws his hands up in the air.

"I don't know," I exclaim, glancing back at the girls. "Don't lean on things. It looks sexual."

"I'm not even going to ask how that's possible. Besides, everything looks sexual to you," he reminds me.

"They may look my age, but they're all sixteen."

He glances back at the girls who are still sizing him up from afar. "No shit. And let me guess, you think I'm going to hook up with one of them. I'm not you, Lily."

Okay, that stings.

"Most guys would go for it," I defend myself. "They're cute girls and men usually think with their downstairs brain. I'm just telling your cock in case it has other plans."

"Leave my cock alone," he snaps. "And while you're at it, leave your sexist attitude on the shore."

Maybe I did generalize the entire male population as being horny, but I'm a little on edge. The last time I was on a boat, I almost ruined my friendship with Lo and then I ended up forming a real relationship instead.

I think boats are my enemy. They make me kind of nuts.

I open my mouth about to tell him this, but Ryke cuts me off, "Get a grip, Calloway."

He's right. I take a deep breath and prepare for the worst. I can do this. It's only a week.

I internally laugh. Yeah. Right.

Ten

While the girls are given a brief tour of the yacht by the chief steward, Ryke and I find the lounge area with a shady overhang. I take a seat on the couch while a server brings us fresh orange juice. As part of the itinerary, my mother told the servers not to carry any alcohol onboard. Last thing she'd want is for one of the girls to fall over the rails and drown in a drunken haze.

"Why didn't you tell me about Lo?" I finally ask. "You've been in contact with him. He said you've actually seen him." The hidden truth doesn't hurt as much as I thought it would. Ryke is stable. Lo needs him. I can understand that.

Ryke hikes his feet on the coffee table while I tuck mine under my legs on the outdoor couch, holding a pillow on my lap.

"I didn't want to tell you because you would have started badgering me with questions the same way Lo does about you. The whole point of being separated is so you can focus on yourselves. If you're constantly worrying about each other, then that's not going to happen."

All this time, I thought Ryke was one hundred percent right. But Dr. Banning said that the solution for me isn't complete abstinence but rather a focus on intimacy. And being intimate with my partner actually requires *my partner*. With the prolonged distance, I can tell she fears I'll revert to porn, masturbation, or worse, other men, to fill the empty space. I won't. She said I have willpower, and I'm trying to exert it to the fullest degree while he's gone. And if he doesn't want to come back to me, well . . . I'm also trying not to think about that.

I stir a cherry in my juice. "You don't trust me, do you? That's why you're here."

Ryke stretches his arms on the back of the couch, his muscles sharpening more than before. He looks like he owns the damn yacht. How do I get that type of confidence? I wish it could rub off on me. On second thought . . . maybe not. That would mean I'd have to get physically closer to him.

"Honestly, I'm worried about you. I'm hoping that if you have some sort of panic attack that I'll be here."

"Because you promised Lo that you'd look after me while he's gone," I say with a nod. "I'm sorry if I'm keeping you from having a better winter break. What would you be doing anyway?"

"I got an invite to go snowboarding in Aspen with some friends, but I already turned it down before Rose called me."

I frown. "Why?"

"I was planning on rock climbing, and my friends don't climb, so . . ." He shrugs like it's no big deal.

I'm still stuck on the 'rock climbing' bit. "You rock climb?"

"Since I was six. I love everything about it, and I spent hours at indoor climbing gyms. I remember I'd beg my mom to let me go *before* school even though I spent all day there the minute the bell rang to release class. My mother hates it, so she put me in track to see if I'd stop, but I didn't. I just found two things that I love instead of one. She was *ecstatic* when I told her I changed my plans this week."

"Do you climb actual mountains?" I squint, trying to picture him harnessed and dangling from a slab of rock.

"Yes, Lily, I climb *mountains*." He shakes his head like that's such an inane question.

"What? You could have spent your whole days in the gym."

"I would have been bored," he says. "I climbed so much that I kept pushing myself for something new and challenging. That's what my trip was supposed to be about. I was going to free-solo climb Half Dome at Yosemite. I've free-soloed El Capitan in the same National Park a couple times before, but never Half Dome."

I have no idea what those mountains are or what they look like, but if he's been climbing since he was *six* and for so many hours, he must be pretty good.

"My mother has been freaking out about it for the past month, but the weather turned out to be bad in California anyway. I would have had to reschedule, even if I didn't come here."

If I had a son, I would be freaking out too. "What's free-solo climbing?" I mean, obviously, *solo* entails being alone, which sounds dangerous enough. If I had the guts to shimmy up a mountain, I'd want someone there to catch me if I fell.

"No ropes," he tells me. "Just me and the mountain and some chalk."

My mouth slowly hangs. "Wha . . . that means . . . if you . . . no." I shake my head at the image of Ryke losing his grip and splatting on the hard ground. "Why would you want to do that?" I pause in thought. "Is it the adrenaline rush?"

He shakes his head. "No, everyone asks me that, but I don't get that feeling like I do when I run. If you have an adrenaline rush when you're climbing, it probably means you're falling off the mountain. When you feel fear, your chest constricts, and you'll probably slip and die."

I gape. "Are you serious? You don't get scared? Not even a little bit?" How is that possible?

"Nope," he tells me. "You have to be calm, and I love raising the stakes and trying to overcome them. Like I said, it's a challenge."

I stare at him like he's an alien species, but I guess plenty of people free-solo climb or maybe not. "Do many people die climbing without ropes?"

"Maybe a little less than half of people who free-solo." He shrugs again.

"You're crazy."

He smiles. "So my mother tells me."

The pack of girls suddenly filters onto the deck in varying shades and styles of swimsuits. Most are string bikinis, but I see a few cut-out one-pieces that expose hips and lower backs. Half of the girls run to the padded chairs on the sun deck, trying to fight for ones with the best light. A few meander over to our lounge area and plop on seats around Ryke and me.

I've met most of the girls before since the majority have grown up with Daisy since preschool, but I can't recall half their names. The strawberry blonde with fair skin and a light layer of freckles is Daisy's best friend: Cleo. Then there's Harper, the Native American girl wearing a black-studded bikini. I can't place the third girl that sits with us. She's already so tan that anymore sun may cause her instant skin cancer. She also wears bright pink lip gloss that matches her neon-blue string bikini, ready to be inserted into a Katy Perry video.

Daisy slides closer to me on the couch. I notice that she wears a string bikini with tons of layered straps, the dark green color matching her eyes. "We need to get some snacks. I'm starving."

At the command, a female server in a white shirt and black pants peels away from the sliding glass door. She hands Daisy a menu with tons of items and a line at the bottom says: *if it's not on the menu, ask us and we may be able to make it.*

"I want chocolate," Cleo says to the server. "How about . . . chocolate-covered strawberries?"

The server nods. "Anything else?"

"I can't have chocolate . . . so . . ." Daisy hums to herself as she slides her finger down the menu. Her features progressively darken, as though frustrated with what she can and cannot eat.

I practically feel Ryke seething beside me. But he needs to shut his trap. She doesn't want chocolate, and he shouldn't pressure her to eat it like he did at the Fizzle event.

I do have some sisterly sway, and I know there are some foods that will be good for her to eat. I lean closer and point to a tuna sandwich. "That's healthy."

"Mom said no mayo," she says softly.

"Well, Mom isn't here." Jesus, my mother has seriously crossed a line somewhere. It's Daisy's birthday. Does she expect her not to eat cake too? That's sacrilege.

Daisy stares off for a long second, thinking about the consequences of cheating, no doubt. She's already a size two at 5'11" which is fucking madness, but until the high fashion industry stops seeking these types of girls, I don't see my mother changing.

"Get the fucking sandwich," Ryke tells her. "You'll burn it off swimming."

"Don't do tuna," Cleo suddenly says. "Your breath will reek."

"Yeah, I hate the smell," Harper agrees.

I already want to strangle them.

Daisy tenses at all the voices. She hands the menu back to the server. "I'll have the tuna, thanks. My friends will have to deal with the smell." She shoots Cleo a look. "It's my birthday, after all."

Cleo shrugs. "Just trying to warn you. What if we meet some hot local boy? You're going to scare him off with bad breath." God, they're already planning on picking up guys. This just turned from slightly fun to terrifying. I hope I'll be equipped to handle them. *Please, let me be equipped.*

"Even better," Daisy says. "The guy will run over to you. See, I did you a favor."

Cleo purses her lips and then her eyes slowly trail over to me. "So, Lily . . ."

I brace myself.

". . . How did you get so skinny? What are you, a size zero?"

Great, she asks me a question I'm not really sure how to answer. The truth—I spend more time consumed by sex than I do taking care of myself. In my defense, I am short. If Daisy became a size zero, she'd fade away and need to be hospitalized.

"She's always been skinny," Daisy answers for me with ease.

"You know, I've never been able to tell if guys are into the whole size zero *skinny* look," Cleo says with a false politeness. She might as well have said "emaciated" instead of skinny. She has to know her words are beyond rude.

Her pretty blue eyes flash to Ryke, who's pretending to be busy watching a basketball game on the hanging television. "Right, Ryke?"

His eyes stay glued to the screen as he confirms with a simple, "Yep."

Cleo holds on to the word like it's bait. "Are you into size zero girls?"

This is so fucking awkward! I shift uncomfortably in my seat, and Daisy lets out a long, exasperated sigh. "Cleo—"

"What?" Cleo says with a nonchalant shrug. "I just want a male perspective on the situation. I only have younger sisters, okay? I'm curious."

Ryke turns a fraction, his gaze still hidden behind Wayfarers. "My brother loves her, so obviously some guys are into skinny girls. Everyone has a different preference."

Harper interjects with a little too much eagerness. "What's yours?"

I imagine he's rolling his eyes right about now. Damn, sunglasses, I'd actually like to see him break in front of a few girls. How is he going to handle all twenty together? He doesn't miss a beat. "I like women. Big breasts, curvy waists, an ass I can grab." He keeps steady, unflinching. I am cringing inside and slightly aghast that he even responded back. Daisy's friends look around at each other, realizing that they all have tiny hips, decent-sized boobs and no butt.

Daisy scrutinizes Ryke for a while and then says, "How big of boobs?" *Ohmygod.*

"How about we change the subject?" I say.

"Big," Ryke tells her.

"You like to grab those too?" Daisy tries. Her friends literally gasp out loud.

Ryke's lip twitches, but he holds back what I *think* is a smile. I'm glad he finds this amusing. I do not. At all. This is like . . . no. If Lo was here, he'd have yelled at his brother for flirting back with an almost-sixteen-year-old. That's what Ryke's doing. Even if his intentions are to start an argument or make someone uncomfortable, it looks like *flirting.* "Only if I hear a woman moan when I do it."

"Ryke!" I shout at him. I mouth, *enough.* My eyes widen to emphasize the severity. I know he's not intentionally trying to flirt back, but he's about to cross a line. And I suspect he knows it exists, and that he's crossed many in his life. Maybe he thinks traditional rules don't apply to him. Or maybe, he just doesn't care.

Daisy opens her mouth to say something back, but he cuts her off. "There's your male perspective." He turns back to the television, closing off to the girls.

Cleo isn't finished harassing me though. "About Loren Hale, he's in rehab, right? My parents heard from some family friends." She nods to the Katy Perry girl. "You remember Greta? Her parents found a dime of coke and she got sent to rehab. It's like they don't understand that we're young, and we want to have some fun. They've done it before."

"Yeah," Katy says. "It's so hypocritical."

I hate that they're comparing Lo to a teenager screwing around. That's how it starts, sure, but his problem has exceeded a small dose of adolescent rebellion. It's not a *shame* that he's in rehab. It's what my father said . . . *admirable*.

"He chose to go," I defend my boyfriend, heat gathering in my eyes. "He wants to get help." Which is a better place than where we were before.

The lounge silences in this awkward layer, and Cleo presses her lips together, avoiding my narrowed gaze. Thankfully, the snacks parade over on a tray, rescuing me from the tense situation. The girls start chatting again, and I look to Ryke. He gives me a supportive nod, which means more to me than I'll *ever* let on. I want to do this right. I want to be strong and fight, and being on this boat is a big step.

Last time I was here, I was a mess. This is my redo.

Daisy grabs her sub, and her long hair sticks to the tuna that squeezes from the sides. She plops the sandwich back on the tray and uses a napkin to wipe the strands. "I hate my hair," she mutters under her breath.

"Ever heard of a ponytail?" Ryke says to her. His antagonizing is not helping. After New Year's I realized her "signature trait" brings up insecurities.

"Yeah," Daisy snaps back, "want me to put *your* hair in one?"

Cleo shakes her head. "He doesn't have enough hair for that." She bites into a strawberry.

"You could always make really tiny ones all over his head," Harper chimes in.

Ryke keeps his gaze trained on Daisy. "You shouldn't bitch about something that you can change."

Daisy's lips form a tight pout. She pulls the hair band off her wrist and gathers her long locks into three sections, braiding them easily. "Happy?" she snaps back.

"Only if you are," he says. "It's not my hair." He returns to his basketball game where he rightfully should stay. He's making me paranoid. I do not want my sister to grow attached to him or think that he's giving her attention for the wrong reasons.

Cleo crosses her ankles, sitting on an ottoman that faces us. Her baby blue bikini washes out her fair skin. "Aren't you going swimming?" she asks me. "Where's your bathing suit?"

"I'm going to put it on later." Though I am not looking forward to swimming with Daisy's friends. Cleo's stares have given me a third-degree burn. She does not like me. Her hatred could stem from anywhere—like the fact that I'm the only one who brought a guy on the trip, or that I'm four years older—so I try not to waste my time questioning it.

"What about you?" Katy asks, scooting closer to Ryke on the couch. "You swimming with us?" Her long lashes flit over the curvature of his body, the angles of his muscles that cut so supremely. Of course he rock climbs. His muscles scream, "I scale mountains!" Not just "I run a shit ton!" I should have known. Silly me.

"I'm going to finish watching this game first." His voice tightens, and he sits more rigid than before.

I want to laugh, but I can't because out of the corner of my eye on another ottoman, I see Harper pulling out a travel-sized vodka bottle, dumping the contents into her *virgin* daiquiri.

"What are you doing?" My brows pinch. Is she serious? I'm

sitting right here. Am I not that threatening? My mother specifically said *no* alcohol. They all heard her warning before she sent them off in the limo.

"Your boyfriend may be an alcoholic, but I'm not," Harper tells me with a dry smile.

"Harper, that's so fucking rude," Cleo says in this pretentious tone that makes it seem like . . . well, not that fucking rude.

I can't take anymore. "I'm going to go put on my bathing suit." I shoot up from my seat, and Ryke, surprisingly, follows suit.

Daisy mouths an apology as we go inside. I shrug my shoulders to try to tell her that it's okay, but my nerves still vibrate in not only frustration but severe anxiety. Ryke shuts the sliding glass door behind us.

"Afraid of being alone with them?" I ask.

"I'm more afraid of *you* being alone by yourself," he tells me.

Oh. He has *zero* faith in me. "I'll be okay. We should get our bathing suits on."

"Sure."

We head to our bedrooms, and I manage to keep a safe distance from all the male servers. If Lo is hounded about being in rehab for alcoholism, how would people react to rehab for sex addiction? I can't even imagine. Maybe it's a good thing that in-treatment facilities turned out to be a bust for me anyway. I wouldn't want to shame my family with the news—that their daughter or sister is some freak.

I close the door to my bedroom, one of the larger ones with a fancy gold bedspread, a fur throw, and a granite-topped dresser. A Victorian cream chaise rests against the right wall, gold-stitched pillows decorated on the buttoned cushions.

I slip on my simple black bikini and comb my fingers through my short hair before taking a quick peek in the mirror. If I inhale a deep breath, my ribs stick out. I feel low, and to combat this sinking emotion, I'd normally jump on my bed and find porn to watch. Masturbate until everything washes into bliss.

Things need to change, I remind myself. So I back away from the bed and stop fiddling with my fingers.

A knock sounds on my door. "You naked?" Ryke asks.

"No."

He walks in. "You okay?"

I swallow the lump in my throat. I wish Lo was here. He'd make me feel better. Maybe not even with sex. He'd just smile, kiss me, tell me I'm beautiful and say, "Fuck them." Because at the end of the day, we were the only thing that mattered to each other. All I needed was him.

"I hate people," I blurt out. Lo and I used to shun the entire world because we were scared of the ridicule. Of how people would perceive us. We created this bubble around ourselves, filling it with lies and misery, until it eventually popped.

"So now you're generalizing the entire world for three catty girls?" He picks up a sailboat decoration on the dresser, overturning it as he talks. "Four girls, if you want to include your provoking sister."

"I exaggerate a lot," I tell him. "And if anyone's *provoking*, it's you."

Ryke lets out a long, dry laugh. "That's funny considering your boyfriend is ten times worse with his words. If anyone can poke at someone's soul, it's him . . . and probably my father, but that's another story, isn't it?" His lips form a pained smile.

"So you don't hurt people with your words?" I question with raised brows.

"You want to know the difference between Lo and me?" Ryke asks, leaning his elbows on my dresser, nonchalant and assholish all in one swoop.

"Sure."

"You remember the Halloween party? Lo stole liquor from the house, and he barely admitted that he took it. Before you came out there, he spent about five minutes telling them all the ways in which they were complete fucking morons. It wasn't even close to being funny, especially not when he told Matt that guys like him are worth nothing in life. That they'll take shit and eat it until they fucking die. It was cold and cruel."

My chest hurts because I believe every word Ryke is telling me. I've heard Lo tear down people in prep school until they cried, not because it made him feel better but because they hurt him first and it was his greatest weapon of defense.

"He walks away sometimes," I say in a small voice. "He's not always like that." I defend him because he's not here to speak for himself. And what I said is partly the truth too. Lo knows when to walk away. Like the first time we were at the Blue Room. If someone's harassing him, he won't stand there and take it for long. He's too used to verbal abuse, and I think he'd rather not be weakened and drained by it. He'd rather just get out of the fucking way.

"Okay," Ryke says, "but in the context of the Halloween party, he didn't."

"And what would you have done, Ryke? Not stolen the liquor? Not started the fight? Congratulations." Rehashing the past puts a bitter taste in my mouth. We can't change that event. Talking about it rubs my skin raw.

"I would have punched him," Ryke says easily. "I would have decked the little shit in the face. That's the fucking difference." He straightens up, and my jaw slowly unhinges, not expecting that.

"You don't seem like a fighter."

"I don't?" Ryke says, his eyes pulsing with something fierce.

"If someone is giving me shit, I'm not going to stand there and take it. Maybe Lo was defenseless all his life, but I wasn't."

"And then what? It would have been four to one at that party. You would have gotten your ass handed to you."

"I never said it would be the right thing." He shrugs. "It's just a different kind of wrong."

His wrong. And Lo's wrong. Neither are better or worse, I realize. Their dissimilar upbringings make them react to situations in opposite ways. That's what he's telling me.

It also makes me incredibly sad. Because he basically admitted to being as damaged as his brother. I picture his fist flying into Matt's face before awful words are spewed, impulsive and brash.

Only it's a different kind of damaged.

Just as he said.

Eleven

I float on a yellow inner tube in the crystal blue ocean. The girls, Daisy, and even Ryke rest on their own brightly colored tubes, each round floating device tied together by a rope so we don't drift from the boat or each other. I catch Harper swigging from *another* mini bottle of liquor she smuggled on the boat.

Dear God, please don't let one of my little sister's friends drown to the bottom of the ocean because they're so fucking intoxicated. Thanks.

The first five minutes were actually fun. I took a nap and listened to music playing from the boat's speakers, and my feet skimmed the cool water.

However, five minutes later, and the girls become so damn restless that their shouts and high-pitched voices scar my eardrums and wake me up.

"Oh my God! Something touched me. Was that a shark?!" Katy screams in fright. She latches on to Ryke's tube, and he nearly topples into the water. Her palm plants on his bare abs to catch herself, but clearly, her grabby hands are no accident. She has been eyeing his chiseled muscles since he strutted off the deck like he built it with his bare freakin' hands. It's mildly infuriating . . . and also scarily accurate.

"Relax," Daisy tells her. "It was probably just a fish."

Ryke tries to disengage from her, but she clutches his bicep now, her panicked eyes darting from him to the water, two seconds away from shrieking, "Save me!"

He carefully pries her fingers off his arm. "I think you'll survive."

"Oh . . . yeah. Right." She raises her chin and situates back on her pink tube.

Ryke unhooks his green inner tube from the pack and paddles with one hand to my lonely rope on the end. He clicks it in and rests his Wayfarers back over his eyes.

"Smooth," I whisper to him.

"That's how it's done," he agrees.

I roll my eyes and sink back into my tube, my butt skimming the water underneath. Ready for nap number two. Naps are great. When I'm asleep, I barely have the urge to jump from the water, go to my room, and perform some self-love acts.

"Seriously, is that even possible?" I hear a girl ask curiously. Now *I'm* curious.

I listen closely.

"I swear on my life it was four fingers," Katy says. "I was really sore afterwards." *Whaaat?*

I glance quickly at Ryke, but with his sunglasses on, I can't tell if he's hearing what I am. Fingers. Sore. This is sexual. I know it's not just my perverted mind.

"How could he do that though? I mean, how would they fit?"

"They wouldn't," another girl adds. "I definitely don't believe you."

Daisy stays quiet in the middle of the pack, kicking the calm ocean with her feet.

"Let's ask Lily," Cleo offers. "She's older and has a boyfriend. I'm sure she'd know. Lily!"

The nearest girl splashes water on my chest, and I hesitate

before sitting up to face the string of girls. I really, *really* don't want to talk about sex with Daisy's friends. This whole trip was about me not thinking about sex, and yet, it still surrounds me, even when I don't bring it on myself.

Harper, the closest to me, explains their debate. "Katy says that her 'boyfriend'"—she uses air quotes—"put four fingers inside of her. Is that possible?"

I squirm a little, my float knocking into the unflappable Ryke who gazes up at the sky, sunbathing during this debacle. While I'm here, two seconds from unclipping my tube and floating down the ocean as far away from this boat and conversation as possible.

"Ummm . . ." My arms turn into a giant red welt. "Everyone has different bodies."

"Did you just call my vagina loose?" Katy snaps at me. *What?!*

"No!" I say. "Of course not. His fingers could have been small." I cringe. That wasn't better. Ohmygod. If I dive from my tube and go underwater right now—will that be really weird?

"Well how many fingers does Lo usually use?" Cleo asks. I must turn a darker shade of red because Cleo adds, "Don't be embarrassed, Lily. It's just sex. How else are we supposed to figure all this stuff out if we don't talk to each other?"

Daisy straightens up in her tube, dropping her feet in the middle and resting her chin on the teal plastic. "How did you learn about sex? Did Poppy and Rose talk to you about it?" She sounds a little bummed, as though she missed out on some monumental sister-bonding experience by being the youngest.

She's mistaken. Poppy never talked to me since she was so much older and spent more time with boys on her own than she did teaching us about them. And Rose—I always believed she'd judge me for sleeping around. *Not* talking to her may just be my biggest regret.

I learned from the internet, porn, and gossip magazines like

Cosmo. Wikipedia helped too. I wonder if it would have made a difference if Poppy or Rose talked to me. Maybe I wouldn't be so ashamed, but then again, maybe nothing would have changed. I'll never know. As much as I hate to even *think* it, Cleo's right. Girls shouldn't be embarrassed to talk about sex.

"Who cares who she learned it from," Katy snaps before I can find a suitable reply for Daisy. "I want to know more about Lo. Have you done it doggy style? I heard it feels better."

"Ew, isn't that, like, in the butt?" One girl cringes. "That's supposed to hurt."

"Doggy style can be in the vag too," another girl pipes in. "Duh."

Secretly, I give Ryke's inner tube a little nudge. He sways and grabs onto mine to steady himself. I face him and hiss, "*Save me.*"

He rests his head back on this tube, *ignoring* me.

I feel myself being left out to dry. "I. Will. Drown. You," I whisper.

Suddenly, he sits up. "I'm going to get some food."

"I'll join." I suppress my smile, and after a short paddle, we end back on the yacht. I spread a towel across one of the lounge chairs on the sun deck and lie back to dry off.

Ryke rubs a towel through his hair and then tosses it on the adjacent recliner. "You sure know how to avoid people. I'll give you that."

"I'm trying to be better about it, but some things still make me uncomfortable." Especially since Lo isn't here to help ease me into this new, terrifying social world. Having him by my side would make for a smoother transition. I wouldn't feel so . . . unhinged by people. "And how can you not be uncomfortable by *that*?"

"It takes a lot for me to get rattled. I wasn't about to swim away from them."

"You just did."

"Because *you* asked me to." He sets his feet on the deck, sitting and facing me while I relax lengthwise on the lounge chair.

"So you really would have stayed there while I described sex with Lo?" I ask in disbelief.

"You're forgetting that I basically watched him grope you," Ryke reminds me. Yeah, I remember now. When Ryke first met Lo it was under odd circumstances. "I'm a journalism major. In my profession, I can't be turned off by weird or uncomfortable situations. I just have to fucking deal. And that's something I've been pretty good at most of my life."

I thought this trip would do a lot of things. Make me confront my insecurities and by the end, boost my confidence for the future. Never did I think it would help me understand the shadowy mysterious figure that is Ryke Meadows.

"Hey." Daisy climbs onto the deck with a towel wrapped around her waist. She sits on the lounge chair opposite mine and holds a decorative pillow to her chest, covering herself while Ryke stays seated in between us.

My stomach lurches. "Are your friends coming up too?" I'm afraid of seeing the mob of girls swarm the deck area and prod for more details about my sex life.

"No, they said they wanted to stay out there a little longer." She stares at her toes for a moment, her nails painted a turquoise blue. "I'm sorry about them. I didn't know they'd nag you. It's stupid anyway."

"What is?" I ask.

"Sex. Who cares how many fingers a guy put in Katy?"

I really, really don't want to talk about this in front of Ryke, and I can tell he's biting his tongue. He wants to say something, clearly, but he needs to hold it inside for two seconds. Please. Is that at all possible?

She elaborates before I can reply. "I can name about three things that are better than sex. People make it seem like it's some terrific experience, and in the end, it's just super lame."

Ryke rubs his lips, curious. *Don't take her bait*, I urge with wide eyes, but he's not looking at me. "What three things?"

Daisy crosses her arms, building up defenses for when he attacks back. He always does. I should end this before it starts, but I see their battle beginning, and I really don't want to be hit in the crossfire. "Oxygen, chocolate and free-falling. There you go."

"Sex is definitely better than chocolate, and Lily would make a strong case that it's more sufficient than oxygen. And when have you been free-falling?"

"Last year, I skydived for the first time."

He nods. "Okay, well, hate to break it to you, but sex is ten times better than skydiving."

"No it's not," she rebuts.

Ryke leans forward on his chair a little. "Then whoever fucked you didn't do it right, sweetheart."

Her cheeks heat, flushing red, but not nearly the same burnt color mine become. Thank God, I wouldn't wish that on anyone. "There's no wrong way to have sex," she retorts.

Ryke looks to me for backup on this question, as though I'm the sex guru. I guess . . . I kinda am. I roll my eyes and sigh heavily. "There can be bad sex," I tell her. "It's possible that he wasn't very good."

"I'm pretty sure he was as good as any other guy."

Ryke interjects, "And do you have another experience to compare it to or are you going on one guy and one time?"

Daisy stares at him with hard eyes, unwavering. "One time, but still, I can't imagine it being any better than that."

"Let me ask you this then," Ryke continues to poke. I want to stop him, but every time I open my mouth to intervene, he speaks and cuts me off. "Did you orgasm at all?"

Daisy's brows cinch as she tries to remember. "I'm . . . I don't know."

"You didn't then," Ryke says.

He pulls his Wayfarers up on his head so she can see his deep brown eyes, honey flecks swimming in them. He actually looks like he comes in peace. Which is nice. But still, he shouldn't be having this conversation with anyone. What did he tell me before she got up here—oh yeah, that very little makes him uncomfortable. Maybe that's a problem!

Interrupting them and ending this severely awkward talk has flashed out of my mind. Mostly because my sister doesn't seem to think it's that awkward, and the last thing I want is to embarrass her or treat her like a child. I'm sure our mother does it enough.

"But I was . . ." she trails off in thought.

"Wet?"

"Yeah . . ." she says softly. ". . . Wait, no, I wasn't."

Ryke's eyes narrow, pissed all of a sudden. "This was your first time?"

She nods and then shrugs. "No big deal."

"Yeah, that's a fucking big deal," he tells her. "What kind of asshole enters a girl on her first time without getting her aroused first? It probably hurt like hell."

"Not really."

"I don't believe you." He points at her. "In fact, you should stay away from any guy who doesn't make you come at least twice before he fucks you. Keep that in mind."

She shakes her head. "I'm not going to have sex again. I have more important things to do. Like wash my hair." She flashes him a dry smile.

"That's a shame then," he tells her. "You'd probably enjoy it with the right guy—maybe even realize that it's better than fucking chocolate." He smiles a little. "That's cute, you know, you should tell that to the next boy you meet."

"Sure," she says, her tone still skeptical, probably knowing that Ryke isn't flirting with her now. "Maybe I'll even tell him to try out four fingers." She shares his smile for a brief moment.

"That, I would not advise," Ryke declares, leaning back on his recliner. "But I'm also not a girl. Lily?"

My turn to interject? Oh goodie. "Yeah, no," I tell her. "I wouldn't either."

"Noted." She stands and tells us thanks before she goes inside to use the bathroom.

I immediately spin around and confront Ryke. "In-appropriate." I break up the word for emphasis.

He slides his Wayfarers over his eyes and rests his hands underneath his head. "I was educating her."

"You were embarrassing me."

"Sounds like a personal problem." His lips twitch into a smile. "Anyway, I'm better than Connor Cobalt. Imagine him here diagramming the reproductive system for her. Would you rather have *that* happen?"

"No, no, I'd rather all penises stay a thousand feet away from my little sister, that's what I'd like."

"Not going to happen, Lily. She's almost sixteen. She's already had sex. And she's a fucking supermodel."

"High fashion."

He laughs under his breath. "Whatever. She's gorgeous, looks older than you, and plenty of guys will see that if they already haven't. She shouldn't be uncomfortable talking about sex just because you are."

Ouch. I let it go because . . . he's right. I cringe as I think it. "Don't tell me you like her."

"Did I mention that she's sixteen?" he snaps.

"Just making sure." I relax a little.

Maybe I'm going about everything the wrong way. Sex is okay to talk about. Sex is not something to fear or to condemn. I just need to find the healthy way to do it. With Lo, of course.

And then, everything will be okay.

Twelve

I usually pop a sleeping pill to battle my warring thoughts, but I do as Dr. Banning suggested and stay far away from prescription drugs. Instead, the darkness and quiet begin to open the doors to my suppressed emotions. I curl up in my bed—the ocean waves not enough to rock me to sleep. I end up staring at the empty place beside me, wishing for the warmness of another body.

Being away from Lo for three months is extremely difficult, but over time, it's become manageable. The part where he returns freaks me out the most. All this anticipation courses through me, and I imagine the moment where he'll stand in my doorway and gently tell me that we'll have to break up for good. That he's moved on, reached a healthy stasis, and figured out that I'm the giant cancer in his life.

I press my forehead to my pillow. *Don't. Cry.* I force, but hot tears seep in the creases of my eyes. I take two trained breaths the way Rose showed me.

Lo made me promise to wait for him. Maybe I should have made him promise to return to me. At least to give me a fighting chance.

Ten minutes later, sex invades my mind like a relentless enemy. These feelings will float away with a better high, and my nagging thoughts will tumble and fall. I welcome the urge, too emotionally drained to care about anything other than drifting away from this state. I crawl off my bed and zip open my suitcase, rummaging around the bottom before I find my black travel bag of toys. They're all the same brand from a luxury line, and it kind of reminds me of Lo's preference for expensive liquors. Great . . .

Quickly, I pick a small pink bullet vibrator and hop back on the bed. I wiggle my black cotton panties to my ankles and then slide the device inside. I debate on whether to concentrate on Lo. On one hand, he's the sexiest guy in my spank bank. On the other hand, tears build whenever I imagine his amber-colored eyes staring at me, with his body thrumming on top of mine. I just end up missing him and wishing he was here. In the flesh. Holding me.

I settle on clicking the remote and clearing my mind of everything. I massage my breast underneath my gray cami-tank. Running my finger over my nipple, I pulse my hips rhythmically against the device. Heat gathers across my arms and legs, and my body throbs for a strong release. I slide my hand along my stomach, past my belly button and to my swollen and tender spot that aches to be touched. My fingers rub against my clit, causing my hips to buck and my breath to catch. *Yes.*

Please make me come. Please make me come. I chant over and over in my head.

Please. I alternate between rubbing slow and fast and speeding up the vibration of the bullet with my remote.

I turn my head and cry into the pillow. *Please.* I beg my mind. *Lo* . . . Too gone to this hunger to think about the sadness that accompanies his name.

Please. And then my insides writhe, my toes curl, and my head floats, a balloon ready to drift away and pop. I pant heavily and stay still for a little bit. The high begins to leave, and I desperately want to catch it—to bring it back and relive it all over again.

It was too quick, too fleeting, too insignificant to replace the hole in my heart.

So I start again.

An hour later and soaked in sweat, I am in no hurry to stop. Each time I come down from an orgasm, I wait a couple minutes and crave the next one before I start again. I'm dripping and wet and sore and none of those things wills me to quit. I just kind of want to exhaust myself so much that I pass out.

An urgent knock sounds on the door, and my heart drops. I fumble with the remote, trying to turn off the vibrator, but it slips from my fingers and onto the floor. I lean over to grab it without uncovering my lower half with the plush comforter, but as I reach, my fingers brush the remote and knock it underneath the bed. *Ohmygod.*

"Lily!" Ryke says loudly. "I'm coming in. You better be fucking decent."

I am not decent. I am not even three-quarters decent. I am semi-freaking-the-fuck-out decent.

"Wait!" I scream back. I have no time to think. I straighten out my tank, covering an exposed breast that somehow popped out. *Oh shit.* The door opens before I can even *search* for my underwear beneath the depths of the huge gold comforter. I hug it to my chest and gulp as Ryke walks in.

I try to give him a glare, but my paranoia ruins its full power. *Why didn't I lock my door?!*

The bullet vibrator silently buzzes inside of me, and my embarrassment hits a new peak. I never thought that was possible. I catch the distressed look on his face as he runs two nervous hands through his brown hair, a little thicker than Lo's. I frown at his rare expression. Something has unsettled him.

"What's wrong?" I ask. *Is it Lo?* What if something happened in rehab? What if he's hurt? I straighten up, my pulse hammering.

He crosses his arms over his bare chest and leans his spine against my dresser, slumping forward a little, his eyes darkening. "One of the girls just crawled in my bed."

Not Lo, but this is still pretty disturbing. "What do you mean?"

"I woke up," Ryke says angrily, "to a sixteen-year-old *groping* me." His fingers go through his brown, messy hair again. "I can't deal with that shit. I trust myself not to do something with a high school girl, but I don't trust *them*. I almost got raped, Lily."

I can't help but snort.

"It's not funny," he says flatly.

"I know. I'm sorry." But this . . . was kind of unexpected.

He goes to the Victorian chaise and squishes a pillow in his hands, tossing each one on the floor.

"What are you doing?" I squeak out. He cannot be staying here. I need to pull this vibrator out. I need *privacy*.

He keeps one of the softest pillows on the head of the chaise. "I'm not going back there." He lies on his back, wearing no more than a pair of drawstring pants that show a little too much definition in the crotch. Seriously, why do Lo *and* his brother wear those things to bed? They're so . . . sexy . . . leaving my imagination to roam towards bad, bad places.

He fidgets a little, smashing the pillow to get more comfortable. This can't be happening.

The vibrations make me lose focus. I can't just sleep here with this inside me all night. Action must be taken. Even if it will be the most awkward (possibly embarrassing) moment of my whole life.

I manage to reach down under the covers and hook my finger on the string to the vibrator, pulling it out and cupping it in my hand. I can't leave it on the bed, not when it makes noises, and in the silence of the night I'm too terrified that Ryke may hear and think I intentionally tried to get off with him in the room.

So now comes the hard part, I try to feel around for my panties without being too obvious. When I touch the fabric, I pull them up around my thighs, trying not to wiggle so much. When they're on, I mumble, "I have to pee."

I grab the plush comforter that weighs a freaking ton and wrap it around my body like I've seen in all the movies. Only when I crawl off the bed, the heavy comforter takes the sheet and an extra blanket underneath it. Basically, I just stripped my bed. *Good job, Lily.*

I'm not smooth at all. I must look like a snowman wrapped in a cocoon. At least it hides my half-waddle and the vibrator in my left hand. Ryke says nothing about my strange behavior. Maybe he's fallen asleep from his traumatic event or I'm stealthier than I think.

Then . . . I face-plant.

"You okay?" Ryke looks over.

My cheeks heat, and I roll over like a burnt hotdog, still clenching the vibrator in my palm and stuffing that hand into my blanket. Out of the corner of my eye, I see Ryke sitting up and staring at me like, *what the hell.*

I glare now, propping my elbow on the floor for support. "I'm a sex addict," I tell him. Saying it feels good. "Maybe you shouldn't be sleeping in here."

He rolls his eyes dramatically and plops back against the chaise. "I can handle you. I have a greater chance of getting raped outside this room."

"You honestly believe they'll rape you?" He's being ridiculous.

"She basically already molested me, and guys can get raped too, Lily," he says. "I thought you had to pee."

I don't, but I desperately need to reach the sanctuary of the bathroom. Standing up feels like a chore, so I end up army-crawling with my blanket around me. After I slide into the tiled room, I kick the door closed and stand on my knees to lock it. Then I collapse on my comforter and stare up at the ceiling. I drop the vibrator on the floor and it moves a little on the marble tiles. I should roll it in a towel and stuff it into a drawer, wash my hands, and go back to bed.

I know this.

But I don't do it.

I feel like I *can't*.

In a quick motion, I grab the device and put it back in. The pulsing kicks up my cravings, making all my nerves stand still for a brief moment. I want more. My fingers skim down my belly and slowly descend over my throbbing clit, and I start all over again. A cycle I just can't seem to quit. I shut my eyes and my breathing quickens. I block out everything from tonight, and I lose myself to pleasure instead of worries and time and even this place. I am nowhere but here.

My body shudders, and I rub harder with mastered urgency.

I wantwantwantwantwant.

No.

I needneedneedneedneed.

PLEASE!

A moan escapes my lips, and my eyes flutter back. The sudden, quick release electrifies my insides.

And poofs away within a few seconds. I pull out the vibrator, and lie motionless on the floor. Tears sting my eyes as my actions swim up and infiltrate the sane part of my brain.

What the fuck did I just do?

Dr. Banning flat out told me that recovering from sex addiction does not mean eliminating all sex. Just the unhealthy kinds.

The things that bleed into my daily life, disrupt my routines, and turn me into a compulsive animal. Some addicts can handle self-love. I suddenly realize that I can't.

My chest hurts as tears spill down my cheeks. I don't understand why I can't masturbate like a normal person. Why do I have to take everything to extremes? I press my palms to my eyes and cry harder. The situation feels too big for me. Everything seems too far out of my control.

I haven't cheated on Lo. I've abstained from real sex, but does it even matter anymore? I'm addicted to masturbating. When do I get a break? I know the answer. And the tears pour full force now, my nose running, my eyes burning. *This battle is a forever sort of thing.*

On my hands and knees, I ditch my comforter and crawl into the bathtub, shivering a little as the air nips my bare legs and arms. Wearing nothing but cotton panties and a tight tank. I sink against the porcelain and clutch my arms to my chest, curling into a ball. I physically try to hold myself together. But I still feel as though I'm breaking apart. Shattering. Into small insignificant pieces.

No porn. No sex. No self-love. What else is left?

Maybe people would find me dramatic and stupid for feeling so empty without those three things. Maybe they'd laugh or spit at me in scorn. But I have no energy left to explain *how* sex fills a deep hole in my chest. How for a single instant, it seems to take everything bad away.

Breathing hurts. Each inhale is like a knife stabbing into my ribs. I shudder against the cold tub and kiss my knees, shutting my eyes tight. I am losing my grasp on everything that has ever made me feel okay. Sex and Lo—they have vanished and left me so very alone.

My head lolls to the side, drifting. My body feels heavy and my tears grow silent, but the pain in my chest intensifies. I'm not even sure what will make me feel better. Not sex. Not Lo. Nothing can make me whole again. The thought steals my breath.

"Lily!" Ryke bangs on the door. "Come on out. You've been in there long enough."

I can't move. I can't speak. My lips have frozen with my hope. Why would Lo even want to return home to me? He just escaped hell, who would want to enter another one?

"Lily! I'm not playing around. Open the fucking door."

I open my mouth to reply, but words stick in the back of my throat, too strenuous to produce. Speaking takes strength that has eked away with my confidence. My bottled insecurities attack me like a parasite with no thought but to destroy until I'm weakened, withered and dead.

Moments later, I hear the door unlock. I assume he grabbed a key from somewhere. Maybe a steward.

"Jesus Christ," he curses and kneels beside the bathtub. I blink slowly, still drifting. My cheek presses to the lip of the tub, but my arms still wrap around my chest. My last safety blanket is myself. Right now, that's not very reassuring.

I listen to Ryke's voice as he dials a number on his cell. "Dr. Banning?"

What? Rose must have given him my therapist's number.

"I'm Lily Calloway's friend . . . I found her in a bathtub. She's unresponsive, and . . ." His usual stoic voice falters just a little. It should pull me up from my stupor, but I am so, so very lost. I just need to return home somehow. I need to find a reason to get up. ". . . I'm worried about her. Can you talk to her for me?" He pauses. "I don't want to touch her, but I don't see blood. I don't think she hurt herself."

I wouldn't. Would I? No . . .

I feel the cold phone being pressed against my ear.

"Lily?" Dr. Banning's calm voice fills my head. "Can you hear me? What's wrong?"

Everything. *This.* I pray for strength, but it won't come. I want to stand, but my legs won't move. I need a reason to continue . . .

"I'm sorry I woke you up," I barely whisper. The words burn my throat, and I shut my eyes as a couple tears escape.

"Don't be sorry, Lily. That's what my emergency line is for, okay? Can you talk to me? What are you feeling?"

"Embarrassed." I squeeze my eyes with two fingers. I'm so ashamed of what I am and what I do. How can I ever stop? It seems . . . like a mountain I have not been tasked or equipped to climb.

"What else?"

"Tired. Ashamed. Upset."

"You're going through a lot right now, Lily," she tells me. "It's normal to feel these things, but you have to stay strong. Before you feel out of control, you need to talk to someone and tell them what's bothering you. It doesn't have to be me, but I'm always here. How did this start? Is it about Loren?"

"Yes. No . . . I don't know," I mutter. I pause and open up a little, forgetting that Ryke squats by the tub only a foot away. As I talk, a weight begins to slowly (very slowly) rise from my chest. It's still there, but it lessens just a little. "I'm going to have to stop masturbating, aren't I?" I lick my chapped lips and cringe at my own words.

"Do you think it's unhealthy or a gateway into other compulsions?" she asks, her tone serious.

"I do it," I choke, "and I always want more. It's never enough."

"Giving something up isn't the same thing as losing control. It's the opposite, Lily. You're taking back control."

I try to relax by her statement. While powerful, the full force of it breezes through me and then drifts away. I imagine Rose saying something similar. I hear them. I see the strength in the words. I feel it, but I can't hold on to it and *believe* it the way they can. I don't know why that is.

"Everything is going to be okay," she emphasizes. "I know it may not feel like that right now, but in time, everything will be okay. You have to start believing you can make it there."

"I know."

"Okay, good. Can you give the phone back to your friend?"

Ryke peels the phone from my ear and presses it to his own. I watch his face as he listens to Dr. Banning. I can sit up now. Even if everything still hurts, I try to numb the pain with her encouragement. *Be strong, Lil,* Lo would tell me. *When I come back, I'll be strong with you.* I wipe the rest of my tears, imagining those last words. Praying that's what his response would be and not the awful *your problems are too much for me right now.* God, please, let him come back to me.

"Yeah, I can do that." Ryke nods, his eyes falling to the tiled floor. "He'll answer. Thanks so much. I really appreciate it. You have no idea." He hangs up the phone.

"I'm sorry," I say in a small, tired voice.

Ryke raises his hand. "I'm going to call Lo. You *cannot* start crying and have a breakdown over the phone. He can't do anything to help you right now, and you know how much that'll kill him."

I nod wildly, my heart lifting at the very idea of speaking to him. "I promise."

He hesitates before dialing.

I lean my arms against the bathtub rim, nearly falling over to be closer to the receiver—to hear his voice.

After a couple rings, Ryke says, "Hey, did I wake you?" He rolls his eyes. "You're such a fucking smart-ass . . . yeah, well, I have someone here who wants to talk to you." He pauses and then glares at the ceiling. "No, she's fine. She just finished talking to her therapist." He rubs his jaw and then nods to himself before holding out the phone to me.

I grab it quickly, but once I have it against my ear, my thoughts start to sink somewhere foreign. I forget what I planned to say. Maybe I had nothing to tell him. Maybe, I just wanted to hear his voice. I whisper, "Hi."

"Hey," Lo replies back. Out of the corner of my eye, I see Ryke kicking my comforter back into the living room. He avoids the vibrator and doesn't ask questions about it, but my cheeks flush, mortified all the same. I sink lower in the tub.

"It's Daisy's birthday," I tell him. "I'm in Mexico."

"Ryke told me already."

Oh.

Ryke props the door open against the wall and nods to me. "Don't close this." He heads to his chaise, plopping down with an exhausted sigh.

Long, silent tension pools over the phone, and I lose track of what I should say. I'd rather not bring up the fact that I'm sitting in an empty bathtub after an emotional meltdown. I don't want to give him another reason to avoid me when he returns home. Because who in their right mind would want to take care of this?

I'm about to mention how we're all going zip-lining tomorrow at Daisy's request, but he beats me.

"So what happened tonight?"

Shit.

"Nothing really, and I don't think we should talk about it. You're all the way over there." Wherever *there* is. No one will tell me his exact location. He could be in Canada for all I know.

"If Ryke handed you the fucking phone—someone who definitely disapproves of our relationship—then I know it had to be bad. I want to know, Lil." This is not how I imagined our conversation. I thought we'd avoid the topic like we've always done in the past. He briefly mentions alcohol. I'll say a little bit about sex, but when things become messy and truly focus on our addictions, we abort.

"It wasn't bad," I mumble under my breath. "Ryke told me not to bring it up. I think we should talk about something else. You need to concentrate on your recovery, not worry about me." I hesitate from going further. Dr. Banning invades my mind, and I can almost hear her saying that Ryke is wrong. That separating from Lo isn't the answer. Finding a healthy way to be together is.

But does he still want me? I'm not so sure. I wipe my eyes.

He lets out a short, bitter laugh. "If you don't tell me, I'm going to be worrying about it all fucking month, Lil. And Ryke hasn't fully comprehended the fact that I'm going to eventually come home. And when I do, I'm going to be with you again. We're going to have to start talking and reforming a better relationship. If I can't handle this shit over the phone when I'm sober *in* rehab, then I shouldn't be returning home anytime soon."

All I hear is: *I'm going to be with you again.* I bring the receiver away from my mouth and wipe uncontrollable, silent tears that stream down in an avalanche. A huge pressure rises off my chest. I feel like I can breathe again.

"Lily?" he says in a frantic voice. "Lily, you there? Lily, dammit . . ."

I put the speaker back. "I'm here."

I hear him exhale and breathe heavily. "Don't do that. And don't make me fucking guess what happened."

I rest my back against the tub. "It's embarrassing," I admit.

"So?"

"So you really want to do this? To talk and stuff . . ."

"If we want to stay together, like *really* stay together and not go back to enabling each other, then yes, we're going to have to talk. I need to know when you're freaking out, and you need to know when I am so that we can stop each other from doing stupid shit."

"Like the opposite of what we've been doing." Dr. Banning said as much.

"Basically. Look, we've spent so much energy hiding each other's addictions from our families. If we put that into helping one another, we just might be able to make this work."

I like the game plan. It starts clearing that haze that has been clouding my future for so long. A picture begins to form of *us* when he returns. And I'm more overwhelmed by the fact that there will be an *us* after a three-month separation.

I finger the hem of my shirt. "We divorced," I mutter. "I thought you weren't going to want me back."

His voice lowers to a pained whisper. "Why would you think that?"

I lick my dry, chapped lips again. "Couples who divorce usually don't get remarried." Of course, we're not actually married. But he'll understand the metaphor. He's used it before when we were teenagers. We played house most of our lives. It's kind of fucked up, but I guess that's just us.

"I'm remarrying you, Lil. Fuck, I'd remarry you a hundred times until it stuck."

I pinch my eyes again. "Yeah?"

"Yeah."

"Even if I make you miserable?"

There's a long pause before he murmurs, "You don't make me miserable. You make me want to live. And I want to live with you."

My throat closes for words. I sniff and rub my nose and wipe the last of my tears.

"Okay?" he breathes. "So about tonight, you need to tell me what happened."

I nod to myself. Right. "These past couple of months, I've just been masturbating a ton. And this boat trip was supposed to be better than last time. I wasn't supposed to turn into this compulsive monster." I fucked up. But telling him this is easier than I thought it would be. Probably because we were always best friends before we ever became a real and true couple.

"Compulsive how?"

"I couldn't stop. I was using my vibrator and then Ryke bulldozed into my room because he was scared he was about to get raped by a sixteen-year-old girl."

"Seriously?" he says in disbelief. I'm not sure what he's referring to, and so my nerves jostle.

"What? Which part?" I scratch my arm.

"The part where Ryke is scared of a high school girl. What a pussy," he says with a laugh.

I relax. "That's mean to say about your brother."

"Half brother," Lo snaps back. *Okaaay*. Obviously there's some issue going on that I'm not aware of.

"I thought you guys were cool."

"Oh yeah," Lo says sarcastically, "I just love being the bastard."

I guess before Ryke showed up, Lo thought he was a child caught in a nasty divorce between his parents. Come to find out, he was the *cause* of their separation: a product of infidelity.

He sighs heavily. "Look, I can forgive him for lying to me because he's been supportive of my recovery, and besides you, he's the only person who knows what it's like to be around my father. But he can be so fucking abrasive."

I smile, glad we agree on something. "I know. He bugs me all the time, but I kind of have to put up with him." Because he means well. And he's one of the reasons we've reached this place.

If Ryke hadn't injected himself in our lives, I'm afraid we would have continued to enable each other.

"About that . . ." Lo trails off, trying to pick his words carefully. "I'm not feeling particularly loving towards him when I'm stuck here and he's over there . . ." He refrains from adding *with you*, but I hear it anyway. "It's just not an ideal situation."

"You wouldn't want to be here anyway," I tell him. "Daisy's friends talk nonstop. Your ears would start bleeding."

"But I would still be with you," he says and then lets out a frustrated groan. "I just want to hold you right now. It's killing me."

"Not as much as me," I breathe.

Lo pauses. "What happened after Ryke walked in on you? He didn't see you naked, did he?"

I blush. "No, no . . ." I quickly explain my comforter snafu and waddling to the bathroom. "I should have stopped, you know. That was the point where I should have ended my self-love for the night."

"But you didn't."

I bite my fingernail to the bed. "Afterwards, I got sad. I broke down. Ryke came in and called my therapist. I talked to her and managed to stop crying. That's it. That was my glorious night."

"I thought you got rid of all your toys," he says, confused. I imagine his brows furrowing and his forehead wrinkling in a bit of disapproval.

Shit. I did tell him that the first time we talked. Along with trashing my porn (which was the truth), I told a lie about ditching my sex toys.

"I lied," I blurt out the truth. "But I really did throw out my porn."

"No more lying," Lo says roughly. "Not with each other and not with our friends. We have to do better."

"Yeah, I know. I will. That was . . . that was all before I met my therapist."

I hear him shift a little, the chair creaking.

"Are you on that ugly orange chair?" I ask.

"No, I'm in my room at my desk."

"Oh . . ." I try to picture his room, and just when I'm about to ask, he pipes in.

"What did your therapist say tonight?"

I cringe. "No more self-love for me." I press my forehead to my knees. "I think it's going to be impossible though until you get back. It's been so long; I can't even imagine . . ." Not touching myself? Not reaching that high just once . . . it seems infeasible.

"How old were you when you started touching yourself?"

I kiss my kneecaps, knowing the first moment well because Dr. Banning made me dig through my memories and give it to her. "Nine, but I started doing it to porn at eleven after I found that magazine at your dad's place."

"Okay, that's disgusting," he snaps. "Please never mention how you *masturbated* to my father's porn ever again."

"It was yours, you jackass," I say lightly, not as offended as I should be I think.

"How do you know?"

"It was in *your* shoebox of porn on *your* shelf and in *your* closet."

"Oh. Never mind then."

I smile. I miss talking to him, even if our conversations aren't normal by any standard. I don't think we've ever been normal. Maybe that's why it works.

"Well, that sounds like a solid plan," I say. "I'll try to minimize now, but completely eliminate self-love when you return home."

"That's the shittiest plan I've ever heard."

"What?" I frown. *This* is not normal. He usually agrees with me.

"It doesn't matter if I'm there or not. If your therapist doesn't think it's a good idea, then it's probably not one."

"But that means . . . I won't be able to have any kind of sex until you come home . . ." My pulse speeds up in sudden fear. I know Lo is cutting alcohol completely from his life, but my therapist said that recovering sex addicts *shouldn't* strive towards celibacy forever. It's an impossible standard to maintain. Sex is a part of human nature.

"Unless it's with me," Lo adds.

Now I'm really confused. "I don't understand. You're not here. Unless you're going to mail me a dildo of your dick," I say hopefully.

"Uh, no. I'm not letting anyone mold my cock for your pleasure. You can have the real thing at the end of March."

"Then how am I supposed to have sex?"

"What about phone sex?" *Ohhhh.* Wait . . .

"Isn't that the same thing as me masturbating?"

"Not if you're doing it to my voice and only my voice. That way, you know when to stop, and it'll set up a system for you. The hardest part about recovering from sex addiction—for you, I think—is going to be establishing limits, right?"

It sounds like a really good idea, and I'm kind of surprised he came up with this on his own. "Yeah, how do you know so much about it?"

"I've been talking to some counselors who know a lot about addictions, some have worked with sex addicts before. They've been giving me some advice."

I smile. "So can we have phone sex now?"

"No."

"What? But you just said—"

"You have to earn it."

Huh . . . "That's kind of mean."

"I never said I would be nice. I'm done enabling you, which means we're not going to have sex whenever you want it. You'll have to find the strength to hold out until the time is right."

"And you get to choose when the time is right. How is that fair?"

"I'm not the sex addict."

Touché. "Jeez. I thought sober Lo would be nicer."

"I'm nice when it counts," he says. "You love me anyway."

"I do," I agree. "But if you wait another month before we have phone sex, I might hate you."

"I'll keep that in mind."

Ryke knocks on the doorframe, and I jump at his sudden presence. I forgot he was even still here. "You done? You're killing my battery charge."

He hates that I'm talking to Lo, but I actually feel a thousand times better. Dr. Banning must have known that he'd be the one to say the right things and in the right way to make me believe the words. He's given me hope again. That I'll kick this addiction. And I won't have to be alone when I do it.

"Lo, your brother wants his phone back," I tell him.

"*Half* brother."

I smile and climb out of the bathtub.

I needed this.

"I'll call you later. I love you," he tells me.

"Love you too." I hand Ryke the phone with an added glare.

He touches his chest. "Hey, I called him for you." He snatches the phone. "You shouldn't be scowling at me. You should actually kiss my toes."

"With this," I say, pushing past him into the room. My comforter lies in a ball at the base of my bed. I tug the tangled blanket out and wrap up in it, hopping on the mattress. I close my eyes but can't seem to wipe the silly grin off my face.

No more self-love, sure. I'll probably be in a world of pain tomorrow, but for right now, I feel like I'm in the clouds.

Thirteen

almost peed my pants. Zip-lining should be banned from all civilized cultures. What I thought was a mild fear of heights intensified to the millionth degree as I propelled across a rain-forest. Never again.

I almost had a heart attack as well. Only it spurned from watching my little sister gliding on the line completely upside down. All her friends kept yelling at me for screaming at *her* as she zipped headfirst over the hundred foot drop. Am I really the insane one in this scenario?

When we decide to go eat lunch back in the village, I could nearly kiss the safe, flat ground. Daisy chose an outdoor café with tiki lights and Mayan-themed masks dangling from umbrellas. We gather around a long picnic table, and I barely concentrate on the menu. My nerves have fried from all the anxiety, and the craving for a release irritates my skin. It's like someone keeps pinching me, and my mind just responds *go to the bathroom. Release. Release and you'll feel better.* I hate it.

And I know that I can't do it anymore. Time to make better choices or at least ones that do not involve ditching a table of girls to masturbate in the bathroom. Thinking the words actually causes guilt to surface. Yeah, I want to avoid that shame. Besides,

Lo says I have to earn phone sex. Giving into the urges the day after I make a commitment to stop will award me zero points.

So I try harder.

I take a deep breath and train my eyes on the menu, debating between fish tacos and a chicken enchilada. The girls start discussing boys in their grade and successfully ignore Ryke and me since we have nothing to add to the conversation.

The sun causes my forehead to bead with sweat, and one of the girls complains about needing a fan moved out here just to cool them down. Ryke orders an extra pitcher of water to shut them up.

As the waiter leaves, Ryke nudges my arm and asks in a low voice, "How was Lo?"

"Mean," I reply. "But good mean, I think. Does that make sense?"

"Yeah. With Lo, it does."

I wish he was here in Mexico with us. Maybe next year or during spring break we can enjoy a trip together. If he's at a place where he can be surrounded by alcohol, that is. Him, sober. Me, not as compulsive about sex. It sounds quite nice even if it's a little hard to picture.

"Hey, has anyone seen Daisy?" Cleo asks.

I look up from my menu and glance frantically around the table, noticing her empty chair.

"I thought she went to the bathroom," Harper says.

"I just came back from the bathroom. She wasn't there. I checked the stalls," Cleo tells us.

My head whips to Ryke, my eyes bugging. And he immediately says, "Calm down. She's probably around here somewhere." He rises from the table. "I'll go ask the hostess if she's seen her." He slips his Wayfarers off and enters the café with stiff shoulders. I see his muscles flexing a little from his red tank. At least if he finds her with a guy, he may be able to intimidate him with pure brawn.

I dial Daisy's number, trying to push away nagging thoughts about how we're in a foreign country. And even though we're staying in the touristy parts, anything can happen. Daisy takes French in prep school. Not Spanish. If someone kidnaps her, she won't be able to understand what's going on.

My anxiety peaks at the fifth ring. *Pick up!*

The line clicks. "Hi, it's Daisy. Not Duck and not Duke. Definitely not Buchanan. I'm a Calloway. If you haven't misdialed then leave your name after the beep, and I'll call back when I return from the moon. Don't wait around. It may take a while."

BEEEP.

I cut the line off rather than leave her a scathing message. She's probably just talking to someone at the bar or something . . . oh God.

"She's not texting me back," Katy grumbles. A couple of the other girls say they can't reach her either.

"That's not like her," Harper says, her brows cinching in worry. "She's a fast texter."

"Do you think she got Natalie Holloway'ed?" Katy whisper-yells.

"You did *not* just use her name as a verb," Cleo chastises.

Ryke returns and throws a wad of bills on the table. His pissed and worried expression unsettles my stomach, a combination that I do not like right now. "Girls." He motions for all of them to rise. "Leave your drinks. We have to call a cab."

I shoot up from the table and walk briskly beside Ryke as we go to the street to hail multiple cabs. "What happened?" I ask. "Where is she?" Cars swerve in and out of the long, touristy strip, and yellow taxi vans pull to the side to collect us. The air is thick with humidity, and the palm trees jut up from the grassy center median, leaning crookedly. Even amid a supposed tropical paradise, something has to go wrong.

He rubs the back of his neck. "The hostess said she saw her leave with a man—"

That's all I hear. I turn to bolt down the sidewalk, about to run and scream her name at the top of my lungs.

Ryke grabs my arm and tugs me back. "Before you go call the fucking Coast Guard," he says roughly, "I think I might know where she is."

"How?" I ask, fear poking me in the lungs.

He motions for the first group of girls to climb into the nearest van. "Get in," he tells them. "Tessa, you too." The Katy Perry girl pouts, obviously hoping to ride in the same taxi as him. But from what Ryke told me, *she* is the one he wants to stay far, far away from.

"Ryke!" I shout. I need answers. Daisy is my baby sister. The girl who trailed Rose and me like a little shadow. We pretended to believe in Santa Claus for five extra years just for her. I can't lose her to Mexican drug lords or kidnappers or rapists or fucking anything. Not on my watch. I'd do more than call the Coast Guard. I'd get the Marines, the Army, the Air Force, parafucking-troopers. I'd have twenty choppers flying around the country for her. Maybe that's excessive and they have better things to do. But I don't care.

"Get in first," he tells me, motioning to the last taxi. I climb in after he gives the address to the first and second drivers. Harper sits to my left. And then Cleo jumps in and squishes to my right. How the hell did I get sandwiched between them?

Ryke takes the passenger seat by the driver. "Follow those cabs," he tells him. "Quickly." And the van speeds off.

Cleo leans forward, her elbow digging into my thigh. "Is she okay?" she asks Ryke, sticking her head in between the seats.

I'm wondering the same thing, Ryke. I need some info here. "The hostess said the guy she walked out with is a local travel agent. She gave me a list of spots he takes tourists to."

"So she hasn't been kidnapped?" Harper says.

"Not until he realizes who she is," Cleo adds.

I shoot them both a glare. "Not helping." My stomach sinks and knots. I stare up at Ryke in the front seat. "How do you know which spot he took her to?"

"I have a feeling—"

"A feeling?" I snap. "Ryke, she's missing, and you barely know her—"

"I know her enough," he says. "She's fucking impetuous and daring, a little too bold and way too fucking fearless."

That sounds about right.

"Trust me, Lily." He cranes his neck over his shoulder to look at me, and Cleo backs up a little, leaning against her seat again. "I promise that I'll find her. I won't let anything happen to that girl, okay?" Confidence and determination pulses in his eyes. I just hope he chose the correct place. I'd rather not chase her around Mexico to find that the tour guide had kidnapped her after all.

I nod once, and Cleo actually takes my hand and squeezes lightly. Compassion—something I'm not used to from people. Especially girls.

I give her a weak smile, and she returns it. The cabs roll to a stop, and Cleo slides open the door. We crawl out, flip-flops hitting cement. Girls pool from the other cabs in front of us, and we all gather together after the vans drive off. I have no idea where we are. At the bottom of a sloping hill, I spot a group of tourists staring at the side of a yellowish brown cliff. I hear the roar of the ocean and the splash as water crashes into the rock. White-capped waves flow into a ravine that separates the tourists' lookout point from the cliff. And the crowd watches the rock and the water. I know what this is, but I don't want to believe it.

Ryke practically runs down the hill towards the tourists, and the girls take their time following. I sprint to catch up to him.

"Did she go scuba diving?"

"No," he says tersely, reaching the bottom. He scrutinizes the faces, trying to find Daisy's among the people, and I follow their gaze towards the cliff.

My heart nearly explodes. Because a set of five bronze-skinned men stand on the side of a forty-foot cliff, some locals even higher at the top, probably eighty feet. And one springs off, his body arched as he dives.

Straight.

Into the ravine below.

Oh. My. God.

He makes a little splash, but all I see is rock and then rock and then the little sliver of water that he could have easily missed. Holy. Shit.

Where is my sister?! And then, I see her. She's not standing with the tourists on the "safe" side where we are. No, she has somehow found her way on the cliff. Barefoot, she clings to the middle of the rock and scoots over as one of the divers directs her where to place her feet.

I cup my hands to my mouth. "DAISY!" I scream until my throat burns. She's crazy. Certifiable.

Ryke freezes by my side and lets out a string of profanities.

"I have to go get her," I say, my ribs constricting around my lungs. She can't jump. She's not a trained diver. We're in Acapulco, Mexico, where the men have probably dived from the ledge hundreds of times, timing the rate of the waves into the rock, knowing exactly which spot to hit. She knows nothing!

"No," Ryke tells me. "I'm going to get her. You'll have a panic attack halfway up the fucking cliff. Just stay here. Watch the girls. Take a fucking breath." He looks like he needs one too. He doesn't waste another second talking to me. He darts off in the direction where we came from, trying to find a way to the cliff side.

I just watch her little speck of blonde hair that's tied in a braid at her shoulder. She nods as a local diver points to the water below and then motions to the rock. *At least he's teaching her*, is all I think. If she jumps she could die or get a concussion. This is not in the itinerary.

"Oh my God," Cleo exclaims, reaching my side. Her fingers curl around the metal safety railing. "Is that Daisy?"

The girls gasp as they huddle around. They all start whisking out their cellphones to record my sister's impending death. Her toes stick off the rock ledge, not much to brace herself with.

She's planning on jumping. She's not just up there for an intimate tour of the cliff. This is her idea of fun.

"She's nuts," Harper says with the shake of her head.

Another local diver springs off the edge and soars in the air with mastered precision. He dives headfirst into the right spot of water, and the man teaching Daisy keeps talking, as though that was some kind of demonstration for her.

Daisy nods, not even a little scared. I can practically see her eyes lighting up in awe and excitement.

"Is she going to jump?" Harper asks. "There are rocks everywhere."

Cleo anxiously clenches the railing. "This isn't an ocean. This is, like, as small as a river. Shouldn't she be jumping into that?" She points to the full blue ocean that hits the northern part of the cliff, but Daisy is on the side, the section where the ocean flows into this little crevice between our lookout point and the mountain she spiders.

"I've seen these types of dives before," Katy (or rather Tessa) says, smacking on gum. She sidles up next to Cleo. "There's a small radius where it's like really, *really* deep and then beyond that it's shallow and really, *really* rocky."

Where's Ryke?!

"Shut up," Cleo snaps at her. "Seriously, shut up."

And then, I see Ryke ascending the cliff, grabbing cutouts in the rock and putting his feet in divots, hiking his body up and then over with endurance and strength. He doesn't need a local to show him the way. He's free climbing, I realize. Free-solo climbing. Without a rope. I guess, in some way, he was able to do what he had planned before coming on this trip.

Still, I am terrified.

A local says something, and their heads swivel in Ryke's direction. The man edges closer and holds out his hand to Ryke when he finds their path. He shakes it as though he's a welcomed guest to their club atop a cliff. Actually, they're not *on* top. That would be too high. But the side of the cliff is already too tall for comfort.

Daisy acknowledges Ryke, and then looks back at the water when his mouth starts moving. His face grows red and veins begin to pop from his neck as he rants. If I was closer, I wonder if I would see spit flying from his lips, beyond furious.

The locals let him say what he needs to, and then Ryke turns to them, speaking a little, but his motions are calm, less irate. They nod and then point to the water, replying back. God, I wish I could hear.

When Daisy begins talking, I think maybe Ryke has succeeded in convincing her to return to the parking lot. But her hands start gesticulating, angry and as irritated as he is.

They're arguing.

He steps closer, his foot halfway on the ledge as they straddle the side of the fucking mountain. His nose touches hers as he gets into her face, shouting. Her chest puffs out and she yells back. Their voices begin to echo through the ravine but not loud enough to make out words or syllables.

And then she puts her back against the ledge and says something to the local man. He nods, and Ryke screams at her, "NO!" We can all hear the fear and anger writhing in his voice.

But it's too late.

She dives.

Right.

Off.

The fucking.

Cliff.

Headfirst.

I hold my breath, my lips parting as my jaw drops. Not even a full second after she dives, Ryke impulsively jumps right in after her.

This . . . is not good. Both Lo and I are going to lose siblings in one day.

I wait for them to come to the surface for what seems like hours. *Waiting. Waiting.* The water rushes in and then back out of the ravine in a systematic cycle. White foam smacking slick black rocks.

Where is she?

Ryke pops up first in the center of the water, hitting the right spot. His head whips around, searching for Daisy. He spins in circles. From where I stand, I can see the panic lacing his eyes, and my stomach does a thousand somersaults.

"Ohmygod," Cleo mutters. "Where is she?!"

The other girls keep out their cellphones, still videotaping. I should have realized that Daisy would be in more danger doing something potentially life-threatening than being kidnapped. I should have had a discussion about *no cliff diving to your death* before the trip began.

And then, her head breaks the surface of the water, a few feet from Ryke.

In what seems to be a deep, safe region.

I let out a small breath of relief.

Ryke looks ready to burst a blood vessel in his neck. He takes his aggression out on the water and splashes her. She splashes back, and they start screaming again. She shakes her head and ends up swimming away towards the rocky bank.

Ten minutes later, they appear near the top of the hill, waiting for us and dripping wet. Ryke runs his hand through his thick, soaked hair. And Daisy's green tank top sucks to her slender frame while her jean shorts sop. We all start walking, and I hear their argument the closer I approach.

"He told me where to land!" she shouts. "I took diving lessons in seventh grade. I was fine, Ryke!" She did take lessons, I remember now. Our mother made her do a ton of things, trying to find her talent until she ended up modeling.

"You left all of your friends at a fucking restaurant!" he shouts back. "Your sister thought you'd been kidnapped! How selfish are you?"

Her cheeks grow red. "I didn't think anyone would care . . ."

"Bullshit," he sneers. "You knew we'd come after you. You knew we'd track you down and ruin our plans to make sure you were alive. You wanted us to chase you."

She shakes her head rapidly. "No. I just wanted to do this, but I knew Lily wouldn't let me. This is why I chose Acapulco—for this cliff. It's famous. And I'm sorry for ruining everyone's day, but it was worth it."

"You could have died," he growls, his eyes narrowing with such anger—I would have already cowered back. Daisy has her shoulders locked tight, her head held high, resolute. Ryke is right. Nothing scares her.

"I know."

He stares at her for a long, long time, and as I reach them, I hesitate on breaking up their heated fight. "Did you want to die?" he finally asks.

Daisy blinks for a couple seconds, not in confusion. It's as though she expected this reaction. She shrugs and then says, "How'd you find me anyway?"

"Free-falling," he tells her. "You said it's better than sex."

Her lips twitch into a smile. "Do you agree with me now?"

"As fun as that was," he says roughly, "it'll never be better than *fucking* someone you love." He adds, "Don't do that shit again." And he turns around and motions to the pack of girls to follow him back to the parking lot.

I catch Daisy's arm before she goes to Cleo. Her weak smile immediately falls to the wayside at my near-tears. I've never been more terrified.

"Lily . . . I'm sorry. My intention wasn't to scare you."

"What if you died?"

"I didn't." She touches my arm and shakes it. "Come on. Be happy, we're in Mexico."

"That's not okay, Daisy," I say. "You can't just sprint away without telling someone where you're going." I have never read the Big Sister Handbook, so I decide to just tell her what I feel. That has to be enough. "We could have found a cliff that was supervised, not one clearly meant for professional, local divers."

"I wanted to jump off this one."

I sigh heavily. "Do you hear yourself? You *wanted* this one? You sound like Cleo and Harper, spoiled and entitled."

She cringes. "I'm sorry. I really am." She shakes her head. "I shouldn't have . . . If I'd known your reaction beforehand, I would have stopped."

The scary thing—I don't believe her. Not one bit.

"Okay." Nothing else can be said. Ryke grilled her. I gave her the disapproving, brokenhearted look.

"I'm not on your shit list, am I?" she asks. "Honestly, I didn't even think you had one."

"I didn't."

She gasps. "So I'm the *only* person on it?"

I can't help but smile. We begin to walk back together, her friends farther ahead of us. "I guess."

"What can I do?" she asks. Her eyes brighten. "I know! Cake. Cake fixes everything." She shouts at the girls, "Cake time!"

They let out cheers and clap and spin around to record Daisy for the end of their videos. I'm sure those will be circulated around her prep school for quite some time. She'll be a superstar. For all the wrong reasons.

Ryke turns his head at the announcement and still looks pissed. He rolls his eyes and shakes water from his hair with a firm hand.

"You know what he said to me?" Daisy says. "He told me that I was going to crack open my skull, bleed into the ocean and be eaten by sharks. And then he goes and jumps in after me." She lets out an irritated laugh. "I didn't need him to be my hero, showing up, scaling the cliff and speaking Spanish to the locals—"

"Wait, they didn't speak English?"

Daisy realizes she let that little part slip. She winces as she flashes an apologetic smile. "They were telling me stuff, and I just replied back with, 'Sí,' over and over again. I got the gist of what they were saying when they moved their hands. You should be more surprised by the fact that Ryke is *fluent* in Spanish."

"I'm not," I snap, "because he grew up with a mom as neurotic as ours."

"He did?" Her brows furrow.

"I don't know her personally," I clarify. "But she kept him busy." I refrain from saying *like you* because she does not need to be attracted to him anymore than I think she already is. Their age difference is no-no territory. Ryke understands this, and I'm afraid that Daisy may not.

"Oh."

I hesitate. "Daisy, you don't . . ." *have a crush on him.*

She meets my eyes and reads them well. "Like you said before, Lily, he's seven years older . . . well, about to be six." She tries to give me a reassuring smile before she breaks from my side and catches up to Cleo, but I'm not satisfied. Because she glances back at Ryke as he peels off his wet shirt and wrings it out. Her eyes flit over his body, and I see a not-so good future.

I'm not sure how Lo would react to a Daisy and Ryke scenario.

All I know is that he wouldn't be happy.

March

Fourteen

Back in the states, the March chill makes it near impossible not to layer up. I devise a plan to stay at the house until the very last second. Usually I arrive seven minutes late to class when I decide to go, but I think everyone should have a ten minute grace period. Seriously. It's cold.

The only other time I brace for the weather is for my therapy sessions with Dr. Banning. Today went decently well, I think. I feel like I'm on the road to uncovering *why* I have this addiction, and she gives me some much needed perspective and guidance.

To preoccupy my thoughts and not obsess over sex, I watch a romantic comedy on Netflix in my bedroom. I closed my canopy so I feel a little like I'm in a jungle, my net keeping me safe from mosquitos. Which is kinda fun. I'd make some safari jokes, but I remember that I'm alone. And no one is around to appreciate them.

The laptop rests on my stomach while I munch on a Twizzler. After abstaining from self-love, I've turned to sugar and sweets and generally anything that will rot my teeth. It barely helps, but it's better than succumbing to the urges.

My phone rings, and I wiggle from my Marvel throw blanket. When I grab my cell, I notice the unknown number on the screen.

My chest lightens as I mute my computer and press the receiver to my ear.

"Hey, it's Lo."

That's enough to make me grin from ear to ear.

"Lo who? My boyfriend's name is Loren."

"Your jokes have gotten progressively less funny without me."

I mock gasp. "No way. You should have been here when I made the *best* giraffe joke. It was hilarious."

"Doubtful," he says, but I can sense him breaking into a smile.

I bite a Twizzler, trying to contain my own silly look, even if he can't see me. "What are you doing? How's rehab?" Before he called, I made a plan to ask more about him. Last time, the conversation revolved around me, and I don't want that to happen again. Even if my recovery takes effort from both of us, it doesn't make his any less important.

"It's fine," he says. I imagine him shrugging. "What about you? Did you go to therapy today?" So I have a boyfriend who doesn't like to talk about his problems. This may be harder than I thought.

"Don't change the subject. I want to know how *you're* doing." I braid three Twizzlers together to form a giant, delicious piece.

"My life is boring," he sighs.

"No, it's not," I refute. "You're probably doing all sorts of cool things. Like talking to people. And . . . playing pool. And . . ." I have no idea what the hell he does in rehab, which I think is the problem.

"And nothing fun," he tells me. "I'm not there. I'm not with you."

"I thought you said we have to start *talking*," I emphasize. "That goes two ways you know. We can't just discuss my addiction and not yours."

Silence bleeds through the receiver for an excruciatingly long moment before he says, "I was talking to Ryke the other day . . . he asked me who Aaron Wells is."

My Twizzler slips out of my hand. I feel like Lo is deflecting, and it's kind of working considering Aaron Wells makes my stomach curdle. And I was planning on *never* telling Lo what happened at the Fizzle soda unveiling, especially while he's in rehab. I didn't want to give him a reason to turn to booze.

Lo says, "I asked him why he wanted to know. And he wouldn't give me a straight answer—just said something about how he went to a family event with you. And I thought, why the fuck would she ever want to bring that douchebag to a party? And then I remembered your mother and how she used to set you up before we were dating." He pauses. "Something happened, didn't it? Aaron knows I'm in rehab. He probably decided now was a good time for payback, right? You're defenseless while I'm basically trapped here."

"You're not trapped," I say. I don't want him to think of rehab as a prison. Not when it's helping him.

He groans, and I picture him rubbing his eyes wearily. "I want to be there with you," he says. "I don't want Ryke to be the one to protect you. That's my job, and I plan to be a hell of a lot better at it than before . . ." He trails off, and I read the rest: *before you almost got raped.* Yeah, he was a little too consumed by alcohol to come to my rescue that night. Thankfully I escaped that, but it still hurts to think about. I've tried to avoid public restrooms since then, and I try not to be plagued by the fear of being assaulted. Sometimes it creeps in, and I sink into myself in large crowds, but I've always been a little recluse in that sense.

I wish I could reply back *I didn't need protection.* But that would be an utter lie. Aaron was aggressive that night, and I did need some sort of reinforcement to help me. "Ryke didn't protect me," I say softly. I open my mouth to elaborate, but Lo has already jumped to conclusions.

"What?" His breath deepens. "If he fucking hurt you, I'm—"

"Lo," I cut him off. "I just meant to say that Ryke wasn't the one to help me . . . your father was."

The silence buzzes through the receiver again.

I elaborate. "He saw Aaron giving me a hard time, and he threatened him. It worked. Aaron left me alone after that."

The phone crackles.

"Lo?"

Then I hear him exhale. "My father?"

Maybe I shouldn't have mentioned anything. It took a great deal of strength to walk away from someone he loves but has hurt him. And to be caught in the grayness of Jonathan Hale makes it difficult to cut him completely out. Even though that may be best for Loren.

"Yeah." Right now, there's a slim, hopeless chance he'll open up about his father, and I kind of think he doesn't even know how he feels about the man. I'd talk to him about it, but he'll end the call before I even begin to prod. So I want to change the topic before he hangs up. "So what about rehab?" I ask. "You can't keep dodging this conversation."

I imagine him squeezing his eyes shut with that familiar agitation, and he groans again in annoyance. "You just put my head on a Tilt-A-Whirl, and you want to know about rehab?"

"Yes," I say, not backing down. I have to push him.

He lets out a long breath. "I'm sober. I just thought it'd feel different being sober for this long."

"What do you mean?"

"I was so miserable drunk, and I convinced myself that being sober would be the flip side of being miserable. I guess, I thought sobriety would be ninety-nine percent knock-your-socks-off

amazing. Don't get me wrong, it is nice. I can think clearer sometimes and filter some bullshit that I'd normally have no problem
saying. But it sucks too. It hurts more."

He has to face the pain now. I'm going through something
similar. All of the situations I'd drown with sex and a high are
things I have to confront head-on. It's difficult and makes the
urges even harder to restrain.

"But I'm not going back to *before*. Not for anything or
anyone . . ."

"Your father?" I ask, knowing that has to be the "anyone"
he's referring to. Jonathan Hale took away Lo's trust fund, his
inheritance, and everything that financially secured Lo's future.
All because Lo won't return to college and live up to his impossible standards.

"Yeah. Him," Lo mutters. "He's my therapist's favorite topic."

Maybe I can ease into this . . . "Are you going to talk to Jonathan when you get back?"

"I don't know anymore . . ." He pauses. "He's one of my triggers to drink, but I didn't need rehab to figure that out."

My chest constricts. "Am I . . ." What if *I'm* a trigger. Oh
God.

"No, Lil," he tells me with a short laugh. "You're the opposite. You're my stability . . . my home."

I inhale, his words pricking my eyes a little. He's always felt
like home to me too. I clear my throat, not wanting to become all
sappy over the phone. I only have so long to hear his voice. And
then I'll be alone again. "When you get back, what are you going
to do?" He won't go to college, and he'll need to earn money now.
Ryke and I both offered to help with his finances, but Lo's pride
squashed the idea.

"I'm not sure. I'll worry about it later," Lo says softly. I wish
I could hold him or hug him. Anything. He sounds a little lost,

but what twentysomething isn't? The only difference between Lo and me at this point is that I'm still in college. But we're in the same place really. I'm no closer to knowing what I want to do with the rest of my life. I wish my future bachelor's degree could magically choose a career path that's perfect for me. If four years of college bought me *that*, I'd be sold.

"Can we steer the conversation away from me now?" Lo asks. "How have you been holding up?"

"I'm a little frustrated," I mutter. "Sexually *and* mentally."

"Mentally?" he asks, worried. "Are you okay?"

"Yeahyeahyeah," I say quickly. "It's just that the therapy sessions drain me. I want to know why I'm addicted to sex so badly. Dr. Banning says the answer might not be so clear. And I just worry that when I find it . . . I won't like it."

His breath grows heavy over the line, and his words come out as a whisper. "Do you think it's me?"

It feels like a stab to the chest. I glance down at the Twizzler braid on my lap. "It's *me*, Lo," I choke. "I can't blame anyone else for my problems. I just have to figure out how it started."

"When we were nine, we did some things," he says quietly. "Do you remember that?"

"Lots of little kids do stupid stuff," I defend, thinking about what Dr. Banning told me. Experimenting, she called it.

"It was wrong," he tells me with added confidence. I imagine him running a shaking hand through his light brown hair. His voice remains firm and determined. "I was older than you."

"By nine months." He's being ridiculous.

"It doesn't matter, Lil," he snaps. "I've been thinking a lot in this place, and I want to tell you that I'm sorry. For everything that I've ever done to hurt you—"

"You haven't hurt me," I interject. "You haven't."

"Lily," he says, very softly. "You remember the night before we split up and I came here? The day before Christmas Eve?"

"The Charity Gala," I say. The night where he broke his short sobriety by chugging mini bottles of tequila from a hotel room.

"I hurt you," he says. "I had sex with you so you'd stop focusing on my alcohol addiction . . . so you'd stop looking at me like I was unraveling. You were crying hysterically, and I *fucked* you. And afterwards, I was a complete dick about it. What do you call that?"

"You didn't . . ." *rape me*, I think, knowing that's what's plaguing his mind. He didn't. "I wanted it, Lo. Please, don't think that." God, we're so messed up. I listen for his reply, but I only hear silence. "Lo?"

"Yeah." He clears his throat. "I'm sorry, Lil. For that night, for when we were nine. I'm *so* sorry."

"You don't have to take all the blame. I was there too when we were younger, you know. I touched you. Maybe I fucked you up."

He laughs now, and it makes me smile. "I can assure you that I'm fucked up, but it's not because of you."

"Likewise." At least, I hope so.

He suddenly lets out a long groan. "God, I just want to kiss you."

I grin. "Welcome to my world. I think I've imagined making out with you about five billion times since you've been gone."

"And how many times have you imagined my cock in your mouth?"

My eyes widen, and I lose my breath, even though he says it so blasé.

"What about my cock in your ass?" I hear the smile behind the words.

Oh my God. I lick my dry lips and squirm a little on the bed. The spot between my legs begins to pulse with his words.

"In your pussy?"

"Lo," I croak. Are we having phone sex right now? I eye the door. Should I go lock it?

"Have you been good?" Lo asks. "Did you touch yourself at all?"

"No, I've waited."

"I'm proud of you," Lo tells me. And I immediately feel a sense of accomplishment wash over me. "You've earned something then."

We are having phone sex! *Yes.* I crawl out of my canopy, struggling with the net for two seconds too long, and then jump off the bed with the phone still braced in my hand. I race to lock the door. Pausing in the middle of the room, I look to my closet. "Do I need . . ." How does this even work?

"Need what?" he asks in confusion. *Great, he can't read my mind.* What I'd give to be dating Charles Xavier—though the *X-Men: First Class* edition where he's played by James McAvoy. Bald doesn't do it for me.

"Never mind," I mutter.

"Need *what*, Lily?" Lo prods again, his voice serious. I don't answer right away, trying to gain the nerve to say the words. "Am I going to have to guess? It better not be lube. You've never had a problem getting wet around me."

"Stop talking," I tell him. "You're making this hard."

"You're making me hard."

I roll my eyes while my lips involuntarily rise. "Please tell me that's not your best dirty talk."

"I've said better," he agrees. "You know you can tell me anything. It can't be that embarrassing." He pauses. "Well, I'm sure you'll be embarrassed anyway, but good news is that I can't see you turn all red."

I wish he could. I'd give anything for him to be here right now. But then I wouldn't. Because coming home early means failure on his part, and I want him to succeed. I just feel so conflicted. About everything.

Maybe that's why I'm still standing in the middle of my bedroom, wavering on whether to venture to my closet or hop right back on the mattress.

"Do you think I should . . . use a vibrator or . . . dildo . . ." I actually *stutter*. My whole face heats, and I swear little beads of sweat gather on my upper lip. I wipe it frantically, panicked as though someone will see me perspiring.

"Are you serious? *That's* what you're fucking nervous to ask me?" he says, slightly offended. "I thought you wanted to use the cellphone or something."

What? It takes me a moment to realize what he's talking about. I gag and cringe. "Ew." Now *I'm* offended.

"That's what you get for not coming clean from the start, love," he says with a laugh. His voice drops to a serious tone. "What does your therapist say about the toys?"

"We haven't talked about them."

"Then let's avoid them for now, okay?"

I can't help but feel a little dejected by the decision. In my head, I heard Lo saying, *of course, go pick out the one that looks like my cock.* I guess those days of enabling are over.

I untangle the knotted canopy and climb back on the bed, the phone now on speaker. "Where are you right now?" I ask, wanting a mental picture in place.

"In my bedroom. I have my own bathroom, no roommate, so the privacy is nice. The comforter is kind of scratchy though."

"How sexy."

I see him grinning in my mind, his amber eyes lighting up. "Aren't I always?"

God, I miss him. A wave of sadness bears down on me, and the crash feels so sudden and abrupt that I have to pinch my nose to withhold tears. I sink back into my pillow and stare up at the top of my canopy. All I can think about is how much I want to see him. How ironic is that? The one time we're about to sort of have sex and I'm turning into an emotional spaz.

"Lily, are you crying?" Lo's worry intensifies.

"No." I wipe my eyes and keep my phone on my stomach. "Let's just do it."

"Well when you say it like that," he snaps.

I haven't had a release in days. I need to collect my bearings because if we call this off then I'm going to regret it badly in a couple hours when the urges start again.

"No, really, I'm okay." I straighten up and the phone thuds to my comforter. "Let's go. Who takes off their clothes first?" I cringe. That could have been way sexier.

"I think we both suck at phone sex," Lo tells me.

I should find this funny, but instead his words bulldoze right over me. It's like someone offered a bag of cocaine to a drug addict and decided at the last minute to yank it away. I picture tonight, alone in my bed, fighting the cravings yet again. And the moment will be my fault. Because I grew mopey and sad and pathetic. Idiot.

"No, we're good at it," I defend us. "Pleasepleaseplease, let's try again." But fear shakes my voice and causes me to garble them out with tears.

"Hey, hey, Lily," Lo says urgently. "It's okay." I can hear him rustling around, and I wonder if he's taking off an article of clothing. Maybe his pants.

"It's not," I refute. "It's not okay."

"Shhh," Lo whispers. "You're fine. I'm fine. I'm still going to make you come, I promise. Just relax and breathe, love."

As soon as he says the words, my computer lets out a *ping!* I sniff a little and mumble, "Hold on a sec." I pop open the Skype menu. Then I see the alert: *Accept call from Hellion616*

My heart immediately jumps to my throat. That's Lo, of course. His username has been his favorite Marvel character since he was fifteen. I'm going to see him, aren't I? Can this be real? I bite my lip and click the button.

The screen fills with Lo. He stares right back at me. He looks the same as I last remember. Almost three months have passed, and he still has the same light brown hair, shorter on the sides, full on top. The same sharp cheekbones that make him look menacing and lose-your-breath sexy. He sits cross-legged on his single bed, the comforter navy blue. He wears a charcoal gray T-shirt, and a pair of black track pants. His amber eyes actually stare into mine. I'm *looking* at him. Not just imagining his body, his eyes, his face. I can't help it—I instantly burst into uncontrollable, happy tears.

"No," Lo prolongs the word and adds a small smile. "Don't cry. You're going to make me start crying."

"I'm sorry." I wipe my eyes with the back of my hand. I let out a long breath and situate the laptop on my bed a little better. Now he's not staring at half of my face.

I meet his gaze again, this time more relaxed, but my chest swells. A part of me feared that he'd return home too changed and too different somehow. All my terror evaporates and shushes to bed. He's still Lo. He's still mine.

"Hi," he says in one breath.

"Hi." The hardest part about the whole ordeal has been being away from him. It has nothing to do with sex, I realize. He's my best friend, my whole world, and losing *that* hurts more than losing a body to grind on at night. Seeing him reminds me that he's not gone forever. Even if it may feel like it sometimes.

"You look good." His eyes flit around my body. "Are you gaining weight?" he asks hopefully. Maybe he imagined I'd be a withered twig, so gaunt and gnarly that he'd have to pick me up before I wasted away. Wow, that would be scary.

Maybe I wasn't the only one with huge, immeasurable fears.

"I am," I say with a smile. I lean back a little and snatch my pack of Twizzlers. I wave them at the screen. "I'm on a new diet. It's called Eat Sweets Avoid Sex."

"That sounds like an awful diet," he tells me, "and an awful way to deal with your addiction."

I shrug and raise the bottom of my cashmere sweater. "I can do this now." I pinch my half inch of fat by my belly button and show it off to him.

"That's nice, but you still have to get healthy the right way. Binge on your Twizzlers and Ho Hos now because when I get home, I'm abolishing that diet."

"How do you know I have Ho Hos?"

He tilts his head, and I see his playful smile envelop his face. Witnessing it lights up mine. "Please, if you purposefully stocked the pantry with sugar, you'd have all the best names. Ding Dongs, Sugar Daddys, Blow Pops."

"I didn't buy Blow Pops, thank you very much," I reply, like I won, even though he's kind of right. I have three packages of Ding Dongs waiting for me in the pantry. I have a penchant for names. Why else did I hire Connor Cobalt as my tutor when I was at Penn?

"Anything else new?" Lo asks gently, but now that I look at him, I spot the fear pulsing behind his eyes. He worries that *I'll* be the changed one. I feel the same, but I know, in time, that I'm going to be different. Everyone eventually grows up. But if there's anything I know for certain in this world—I never want to change without Loren Hale. We have to try to evolve together.

"I found a new freckle on my shoulder." I try to show him, but I bump into the screen. "Oops . . . sorry." I feel like I smacked him in the face or something. I tilt the computer back up and catch Lo grinning at me.

"Cute," he says.

I flush, and he rolls his eyes at my reddening cheeks, but he's still smiling. So that's good.

"I have something new too."

My eyebrows rise. *Really?* He grips the hem of his T-shirt, and then his eyes teasingly flit up to me, prolonging the moment. *Please don't let it be a tattoo.* Lo hates them, and the last thing I need is for him to declare his undying love with something he dislikes. And I don't necessarily want to stare at my name inked on his chest while we have sex. That's a mood killer for me.

I realize I'm progressively moving closer and closer to the screen. I lean back so I don't come across as a complete weirdo. "Come on," I say with a groan as he just *waits* there with a silly smile. He's killing me!

Finally, he tugs the shirt over his head, and he fixes his hair with his fingers, watching my expression which goes slack-jawed. I squint, hoping this isn't some sort of Skype Photoshop enhancement. "Are those real?" I end up asking, my fingers subconsciously running over his muscles on the screen. As though I can *really* touch them. Damn, I want to. I have to back away from the screen again. I think Lo received a pleasant view of my nose hairs.

He gives me a strange look and then laughs. "No, I painted these on just for you." Now shirtless, Lo cannot stop grinning. I cannot stop *staring*. His abs are ripped. Six-pack definition. He was muscular before, but they were not sharp like *that*. His lean muscles curve and even have that sexy dip by his waist, as though leading my way to his cock.

This is *so* much better than a tattoo.

"I've been working out," he explains. "We have a lot of recreational time. I spend most at the gym." He licks his bottom lip, his eyes grazing my body. "Your turn."

"I knew this was a trick to get me naked," I say with a smile. "Just don't get your hopes up. My boobs have not grown."

"I love your boobs how they are."

His husky voice makes me breathless. I blink a couple times and concentrate on "disrobing."

I stole Rose's cashmere sweater because I'm all out of clean clothes, and laundry is very low on my list of things I like to do. I situate myself on my knees and tilt the screen up so he has a better view of my top half. My heart thrums as I watch the rise and fall of his chest in anticipation. I've been naked so many times with Lo, but never over a computer screen. It's a little different—the distance, the inability to physically touch. But maybe it's a good different, almost more exciting.

I gradually pull the sweater over my head, my breasts pushed up in a black bra. My breathing deepens as I watch the way he stares, his eyes lowering and then trailing back up, as if his lips make their usual descent along my breasts and belly.

I want him to take me in his arms and push his whole weight on me. I want to feel his hardness against me—his muscles pin me to the mattress. To be buried beneath his love and his warmth.

"Where are you?" I whisper, plans to find him, to curl up in his arms, invade my mind.

"Right here. With you," he whispers back, not offering me any more, but *those* words are enough to steal my breath and cause my mouth to open. I keep my eyes on him and imagine his hand doing what mine does. Unclipping the clasp of my bra. Letting the straps slide down my shoulders and to the keyboard.

He looks at me like he wants to tug me into his hard chest and hold me tightly, like he's seconds from sucking on my bottom lip, from biting and then plunging his tongue inside. He'll rock against me and whisper my name until my back arches. Until I cry into his shoulder.

My nipples stand at attention, his gaze intensifying parts of my body that haven't been lit up in months. His eyes return to mine, and they're swimming with eagerness. Phone sex could never work with us. I would miss the looks and glances and the way he devours my body with his amber eyes. He makes me feel utterly and unequivocally gorgeous.

He alone can claim that feat.

Slowly, he begins to slide off his track pants, and I start unbuttoning my jeans. We glimpse each other often, trying to catch the other's sensual, measured, unhurried movements. Everything below my waist is blocked from his sight, and likewise, the screen cuts him off at his lower abs. The allure of what lies beneath heightens my pulse, heat gathering across my brow.

Clumsily, I wiggle out of my jeans and kick them off the bed. Now that I'm on my knees, Lo has a nice view of my green cotton panties. I plop back on my butt so he can only see me waist-up. While Lo undresses, I catch a view of the bulge in his black boxer briefs. The spot between my legs starts to throb again, aching for something hard to fill it and to thrust for a long, long while.

The silence drags out the tension, nothing but our heavy and shallow breathing. I wait motionless while he removes his last piece of clothing. My eyes fix on the screen in case I can glimpse his cock. But it doesn't make an appearance. Lo successfully strips off his boxer briefs without flashing me. *Boo.*

He raises his boxer briefs to the camera, dangling them from a finger victoriously before tossing them aside. His eyes meet mine in challenge. *My turn.*

With one hand, I brace myself on the mattress, and with the other, I roll my panties down my ankles. I bend forward to pull them over my feet, and I think I end up giving Lo a full-screen shot of my boobs in the process. He's getting way more out of this deal than me. That's for sure.

My panties rest in my hand, but they are *way* too soaked for me to lift them up in triumph. I'm about to fling them on the floor when Lo says, "You're not going to show me?"

Great. I turn them around so he has a view of the butt and hold them to the camera for a split second.

"Let me see the crotch," he urges in a soft voice. So demanding.

My eyes widen, and I shake my head quickly. No, no that will not be happening.

The corner of his lip rises. "Come on, Lil," he breathes. "I can't touch you. How else am I going to know how wet you are?"

I exhale a long, deep breath. I swallow hard and have the sudden longing to run my fingers right over my sweet spot. To feed the monster inside of me.

I take a trained breath and focus on Lo. "Let me see your cock first." My voice comes across more pleading and desperate than I intended. I don't even know why I want to see it. It's not like he can enter me through the computer screen. Really, it'll only torture me more.

"Not yet, love," he tells me sweetly.

"Then I'm not showing you my panties again," I refute stubbornly. I cross my arms over my breasts. For as long as I can remember, I always get what I want during sex. Or at least, I try to. And since I've been with Lo, he's been more than welcoming to give in to my desires. I didn't realize how difficult succumbing to his orders would be until now. I have to relinquish my control to him—to trust him, to put all my sexual needs into his care.

It's not so easy for me.

"That's not how this works," Lo says. "I'm in charge. If I tell you to come, you'll come. If I tell you to stop, you'll stop."

I need boundaries to harness my compulsions. *We've talked about this*, I remind myself. I drop my arms, exposing my breasts again for him. That's a start. Lo will provide the guidelines for my limits so I don't overdo it. I just need to learn how to accept them.

Lo has given himself completely to me. It's my turn to let him have me.

I obey his first command and turn my panties inside out and raise them to the screen, silently hoping the computer isn't high-definition. Though, clearly, they're soaked.

"Satisfied?" I ask after a few seconds.

"Immeasurably." His grin softens my heart, and my stomach flutters, weakening my resolve. This taunting can't go on for much longer.

I toss the panties on the floor, and he shifts a little on his bed. But I still can't see below his waist.

"Hold up your hands," Lo orders.

I frown and raise my palms to the computer. He gazes at me for a long moment, and I suddenly realize what he's about to do. I open my mouth to complain, but he cuts me off. "I want us to come together," he says seriously. "Keep your hands up and when I tell you to touch yourself, you can."

I surrender at the words *come together*. I can't stop nodding, and another smile quirks his lips. Slowly, his hand lowers, and his eyes flicker down a little. His camera is still angled so I can't see anything below his waist. Maybe that's the point. Some things are hotter left unseen.

His eyes rise back to mine, penetrating me, not tearing away even as his breathing deepens, the rise and fall of his ribs quickening. His body rocks forward a bit, and small grunts escape his parted lips. My eyes dance around his arm that moves in fast succession, his chest glistening with a layer of sweat, sultry and hot.

"Hands up," he says in a hoarse tone. I raise them again, not realizing I even dropped them.

I squirm on the bed as I feel the wetness slide down my inner thigh. I grab a pillow and press it between my legs, the spot throbbing for more pressure, more weight, more friction—begging for touch.

"Hands," he orders.

I raise them for the third time, practically tearing out my hair. I tremble and let out a small whimper.

I can't wait anymore.

"Lo," I cry out.

"Hold on, love," he encourages kindly, but his eyes say something different. *Hold the fuck on.* He's testing me. I know it. And I want to pass and succeed and show him that I can fight my compulsions.

I keep my eyes on his and try not to look anywhere else. It barely helps since he stares at me like he wants to be deep inside of me. God, what I'd give for that . . .

After another long moment he says, "Drop your hands."

That's all it takes.

My hands fall and slide down, feeling the wetness for the first time. I gasp and moan all at once and nearly collapse backwards onto my pillow. *I need you*, I want to scream. *Please.*

"Eyes on me, Lil."

I prop my body on a weak elbow and try to keep my focus on him without tilting my head back, without my eyelids fluttering closed. I am so . . . close to being completely and utterly gone. I alternate between rubbing and sliding my fingers inside. The pressure mounts, spiking my nerves on every surface of my skin. Even though he wants me to look at him, his eyes begin to drift from mine. They lower from my breasts to my abdomen to my wrist where the screen ends.

At the same time my hips buck, he jerks forward a little. Our breathing synchronizes with our heady movements. And all of a sudden, it feels as though he's really here. Inside of me.

He reaches up and tilts the screen down. For a mere second, he lets me see what he's doing—his hand grips the base of his cock and runs up and down along the shaft. The camera moves back up to his face, and I'm lit on fire. I need to come. I need to release *now*.

His arm quickens, and my moans grow louder. I hear him groan in a deep husky breath. My body tightens, clenches and squeezes while my toes curl. The whole world rotates. I claw at the sheets with my free hand and ride the high out.

A few moments later, I flop against the bed, my elbow giving way to exhaustion and my staggered, heavy breathing. My stomach, breasts, thighs and ass are slick with sweat. God . . . that was incredible.

I want to feel it again.

Impulsively, my hand trails down my body and touches my tender mound. A moan escapes my lips, and I rub harder.

"Lily." Lo's voice fills my head. I close my eyes and slip my fingers inside.

Yes.

"Lily. *Stop.*"

My eyes snap open, but I keep my hand between my thighs. Gently, I prop myself up to look at the screen. In the little box to

234 · KRISTA RITCHIE and BECCA RITCHIE

the left, I see myself sprawled on my bed in this position, but Lo only has a view of my belly button up, my legs drifting past the computer. But I suppose it's obvious what I was doing.

I avoid his gaze. "Give me a second," I tell him in a soft, guilty whisper. I lie down and disappear fully from his sight, the screen tilted towards my headboard, not the mattress. My fingers move once more. I *need* to feel it again.

"Fuck," Lo curses. "Lily! I said *stop*." I hear him. I do, but listening is so fucking hard. And a selfish, horrible part of me wants to kick the computer closed to drown out his demands. The pressure intensifies as I stand on another precipice, preparing to jump. Oh God . . .

"Lily, sit up so I can see you," he orders.

I can't. I rub faster and harder and longer. I need more. I've always needed more. I cry, my bony shoulders digging into the mattress, my body writhing. I want his hands to pick me up, to throw me into his chest, his muscles to meld into *me*. My eyes clench closed, and I imagine it all. That he's hard against me— that he's inside, waiting for me to come, whispering in my ear that everything is going to be okay if I just release while I'm filled with him.

Yes! I scream, my spine arching, my body prickling with a fire so hot that I can barely breathe. I hit it. Again. And then . . . I begin to come down. My open mouth closes, and my heartbeat slows, moving past the irregular, erratic pace and towards something I hate.

"Goddammit, Lily," Lo snaps. "Sit the fuck up, *now*."

My eyes widen in horror at what I've done, burning with guilty tears. Everything feels different this time. I pull my hand away and mechanically hoist my sluggish body to a sitting position. I hunch forward and hold a nearby throw blanket to my chest. "I didn't mean . . ." I bite my fingernail and wipe an escaped tear. Shame crashes into me like a hundred pound wave. I can't even look at the screen to meet Lo's disappointed gaze.

I understand now. Why he wanted me to listen to him from the beginning. So we could avoid *this*. What's even worse is beneath the festering shame and guilt, there's a small part of me that wants to do it again. Maybe after we end the Skype conversation . . . *no!*

"Did that feel good?" he asks in a tense voice.

Which part? And why do I have to ruin everything? I stare pathetically at my hands. "Don't look at me like that," I whisper.

"You haven't even looked at me yet," he murmurs.

I inhale a strained breath and finally gain the courage to meet his gaze. No judgment crosses his features. Instead, his amber eyes swim with empathy that I do not deserve. And I see the worry, as though I broke his heart, as though the extremity and horror of my compulsions just fully registered in his head.

"I'm sorry," I choke. I rub my tears before they fall. "You don't have to . . ." *be with me.* I am a monster.

"I love you," he says. "We're going to work on this together." Translation: *I'm not going anywhere.*

"I want to do it again," I admit in a small voice.

"I know." He rubs his lips in thought.

"So . . . then can we do it together again . . . tonight?" He's just mad I did it without him, surely.

"We're done for today," he says, each word like a mountain he has to climb.

"But I only came twice." Fear pushes into my chest, making it difficult to breathe.

"And I was only going to let you come once," he says. "I tried to exhaust you, but it's hard. I should have made you wait longer, and you should have listened to me afterwards. We're going to get better at it though, but it'll take time and practice."

So that's it for me. I'm not allowed to have any kind of self-love, and Lo is done for the night. I don't want to do something moronic when he leaves. *Don't think about it, Lily.* I let out a deep breath, but it barely calms me.

"Talk to me," Lo says urgently. He rests his forearms on his bent knees. "What are you thinking, Lil?"

"I'm scared," I mutter. ". . . I'm so terrified of what I may do." I feel hot, searing tears scald tracks down my cheeks.

"I know it's difficult. I can't imagine someone giving me one beer and forcing me to stop there. I get it, Lil. I so fucking get it," he says. "But you have to find the strength to wait. I know it's there. You just have to dig."

I let his words sink in for a full minute. A pain weighs on my chest, and it explodes with my next proclamation. "I wish you were here." My chin quivers, and my voice gives out. I press my forehead to my knees, hiding my shattered expression.

"I am there, love," he murmurs. "I'm right there with you." I hear the hurt in his voice. He tries to relax as much as possible, but it's as though I'm gripping his heart as much as he's clenching mine. "You're in my arms," he tells me, "and I'm kissing your lips, your cheek, your nose . . ." I shut my eyes and drift to his voice that begins to settle my torment. "Your head leans against my chest, and you listen to the beat of my heart as it slows. I hold your wrists, allowing you to gently come down from your high on my terms. You collapse against me."

I look up to meet his gaze. It's filled with hope, with longing and something more. Something that I think can only be shared between two broken people.

"And you stop struggling," he whispers. "I watch your body relax against me, and then I kiss you on the top of your head. I tell you how proud I am of you, and how making you come once lasts a *lifetime*."

My last tear falls. I can't move to wipe it. I am transfixed by Loren Hale, my *everything*.

"I love you," he says again, "and no other man will ever say those words and mean them the way I do."

My chest hurts so badly. His words are beautiful and painful at the same time. Like us, I suppose. I have to be strong. For him. For me. For *us*. My throat has swollen, but I find the resolve to reply. "I'm going to spend the rest of the night with Rose." I nod, solidifying the plan in my head.

"That's a good idea," he agrees. "How about you clean yourself up. Get dressed. Tell me goodbye, and then I'll call Rose and make sure you're with her."

I nod again. I'd like that. So much. Having him on my side makes the unbearable feel tolerable. I just hope in the future our struggle will become easier.

Hope. Such a silly thing.

Sometimes it doesn't come true.

Fifteen

A few days later Rose has finally finished decorating our house and decides that we need a proper housewarming party to commemorate the event. She also wants this to coincide with a "Lily Vow Day" or LVD for short. She coined the term and also proposed the idea.

Writing down my vows on a piece of paper and reading them aloud is supposed to reinforce my long-term goals. I was all on board until she invited Connor and Ryke. I reminded her that she's a feminist and supposed to be on *my* side. I'm the girl.

She responded with "you shouldn't be ashamed of your addiction" and "it'll give you more incentive not to break the vows." Because apparently I'll feel way more guilty breaking vows that three people hear rather than just Rose . . . okay, she has a point.

"I don't understand why we had to do this outside," I complain, wrapping my arms in one of Rose's fur coats, which are way warmer than anything in my closet. Topped with my *Star Wars* Wampa cap that has large ear flaps, I literally look like some sort of furry monster.

"I didn't want to start a fire in the house," she says. A light layer of snow coats the ground, but grass still manages to stick out of the powder. A fire roars in a metal trash can a couple feet in front of us. The flames lick the nippy air, and I question how Rose even started it to begin with.

Though it can't be rocket science. Hobos do it.

The glass back door slides open and Rose says, "Finally, what took you so long?" After the Fizzle event in January, Rose and Connor have shockingly stayed together. But I'm waiting for their next twenty-four-hour breakup.

Connor's loafers crunch against the snow as he walks towards us. "Driving generally requires time," he tells her. "Simple physics really. Time equals distance divided by speed."

"I know the formula for time, Connor."

"I know, you know," he replies with a smile. "I just like the way your forehead wrinkles when you think I'm insulting you."

"When you *are* insulting me."

"That's your perspective," he says and looks to me. "Hi, Lily. Big day."

I shrug nonchalantly, and Rose gives me a hard stare. "It is a big day, Lily," she reinforces. "This is when you commit to getting better."

"Right," I say with a nod. "I think I'm just nervous."

Connor frowns. "Why? Isn't this the easy part? You've been away from Lo for nearly three months and you haven't cheated." He pauses and adds, "According to Rose."

"I haven't cheated," I affirm. "I'm just not a hundred percent comfortable talking about this stuff yet." I've kept my addiction a secret so long that *sharing* requires a lot more courage than someone like Connor or Rose could ever understand.

"It will feel better when you get everything off your chest," Rose assures me. She turns to look at the house and then glances anxiously at her watch. Her lips purse before she says, "Ryke better be here soon. The housewarming party starts in fifteen minutes."

Daisy, Poppy, my parents and basically the whole brood are invited, and they cannot witness this act of symbolic declaration. The rest of my family will remain in the dark about my addiction until I decide I'm ready to tell them. I'm not sure if that day will come anytime soon.

"Shouldn't you have waited for Lo to have the party?" Connor asks. "He's going to be living here, right?"

Lo will move into our little secluded house. I talked with Dr. Banning and she agreed that we should live together if we want to continue to have a relationship. The only stipulation and change from our normal routine is that we actually have to *live* together. No more separate rooms and secret lives. At this juncture, we may be co-dependent but our addiction to each other may very well kick our other ones. Helping rather than enabling. If Dr. Banning thinks Lo is a huge key to my success (not an obstacle), then I believe it. She's smarter than me after all.

Rose will still be living at the house too, making sure Lo and I mingle with the family instead of resorting to our reclusive ways. The plan actually seems feasible. But I know it may not be easy. Nothing ever is.

I asked her if she was going to invite Connor to stay with us. There's an extra bedroom for him if she wanted to still have privacy. But I forgot that Connor attends Penn, too far away to permanently reside here. However, her answer didn't involve distance. She told me that their relationship hasn't progressed to *that* status yet, and she wouldn't be comfortable asking him. I read between the lines.

They haven't had sex.

Rose may be the most confident woman I know, but when it comes to talking about *her* sex life—she might well turn as red as me. She can read textbooks and clinically diagram the reproductive system without blushing. Hell, she *impersonated* me, acting as though she had a sex addiction to dozens of therapists. But telling someone about herself is like pulling rotten teeth. She tries to keep her private life private, but I think it's more than that. I think she's scared to admit how she feels. She wants people to think she's this ice queen, but in reality, she *fears* just like the rest of us.

Sometimes I think we're more alike than different. Maybe that's why we're sisters.

Rose turns to answer Connor's question. "Lo would hate this party. I'm doing him a favor."

She has a point.

"Do you think he's going to be pissed you're living with us?" I ask Rose with a smile. She's never been his favorite person. Honestly, I just hope I can survive in the same vicinity as them. They may kill each other or kill me in the crossfire.

"He'll have to deal," Rose snaps.

Connor looks to me. "You and Lo need to live alone together like a fat kid needs to live in Candy Land," he pauses, realizing this could be taken as either good or bad, depending on "perspective." So he adds, "He'd die."

I gape, an image of a chubby kid's corpse popping in my head, his cheeks stuffed with candy corn. My open mouth contorts into an extreme downturned frown, grossed out at the disturbing metaphor. "Ewwww . . ." I cringe and wiggle my arms to shake off the image.

Rose rolls her eyes, but she's *smiling* at his response. *That's why they're together*, I think.

The back door whooshes open again and Rose gives Ryke a cold scowl as he bounds over. "I said to be here at five o'clock."

"There's fucking traffic everywhere," he snaps back and stuffs his fists in his black North Face jacket. When he sidles next to me, his eyes immediately rise to my cap. "What the hell is on your head?"

"Wampa."

He stares at me blankly.

"Star Wars."

"You look ridiculous," he says and then turns to Connor. "Did you know what that was?"

"I didn't care, so I didn't ask," Connor tells him dryly.

Ryke glowers and I sense something bad coming. The two of them are still not warming to each other. I'm really not sure what it will take.

"You're a tool," Ryke says, blunt but not in a Connor Cobalt endearing way. He's just kind of mean.

"Why are you here again?" Connor asks.

Ryke's jaw hardens. "I'm Lily's friend."

"Well, I'm Rose's boyfriend *and* Lily's friend," Connor says. "I don't know if you're good at math but . . ." He flashes his prep school smile. Oh . . . Connor . . .

Rose smacks him lightly on the arm. "Stop, we're here for Lily. The two of you, get a grip. We don't have much time left."

She hands me a black plastic bag and I take a quick peek inside, already knowing it contains the *very* last of my porn. I forgot about one of the shoeboxes in the back of my closet the last time I threw everything away.

"So I guess I just toss this stuff in?" I turn to Rose for instruction. She nods and I take a couple steps forward.

"Don't catch on fire. You're made of fur," Ryke warns me. Oh yeah. I stop a foot away and slowly pull a couple of the magazines from the bag. I roll them up so that Connor and Ryke can't tell what they are. I really don't need to add to my embarrassment today.

"Goodbye, porn," I say under my breath and toss them in one by one as quickly as I can. The fire cracks and sparks and I step back a little. Now I am kind of scared I'll catch on fire.

Hurriedly, I finish with the magazines and throw the empty bag in last.

"Now your vows," Rose announces. "Read them out loud."

Right. I stuff my hand in the pocket and pull out a slip of paper. My fingers are already pink from the cold, but I manage to fold it open quickly anyway.

I only have a few items on my list, but each one is a little painful to say. At least in front of Rose, Connor and Ryke. They move around the trash can so that I can see them clearly, which makes this even harder.

"One," I say in a small voice. "I will not look at porn."

"I thought this was supposed to be a proclamation." Ryke rocks on the balls of his feet. He leans forward and says, "I can't even hear you."

"Say it like you mean it," Rose agrees with a supportive nod.

"Scream it," Connor adds.

The fire lets out another loud *crack* and it triggers something in me. Or maybe the unbridled confidence of my friends does. I take a deep breath before I yell, "I will not look at porn!"

Ryke starts clapping. Connor lets out a whistle with his fingers, and Rose gives me a smile. The pressure on my chest builds but also lightens with each word. In this moment, maybe their confidence is contagious.

"Two. I will not masturbate!"

They're still cheering and I focus on the paper in my cold fingers.

"Three. I will not be compulsive about sex!" I scream it, and yet I know this will be the hardest vow to live by. The most difficult to control.

"And four," I pause as I look at these final words. They mean the absolute most to me. "I will not cheat on Loren Hale!"

My blood is pumping from the fire, my friend's supportive cheers, and my words—so much so that I toss the paper triumphantly into the flames.

"What the hell?!" Rose shrieks. I jolt backwards and check my arms to make sure I haven't caught on fire. I'm okay though. I touch my cap. Wampa's fine too.

"What?" I ask, confused now.

I look back up and see Rose about to faint in distress. "You burned it," she says like I'm the one who lost my mind.

"I thought I was supposed to."

"Why would you burn your vows? They're supposed to help you."

"Then what's the fire for?" I point at it accusingly.

"For the porn, Lily." Rose groans into her hands and looks up. "Okay, we have to do it again."

"No," we all say unanimously.

Rose turns on Connor first. "This is important," she complains, her hands going to her hips. She means business, but I have no intention of repeating this. I think one LVD is enough for a lifetime.

"She read it aloud. Isn't that the point, Rose?" Connor asks.

"It's bad luck."

"Please tell me you're not superstitious." Connor tilts his head, scanning the length of her. "Are you going to tell me you practice witchcraft and sorcery too?"

"This isn't the seventeenth century, Richard," Rose snaps. "If it was, I suppose you'd have me burned at the stake."

"I wouldn't have the chance. I'd already be dead."

"For what? Being a smart-ass?"

He edges closer to Rose, only a couple feet away, and I'm surprised when she stands her ground, not taking one step back. His eyes flit across her porcelain cheeks, her nose pink from the cold, and her striking cat-colored eyes. "I would mention how the Earth revolves around the sun, and they'd cry *heretic*. You, of course, would be accused of heresy or witchcraft by eighteen."

"I'd survive," she declares.

"You would." He nods. "You'd cut your beautiful hair in order to." His fingers skim her brown, glossy locks that stop at her chest.

"You think if I cut my hair I would look like a boy?" she retorts, defensive. I guess to protect herself back then, she would need to be a man. She jerks out of his grasp, eyes as cold as ice.

He doesn't shrink back. He takes the challenge with a fervent smile. "I think you would make an effort to, and I'd keep my smart-ass lips shut so I didn't die." He looks her over. "Then I'd pretend to be with a man just so I could do this." One of his hands slides across her neck, the other cups her face, and he presses his lips to hers, drawing her closer as they kiss.

Her hands hang loose by her side, and as he melds his chest to her, closing every gap, she relaxes her arms around his shoulders. Internally, I'm waving Connor Cobalt and Rose Calloway flags, cheering them on.

When they part, their warm breath smokes the cold air. Rose's eyes are surprisingly soft, but her words remain fiery. "And then we'd both be dead," she reminds him. "We'd be hung for sodomy."

"Then I'd die with you. Happily." He grins, and her lips rise in an equally infatuated smile.

And then the doorbell rings, breaking their moment and successfully ruining Rose's pleasant mood. "I still have to put out the fire," she says in distress.

Connor squeezes her arms lightly, and her attention returns to him. "I'll go mingle with your mother. Take your time, hun." He kisses her softly on the cheek and disappears inside the sliding glass doors.

It's in this moment that I realize how well Connor knows my sister. Most guys would choose to save the girl from manual labor. But Rose would rather delay any conversation with our mother. As she walks off to find something to smother the fire, Ryke approaches me with a stiff gait, his hands still firmly pocketed in his jacket.

I lick my chapped lips, as hesitant as him. "What?" I wonder if he's going to chastise me for something I did with Lo. Maybe talking to him again. He's never been on my team. Not really. He's sided with Lo far more often.

"I'm sorry," he says, the words sounding so sincere that I almost stumble back in shock.

"Huh?"

He rolls his eyes, his features darkening. "Don't make me say it again."

My brows crinkle, and I tug the flaps of my Wampa cap lower to shield my flush and the incoming gust of wind, not sure what else to say since he's left me in a state of confusion.

He runs a hand through his hair. "I thought you'd cheat on him and break the guy's soul," he admits. "I didn't think you could do it. And I was wrong." He pauses and then his eyes meet mine, and I see Lo in them. "I'm sorry for being an asshole, for not understanding . . . I think that he needs you as much as you need him." He nods to himself, as though realizing how *right* those words are as he says them.

So, he may not be rooting for me exactly. But he's supporting our relationship. That's even better. I can't help but smile.

Ryke actually smiles back. "You're okay, Calloway." With this he pats my shoulder and then turns around, heading for the warmth of the indoors.

Rose shovels a light layer of snow into the trash can, and the fire hisses and smoke plumes in the air. She tosses the shovel to the side and smacks her hands together to clean off the dirt. When she sees me watching, she nears and tightens my coat around me, finding the hooks to snap it closed.

"Thank you," I tell her, "for these three months."

Her eyes flicker to mine. "You did all the work."

"Not true," I say with a small laugh. She found my therapist. She decorated the house. She spent more time helping me than I can even add up. "I'm happy I'm here."

"Me too," she says, her eyes softening again. She's starting to get good at that. Her arm wraps around my shoulder. As we go inside, I know that the future may not be so easy. I know that there will be more issues to deal with.

But I can't imagine going back to how things were.

Now it's time to start building relationships.

I think I'm ready.

Sixteen

Lo comes home tomorrow.

I don't think my brain can process anything else for the day, yet I'm sitting in Dr. Banning's office trying to go over some heavy topics before Lo returns. My poor brain is about to emergency eject right out of my skull.

But I don't want to quit, not when I'm so close to having some sort of breakthrough about my addiction. I feel like I'm on the verge of answers. I just need something to *click*.

Dr. Banning runs a hand down the side of her short black bob, her eyes intent on her notepad for the moment. My fingernails are bitten down to the beds, and I rub the tops in an attempt to ease the sting. It only hurts more.

"Lily." Dr. Banning finally looks up and I meet her gaze. She gives me a warm consoling smile and I relax a little. "You told me you were having a housewarming party. How did that go?"

"Fine," I say, running my hands on my jeans and inwardly cringing at the word. *Fine.* Such a stupid word really. It feels empty and weightless. It's the kind of word you use to hide the truth.

"And your parents know that Lo will be returning home from rehab. How do they feel about him living with you after all of this?"

I mull over the question, hearing my mother's response instead of my own. *Work it out.* Three words that had me more confused than anything.

"They've always approved of our relationship," I tell Dr. Banning. "Rehab didn't change that. I'm not sure anything would."

"What if you told them about your addiction?" she questions.

My stomach churns at the very thought, but I imagine my mother with her cold judgment and my father's shame for having a dirty, disgusting daughter. I couldn't . . .

"They wouldn't understand."

"How do you know?"

I try to think of an answer better than *I just know.* But I can't.

Dr. Banning leans forward a little in her chair and asks, "What about the housewarming party, really? You're in your new home with your friends and your family, but Lo isn't there. That has to be difficult."

"Shouldn't you be asking me about sex?" This question has been my go-to digression tactic.

"We'll get to that later. Right now, I want to talk about the party." Obviously, she's picked up on my strategies. I end up giving in.

"I felt awkward," I mutter. "But I always feel awkward so it really wasn't much different." I scratch my arm, but without any fingernails it's more like rubbing than scratching.

"Why would you feel awkward around your family?"

I have so many secrets, sometimes they feel like they're crushing me from the inside out. Keeping my addiction from my family has always put this intangible gap between us. But something stops me from telling Dr. Banning. A lump lodges in my throat as I blink a couple times, utterly confused.

Because I think I know . . . I think I know that I've always felt this way, even before my addiction. Before there were any secrets at all.

I try to remember the mornings where I woke up in my own house. Where I clambered downstairs in my pajamas to have breakfast with my family. I can smell bacon and eggs, and I can see Lucinda standing over the stove asking me if I want mushrooms or tomato in the scramble. It's not the right memory though. Our chef was named Margaret. Lucinda cooked for Jonathan Hale.

"It's not right," I mutter under my breath.

"What's not right, Lily?"

Let me think. Nights. Nights were at my house. But that was before I left for Lo's to hang out and sleep over. *Yes.* I'm what . . . seven. I can see the television screen with silly cartoons, and I hear Poppy playing the piano in the background. Rose was on the floor, reading the first *Harry Potter.* My mother's heels clapped into the room and she looked between me and Rose. She strode to the bookshelf and came back to jerk Rose's novel from her grip, replacing the magical world with *To Kill a Mockingbird.*

Our mother tucked the fantasy novel under her elbow and walked right out of the room without another glance.

"I can't . . ." I shake my head, tears pricking my eyes. I don't like this answer. *Take it back.*

"Lily," Dr. Banning says but I'm still shaking my head.

I see all the years flash in and out. I see each of my sisters suffocating, being silently molded by a mother who just wants the best. I see me being free of *that.* But why does it hurt? It shouldn't fucking hurt.

"It's stupid. It's so stupid," I complain and touch my hands to my eyes.

"Lily," she says slowly. "You have to let it in."

"Let what in?"

"The pain."

My bottom lip trembles and I just keep on shaking my head. "It's stupid."

"Why do you think that, Lily?" she asks fervently. "Your pain isn't worth less than anyone else's."

"You don't understand. I *shouldn't* feel this way." I point to my chest. "I have money. I come from a privileged life. I refuse to throw a pity party for myself."

"You can't refuse to feel hurt just because you think that you don't deserve to feel it."

I don't know if I believe her. I think I should. "My sisters got the raw deal," I say in defense, my cheeks stained with tears. "I got off." No controlling mother. No piano lessons or ballet recitals.

"You never give yourself a break," she tells me. "You've never given yourself a chance to feel. Do you understand?"

The emptiness. I guess it's where that pain should be.

"It's just you and me," Dr. Banning says. "I don't care about your last name. I don't care about what your sisters went through. All I care about is you, Lily."

It takes me a few moments to gather the strength to start talking about the thoughts that unsettle my head. A couple tears fall onto my hands and I manage to say, "When I was *really* little, my mother used to put me in classes like she did the other girls. Art. Singing. Piano . . . Everything." I bite my lip, nodding to myself as I remember. "I lasted about a day in each. I just never picked up talents like Poppy and Rose." I pause and cringe at my own words. *So what Lily Calloway? You're not talented. You don't need to cry about it.*

"Keep going," Dr. Banning urges.

I shake my head now, but the memory continues to spill.

"When the school sent me to remedial math in third grade, I think that was the last time my mother paid attention to me. I wasn't sociable and congenial like Poppy. I wasn't smart like Rose." I wipe my eye. "And I never grew tall and beautiful like Daisy. I think . . . I think I was something she wished she could return. Like a generic handbag. But she couldn't. So she just acted like I didn't exist . . ."

She let me spend nights at Lo's. Let me do whatever I wanted. And that freedom turned out to be as suffocating as her control.

"I never felt like she loved me," I mutter under my breath. "I never felt worthy enough."

I shake my head again. I don't want this to be the answer. It should be something *more*. It should be a horrific, life-threatening event. Not these stupid feelings.

"When are you going to stop punishing yourself for what you feel?" Dr. Banning asks me.

"I don't know how," I choke out.

"You're human, Lily. You hurt just like the rest of us. It's okay."

I nod now, changing course a little. I want to get there. To allow myself to feel pained by my childhood without feeling irreparable guilt at the same time. I just don't know how to compartmentalize these emotions. How do I bear the hurt of being lonely without hating myself at the same time? Because my sisters would have given anything for the freedom I had. Because the world would give anything for the life I was born into. I feel selfish and stupid. Worthless and pathetic. Ugly and used.

Sex made me whole again.

One time turned into two. Two turned to three. And then I just couldn't stop.

Dr. Banning passes me a box of tissues and I pluck a few from the carton, blowing my nose and trying to compose myself.

When the quiet lingers, I say, "I don't want that to be the answer. No one will understand." I'm some girl who decided to fill the emptiness in her heart with sex. Neglect and loneliness drove me to this place. A single choice to start and then the inability to stop.

"I understand," Dr. Banning tells me. "Rose will understand. And in time, your family will too. You just have to give people the chance, Lily, and you have to learn not to be ashamed of how you arrived here. It's not your fault."

Her voice soothes me, relaxing my turbulent thoughts to mush. She scribbles something down in her notepad and my brain screams at me for not hitting eject earlier. But there's unfortunately still more to discuss, especially with tomorrow looming.

"What about Lo?" I ask, clearing my throat. I sweep the last of my tears away. "What should I do now that he's coming back?"

She unlocks her cabinet drawer and I watch her pull out a small white envelope. "Before I give you this," she says, "I want to congratulate you on your ninety days of celibacy."

I think I hear her wrong. "I haven't been celibate."

Her smile is warm. "Have you had sex with another partner?"

"Lo and I had . . . Skype sex," I say, flushing a little at the words.

"But he hasn't actually penetrated you," she reminds me. I turn even redder at the word *penetrate* and silently wonder how she didn't even blink when she said it.

"So I've been celibate?" I say, a little unbelieving.

"For your personal treatment and what you needed to do, *yes* you have completed your celibacy period. You should be proud of yourself."

There's really only one thought on my mind. "So I can have sex with Lo?" I want to jump up from the chair and do a jig or something silly. I also feel a little bipolar. A second ago I was crying and now I'm more excited than ever.

"Yes and no," Dr. Banning says and crushes me yet again. This emotional roller coaster is killing my stomach.

She slides the white envelope towards me. "Based on our sessions, I've listed your limits. Sexual acts that you should never participate in and acts that you should limit for yourself. Think of these as guidelines or rules for sex." I always thought the words sex and rules should never be synonymous. I guess things will definitely be changing for me.

I take it quickly and press my finger against the crease to rip the seam.

"Before you open it," she cuts me off. "I'm going to advise you *not* to look at it."

I frown. That doesn't make any sense. "How will I know what not to do?"

"Have you ever heard of the saying 'people want what they can't have'?" she asks. I don't like where this is going. "In my experience, every time someone chooses to read that envelope, it's much more difficult to abide by it. They get scared and they usually never share the information with their sexual partner. You have a choice, Lily. You can either look inside the envelope now or you can give it to Lo and let him take care of it."

That sounds like a huge decision, one that could change everything. Reading it now could seriously terrify me. I can just imagine the words *sex once a month* written in clean scrawl. I think I'd have a panic attack. With Lo around, abstaining from sex will be a thousand times more difficult, and I know how draining telling me *no* will be. But that's exactly why I should give it to him, so I don't punk out and toss the letter in the trash.

Let him decide my fate.

My nerves spike at the thought of being in that unbearable unknown. But maybe Dr. Banning was right.

Giving up something isn't the same thing as losing control.

"You don't have to decide now," Dr. Banning says, "and when you and Lo feel ready, you both can see me together."

Great. I've never had a one-hundred-percent heart-to-heart about addiction with Lo. Not sure how therapy *with* him will turn out. Another hurdle to look forward to.

I slip the envelope into my back pocket and give Dr. Banning a quick thanks and handshake before I leave. On the way out, my stomach overturns. I know how well choices can alter the future.

We started a fake relationship. We ended it. We dated. We loved. And then we separated. Pain, happiness, joy and hurt ricochet from each path taken and from each memory uncovered.

One decision can change my life forever.

I hold the strap to my Captain America plush backpack, which can easily alternate as a pillow if need be. Every time I've spent the night at Lo's house, I stuff my toiletries and clothes into the little inside pocket. With my seventeenth birthday in a couple days, I should probably retire the backpack for a more *mature* option. Like Batman. But Lo would kill me if I went DC on him.

I shift on his doorstep, not used to entering his place by the front door. I usually go through the window. Much cooler. Having to wait on the stoop of the enormous mansion just reminds me that tonight is a little different than most. I raise my knuckles to the door but decide to use the lion metal knocker instead. I slam it a couple times and twiddle with the strap to my backpack. Waiting.

After a solid minute, the door swings open, more lights streaming onto the stoop. And my mouth falls and my face scrunches. Lo stands before me, but he's . . .

"What are you wearing?" we both say at the same time.

What am I wearing?! He has on black slacks and a white button-down, looking nearly twenty-two. His light brown hair is still a little messy, but it's systematically disheveled. He's clean-shaven, and his cheeks sharpen, pouting his lips as he stares from my toes to my head.

"What the fuck?" he says lightly, shrugging at me like *I've* turned into an intergalactic alien. I am *exactly* the same. He is the one who's different.

"I didn't know there was a dress code tonight," I refute.

He crosses his arms and cocks his head to the side.

"Don't give me that look," I snap back, pushing my way through the door since he has rudely not invited me in yet. The living room awaits to the right of us, the vaulted ceiling and crystal chandelier shining a great deal of light onto leather furniture and expensive animal-skin rugs. I try not to think about *what* animals I may be stepping on when I'm at his house.

He locks the door, and I throw my backpack on the nearest couch. When I turn back to face him, he still wears that same crazy look. "What?" I say.

"You're wearing dinosaur slippers and long johns," he says like I've gone crazy.

I glance down at my nightly wardrobe. My baggy long johns sag at the crotch, and my green dinosaur slippers make my feet look huge. I also wear one of Lo's long-sleeve shirts that he left at my house the other day—the Philadelphia 76ers logo printed on the front. I shrug. "I wear this all the time when I spend the night here."

"That was before," he tells me.

I hear his unspoken words: *that was before, when we weren't dating and in a fake relationship.* Two weeks ago, Lo was suspended from school, and his father went apeshit, threatening to ship Lo off to military academy, actually showing him the forms. I spent the whole day anxiously pacing my room as we tried to find solutions on how to pacify his father.

And this was it. Make his father believe that Lo is a changed man by dating a girl he thought he'd never be worthy of. Me. A Calloway. When in fact, I'm just as fucked up as his son. Go figure.

When we made the announcement of our new relationship status, his father hadn't really believed it. Which is why I'm in Lo's living room tonight instead of his bedroom where we usually pour over comics and I watch him drink himself to sleep. Tonight, we're supposed to *prove* how in love we are.

And then everything will be okay again. Lo will stay here. He'll be a "changed man" and we'll both continue to go on as normal. Except for the fake relationship part.

I shift anxiously. "Sorry," I mutter, all of a sudden self-conscious. He dressed nice for me, and here I am, in baggy long johns and his oversized tee. The slippers are still cool.

"You're right," he tells me, his amber eyes grazing my whole body. "It doesn't matter." He undoes the top three buttons of his shirt.

My breath sticks to my throat.

"You look cute," he says. A smile plays at his lips, and he laughs at my long johns again. "Are those mine?"

I'm still frozen on the *you look cute* part. I can't tell if that was all show or not. I mean, no one is here to witness the performance of our romantic rendezvous, but at the same time, we *are* supposed to be practicing before his father walks through the door.

"Yeah," I manage to say. "I stole them after the camping trip in October." Almost a full year ago. He didn't notice then, so I'm surprised that he does now. Or maybe he just never mentioned it before.

"That's my shirt too," he says, pushing through his last button. My eyes rake his lean muscles, and I realize that I'm going to be given permission to touch them for the first time since we had sex. And that was a long, long time ago. Well, almost three years to be exact.

"Good eye," I whisper as he nears me. Usually I'm in complete control during sex. I know how it will end and how it will start, but with Lo and this new arrangement, I am at a total loss for where this will go.

I take a few steps back, down a couple stairs into the living room. He follows, as though he is the hunter and I'm the little doe he wishes to ensnare. My breathing deepens, not used to the way he's staring at me. As though I am his and he's mine.

This has to be pretend, right? *Of course it is*, I remind myself. *The deal, don't ever forget. It's all pretend.* But that doesn't mean I'm not allowed to enjoy it.

The backs of my knees hit the mahogany leather couch. "You're wearing my clothes," he says, his voice husky and deep.

I swallow hard. I want to wrap my arms around his neck and run my hands through his hair, bringing him close. This is wrong. But it feels right. And the way he's staring . . .

His fingers slip into the waistband of my long johns, tugging me to his chest. His forehead nearly rests against mine, his warm breath entering my parted lips.

"Lo . . ."

He folds down the band, discovering my hipbones, and his body stiffens against mine. My hand quickly clasps his, my eyes bugging all of a sudden.

"I'm not wearing any . . ." I trail off, more nervous with a guy than I think I've ever been.

My words only cause his chest to fall heavier. "You forgot your panties or you just realized you forgot to steal a pair of my boxers to wear?"

My eyes fall to his lips. I want to kiss them so hard that they'll swell and redden, where he'll feel me on him for days. "You don't wear boxers," I say, breathless.

"I don't?" His lips brush my ear. "Then what am I wearing, love?"

Oh God. My body throbs and pulses, and I desperately want his hands to run over every inch of my skin. I should take his invitation, but I hesitate, worried about crossing a line even though I know that's why I'm here. We're stepping into brand-new territory, all for the purpose of declaring our "fake" love. But for some reason, this feels so, so real.

He watches me waver and decides to help me by gathering my hands in his. He places my fingers on the band of his black slacks and the other on his zipper, guiding me to the right actions. I unbutton, my heart beating wildly in my chest. I've never been this anxious, this excited, and this fucking scared all at once. I'm riding a roller coaster at high speed, and any second now, I may run off the tracks.

I begin to tug his pants down, and my eyes refuse to peel away from the bulge in his black boxer briefs. If that's how big his cock looks now, I can't imagine what it'll look like when he's hard. But I know I want to see.

I open my mouth to ask how far we're going to go, but the words won't form. I'm afraid if I say them, then he'll stop. And a part of me wants him inside of me again. The other, more reasonable, part is screaming about keeping things as chaste as possible. So he's not like all the guys I'm with. So I don't break his heart when I undoubtedly will seek out another man in the future.

And then all thoughts whoosh out of my head. He cups my face in his hands and kisses me so forcibly that air pushes into my lungs and locks there. That my legs quake beneath me, and my arm wraps around his waist, gripping for dear life. I am succumbing to his body, to this passion that he pours with each kiss.

He parts my lips, his tongue exploring my mouth, his chest thrumming against mine.

I moan, and the sound drives him deeper. He hikes both of my legs around his waist and pushes me to the couch cushions. Lo hovers on top, but his pelvis digs into mine, my whole body ignites with something foreign and yet so familiar. I can barely breathe.

I kiss back with the same urgency, as though this will poof away in a matter of minutes. As though it will all disappear before our eyes, and I'll be left without this feeling tomorrow. He pulls off my shirt, leaving me in a blue bandeau and cold skin that he warms with his hands. His fingers find their way to my breast, and I lose myself to the way he flicks my nipple. I need his mouth on . . . and then his lips find the same spot, licking a circle around the tender place of my breast.

"Lo," I gasp. "Lo . . ." I moan and writhe beneath him. This can't be real. I have to be dreaming.

His hardness presses near the wet spot between my legs. Only fabric keeping us apart. I ache for him to move it. I silently plead for him to fill me, even though I know it will be so, so wrong. *This is pretend.* But why does it feel so good? Why does it seem so fucking real?

And then I hear the click of the door. We both freeze. Lo lifts his head and adjusts my bandeau so my breasts are covered. Expensive loafers clap against the marble floor, and keys jangle as they're slipped into a pocket.

Jonathan Hale stands right in the foyer with a full view of the living room—our couch angled in perfect sight. He sets down his briefcase and begins to take off his tie, and then his head turns and he solidifies as much as we have. This is what we've waited for, but it doesn't make it any less awkward.

I turn cherry red and shield my face behind my hands, looking at Lo's father through the cracks in my fingers.

"Dad," Lo says, sitting up only a little. My legs still wrap around his waist. His pants still lie in a heap on the ground. Maybe this was a bad idea . . . "I thought you weren't coming home until late."

"It is late," he says, scrutinizing our position on the couch. I want to disintegrate into it. "So you two are together now?"

"Yeah," Lo snaps. "I told you that five days ago."

"Don't talk to me with that fucking tone, Loren," he retorts with the *same* hostility. "I heard you before. I just didn't think you two were serious. When you were seven, you said she was your fucking wife."

I blush, remembering our "pretend" wedding. Rose told me that I was stupid during the whole ceremony. I suppose not *everything* changes.

"I'm not seven anymore," Lo tells him.

"I can see that." Jonathan eyes me for a little longer than I like, and I shrink farther into the cushions. Lo shifts so my half-naked body is hidden better from his father's view. "Do you agree with what my son did, Lily?" he asks. "You think it was right of him to fuck with another person's property?"

I shake my head repeatedly. "No, sir. In fact . . ." I clear my throat, willing on a bit of confidence. "I've told Lo that if we're going to be together, he's going to have to change." The lie tastes gross in my mouth, but I better get used to it. There will be far more from here on out.

Jonathan mulls this over and then says to Lo, "Hopefully a woman can knock some fucking sense into you." So he's going to let Lo stay?! We watch as he takes measured steps to the liquor cart, ignoring our not-so-innocent position on the couch. He pours himself a glass of bourbon. "I paid for the damages you incurred on the Smith's house, but I'm taking a portion out of your allowance."

Lo drills holes into the couch arm above my head, glaring at the object instead of his father. I think that's a wise decision. "Thanks," he says.

Jonathan swishes his glass. "I talked to that bitch principal of yours. She's going to take your suspension off your record. You'll stay at Dalton unless you fuck up again." I can barely celebrate the news because he tops the statement off with, "Stop tarnishing *my* name."

Lo grits his teeth, his nose flaring to bridle his emotions. His father refuses to even acknowledge *why* Lo retaliated against Trent Smith. Maybe if he heard the reason, he would understand.

"Okay," Lo says through clenched teeth, choosing to drop it. "You can leave now."

After a long pause, Jonathan asks, "You have protection?" Oh my God! I nearly scrunch into a ball, but Lo keeps a hand on the outside of my thigh that hugs his waist.

Lo closes his eyes and then opens them, his glare deepening. "Yeah," he replies with the same hard-edged voice, as though each word is lethal.

"Good. I'd rather not explain to her father why my son couldn't keep his dick in his pants." *If only he knew.* He goes to the archway that'll lead him *away* from us. "And, Loren?"

Lo cranes his neck over his shoulder to meet his father's hardened eyes. In all my life, I've never seen them soften.

"Don't be such a sick fuck." He watches the way Lo's face contorts into anger and pain, and I look for the glimmer of remorse in his father's eyes. But I see none. He drowns it with the liquor in his palm and disappears into the darkened hallway.

Lo sits up for a second and sets his hands on his head,

breathing heavily as if his father chased him around the room with a gun.

"You're okay," I whisper. "Lo, you're not sick."

"I doused his door with pig's blood."

I cringe. "It was supposed to be poetic, and what he did wasn't much better." I flush at the raw memory where I opened a package sent to my house, addressed to me. Lo sat with me on my bed, thinking we ordered a comic book we'd forgotten about. And when I pulled the flaps of the box, I screamed at the contents inside.

A dead white rabbit.

Lo found a note spotted with blood, and I pushed the box away, the smell as ghastly as the image. "*Here's something you can hump,*" he read. Trent signed his name at the bottom. What an idiot, I thought with thick tears. Apparently his girlfriend broke up with him because we had sex at a hockey game *months ago.* He was on the "away" team, driving in town a couple hours to beat Dalton Academy.

And Trent blamed me for the breakup. As though he had no part in it, as though I was a siren who seduced him.

The next day after I received the "hate" package, I spent the night at my house. Rose wanted me there since my mother's book club usually ran late. She didn't want to be alone with her, so I stayed. Lo got wasted, and then I heard, he was thrown in jail for vandalism and underage drinking.

All I could think: *At least he took a cab. At least he had enough sense not to drive drunk.*

"Maybe it was fucked up," Loren whispers.

"I liked your note," I murmur.

His brow rises. "*Drink up, pig?*"

I smile. "Yeah."

His eyes drift to my lips. "You're strange."

"So are you."

"Good." He leans closer. "We can be strange together."

His heart thuds against my chest while his hands fall on either side of my shoulders, pressing me to the cushion. His head dips low, and his mouth hovers an inch from mine. He stays still for a moment, and my nerves prick at the way we're melded together, the way he seems to fit perfectly against me.

My chin tilts up, my eyes closing as I fantasize about where this could head. He could take me here. Now. And never let go. He could rock until my hips buck and my thighs clench around his waist. I could be so full of Loren Hale that I'll ache when he decides enough is enough.

His large hand caresses my cheek, holding my face with security. "Open your eyes," he whispers.

My lids flutter, and I see him staring so intently, absorbing my tiny, sharp movements. Full of lust and power and *soul*. And then I begin to wake up from my dream. He'll see what a fiend I am. He'll realize how needy and gross I can become, and he'll toss me away as a friend and as a lover. If I cross the line—if he fills this need inside of me—what will become of us?

What will become of *me?*

The fear washes me cold. And my breathing deepens in alarm. "Your father's gone," I remind him. There's no reason to pretend anymore. Not when we're alone.

His forehead wrinkles in a deep frown. He licks his bottom lip and shakes his head. "He may come back." *He won't*, I should tell him.

But his other hand disappears between our pelvises, and his fingers touch outside my long johns, to a spot that causes me to tremble beneath him and I let out a sharp gasp.

"You're wet," he breathes.

"Lo . . ." I start, shutting my eyes as I begin to drift off again.

"Look at me," he says.

Tension wraps us in a tight, uncomfortable cocoon, and I succumb to this one wish, opening my eyes for the second time.

His two hands hold my face again, cupping me with intensity and purpose and deep passion. My parted lips nearly meet his.

"You need me," he whispers, his breath filling my lungs.

Yes.

But the word stays buried beneath fear. I stare at him, drowning in his amber eyes.

He stares at me, swimming into my heady gaze.

It's what we don't say that hurts the most. Neither of us will speak to unwind the things that cause this friction to build and torment. So we watch and wait and listen to each other's heavy breath.

Some choices define us. And in this moment, I make a decision that will change the course of our lives forever.

Or maybe, I just prolong the inevitable.

Either way, in my heart, I know this feels right.

BONUS SCENE

Addicted for Now

Lily Calloway

O f all the days in the month, I have to be stuck in traffic on the one that means the most to me. I try not to badger Nola, my family's driver, on our ETA to the house I share with Rose. Instead, I anxiously shift on the leather seat and rapidly text my sister.

Is he already there? Please say no, please tell me I haven't missed his homecoming. I'm supposed to wait on the white wraparound porch of our secluded house in Princeton, New Jersey: many acres of lush land, a crystal blue pool, black shutters. The only thing it's missing is the picket fence. I'm supposed to give him a tour of the cozy living room and the granite kitchen, leading him upstairs to the bedrooms where I sleep. He won't be in one of the two guest rooms. Nope, he'll be making residence in mine for the first time ever.

And maybe awkwardness will linger at the idea of sharing a bed and a bathroom day and night, at the idea of cohabitating beyond a kitchen. Our relationship will be one-hundred percent real, and there'll be no nightcaps of bourbon or whiskey. I'll be able to say *don't do that*. And he'll be able to grip my wrists, keeping me from compulsively climaxing until I pass out.

We're supposed to help each other.

For the past three months, that's what we've planned. And if I'm not there to greet him—then I've already messed up in some way. After three whole months of being physically apart, I thought I'd be able to get this right—the celebration of his return from rehab. On top of desperately wanting to touch him, for him to hold me in his arms, I feel a sudden wave of guilt. *Please be late like me*, is all I think.

The text pings, and I open the message, a knot tightening my stomach.

He's unpacking—Rose

My face falls, and a lump rises to my throat. I can just picture his expression as he opened the car door, expecting me to fling my arms around him and start sobbing into his shoulder at his arrival. And I'm not there.

Was he upset? I text back. I bite my nails, my pinky starting to bleed a little. The habit has made my fingers look ghastly these past ninety days.

He seemed okay. How much longer will you be?—Rose

She must hate being alone with him. They've never been good friends since I chose to spend time with Lo more than I did with her. But she's been kind enough to allow him to stay with us.

Maybe ten minutes. After I text her, I scroll through my contacts and land on Lo. I hesitate before I type another quick message. I'm so sorry. I'll be there soon.

Five slow minutes pass with no response, and I've squirmed so much on the seat that Nola asks if she needs to stop somewhere so I can use the bathroom. I decline. I'm so nervous that my bladder probably won't function properly anyway.

My phone buzzes in my hand, popping my heart from my rib cage. How was the doctor?—Lo

Rose must have clued him in on the reason for my absence. I scheduled my gynecologist appointment four months ago because she's crazily booked, and I would have canceled if I thought I'd be able to nab an appointment sometime soon. But that's doubtful. And it didn't help that my gynecologist is near the University of Pennsylvania in Philly, not even close to Princeton where I now live. Having to drive back has eaten up all of my time.

I had to wait for about an hour. She was running behind, I text.

After a long moment, a new message flashes. Everything's okay though?—Lo

Oh, that's what he was asking. I'm so hung up on missing his homecoming that I didn't think about him being worried. I type back. Yep, looks good. I cringe, wondering if that was a weird reply. I basically just said my vagina looks good—which is kinda strange.

See you soon—Lo

He has always been a brief texter, and right now, I'm cursing him for it. My paranoia grows and the pressure on my chest does not subside. I grip the door handle, about ready to stick my head out of the moving vehicle to puke. Dramatic, I realize, but with our situation—recovering alcoholic and a struggling sex addict—we're anything but mundane.

Ninety whole days passed and I stayed faithful to Lo. I saw a therapist. But sex still has a way of making me feel better, masking other emotions and filling a deep hollowness. I'm trying to find the healthy kind and not the compulsive "I have to fuck every day" type of sex. I'm still uncomfortable talking about it, but at least I made progress the same way Lo did in rehab.

My mind whirls right up until Nola pulls into my driveway. All thoughts vacuum out into another dimension, and I dazedly say thanks and drift from the car. Purple hydrangeas frame the three-story house, rocking chairs lined in a row on the porch, and an American flag clings against a metal pole near a weeping willow.

I try to inhale the peacefulness and bury my anxiety, but I end up choking on springtime pollen, coughing into my arm. Why does the prettiest season also have to be the most foul?

I shouldn't hesitate in the front yard. I should rush right inside and finally touch the man that plagues my fantasies. But I wonder how different he will seem up close in person. I worry about the awkwardness from being apart for so long. Will we fit the same way we used to? Will I feel the same in his arms? Or will everything be irreparably different?

I muster a bit of courage to walk forward. And by the time I climb the porch, the door swings open. I freeze on the highest stair and watch the screen door clatter into the side of the house. Then he emerges, wearing a pair of dark jeans, a black tee, and an arrowhead necklace I gave him for his twenty-first birthday.

I open my mouth to say something, but I can't stop my eyes from grazing every inch of him. The way his light brown hair is styled, full on top, shorter on the sides. The way his cheekbones sharpen to make him look deadly and gorgeous. The way he reaches up and rubs his lips, as though hoping they'll touch mine. He rakes my body with the same impatience, and then his head tilts to the side, our eyes finally meeting.

"Hi," he says, breaking into a breathtaking smile. His chest falls heavily, nearly in sync with my uneven rhythm.

"Hi," I whisper. A large distance separates us, reminding me of when he first left for rehab. Picking up a foot and closing the gap feels like crawling up a ninety-degree angle. I need him to help me reach the top.

He takes a step near me, snapping the tension. All these sensations burst in my belly. I love him so much. I missed him so much. For three months, I felt the pain of being separated from my best friend while trying to fight my sexual compulsions. I needed him to tell me everything was going to be okay.

I needed him by my side, but I would never take him from rehab for my benefit, not when it would be detrimental to his recovery. And I want Lo to be healthy more than anything. And I want him to be happy.

"I'm back," he murmurs.

I try to restrain my tears, but they flow unwillingly, sliding from the creases of my eyes. I should be emerging from the doorway to greet him, and he should be the one lingering on the porch stairs. Why are we so backwards all the time?

"I'm sorry," I tell him, wiping my eyes slowly. "I should have been here an hour ago . . ."

He shakes his head and his brows pinch together like, *don't worry about that.*

I stare at the length of him again with a more confident nod. "You look good." I can't tell that he's sober exactly. He hasn't lost that look in his eye—the one that seems to kiss my soul and trap me altogether. But he's not beaten or withered or gaunt. In fact, he has more muscle to his name, his biceps supremely cut. And after a Skype session some time ago, I know his whole body matches those arms.

I wait for him to say *so do you*, but his eyes trail me once more, and I watch the way his chest collapses and his face twists in pain.

I blink. "What is it?" I glance down at my body. I wear jeans and a loose-fitting V-neck, nothing out of the ordinary. I wonder if I spilled coffee on my jeans or something, but I don't see what he does.

Instead of telling me what worries him, he inches forward, the deep hurt in his eyes frightening me. What did I do wrong? I shuffle back—a reaction I hardly would have predicted for today. I nearly stumble down the stairs, but his arm swoops around my waist, drawing me to his chest, saving me from a plummet into the grass below.

His warmness snares me, and I clutch his arms, afraid to let go. He stares intensely before his gaze drifts to my arms . . . my hands. He peels one off his bicep, his fingers skimming over mine, stealing the breath right from my lungs. He raises my hand in between us and then lifts my elbow, giving me a good view of my arm.

My chest sinks, realizing the source of his confusion and hurt.

"What the hell, Lil?" he says.

I scratched my arm raw during the last therapy session yesterday, and an ugly red welt will most likely scab tomorrow. Even with gross, bitten fingernails, I managed to irritate my skin.

Lo inspects my nails, his nose flaring to hold back even more emotion.

"I'm fine. I was just . . . anxious yesterday. Therapy was harder. You were coming home . . ." I don't want to talk about this now. I want him to hold me. I want our reunion to be epic—*The Notebook* worthy. And my stupid anxiety and bad habit has ruined the perfect outcome I imagined. I reclaim my hand and touch his jaw, forcing him to stop focusing on my problems. "I'm okay."

The words feel a little false. I am not one hundred percent okay. These past three months were a test I could have easily failed. At times, I thought giving up was better than fighting. But I made it. I'm here.

Lo's here.

That's all that matters.

His arms suddenly slide around my back, and he melds my body to his. His lips brush the top of my ear, sending shivers spiraling across my neck. He whispers, "Please don't lie to me."

My mouth falls. "I didn't . . ." But I can't finish because tears begin to pool, burning on their way down. I grip his shoulders, holding him tighter, afraid he plans to pull away and leave me broken on the porch. "I'm sorry," I choke. "Don't go . . ."

He edges back, and I cling harder, desperate and afraid. He's a lifeline I cannot quantify or articulate. I depend on him more than any girl should depend on a boy, but he's been the backbone of my life. Without him, I will fall.

"Hey." He gathers my face in his hands. His glassy eyes bring me back to reality. To the fact that he feels my pain just as I feel his. That's the problem. We hurt so much for each other that it's hard to say no. It's hard to take away the vice that will numb the agony of the day. "I'm here," he says, a silent tear dripping down his cheek. "We're going to beat this together."

Yes. "Can you kiss me?" I ask, wondering if that's allowed. My therapist handed me a white envelope filled with my sexual limitations—what I should and should not do. She advised me not to read it and to give it to Lo instead. Since I'm supposed to strive for intimacy, not celibacy, I need to relinquish my control in bed to him. He'll set the guidelines and tell me when to stop.

I handed the envelope to Rose yesterday and told her to deliver it to Lo just in case I chickened out. As concerned as Rose has been for my recovery process, I'm sure that was the first thing she did when Lo walked through the door.

I have no idea how many times I can kiss him. How much I can climax or if I'm allowed to have sex anywhere other than a bedroom. I'm so compulsive about intercourse and foreplay that *limits* have to be set, but following them will be the hardest part of my journey.

His thumb wipes away my tears, and I brush his. I wait for his answer, my eyes glued to his lips that I want to kiss until they sting and swell. His forehead lowers, dipped down towards mine, and I become so aware of how his fingers press into my hips, of the hardness of his body. I need him to close that gap between us. I need him to fill me whole.

Hastily, I meet my lips to his, expecting him to lift me up around his waist, to plunge his tongue in my mouth and slam my back into the siding.

But he doesn't give in to my desires.

He leans back and breaks the kiss in a matter of seconds. My stomach drops. Lo rarely tells me no when it comes to sex. He'll play into my cravings until I'm wet and wanting. Things, I realize, are about to really change. "My terms," he whispers, his voice husky and deep.

My whole body already pulses from his nearness. "Please," I beg. "I haven't touched you in so long." I want to run my hands over him. I want him to thrust into me until I cry. I imagine it over and over, torturing myself with these carnal thoughts. But I also want to be strong and not throw myself at him like he's only a body I missed. He means so much more to me. Maybe he's hurt by my persistence to kiss him? Maybe he sees it as a bad sign? "I'm sorry," I apologize again. "It's not that I want you for sex . . . I mean, I do want sex, but I want you because I miss you . . . and I love you, and I need . . ." I shake my head. My words sound stupid and desperate.

"Lil," he says slowly. "Relax, okay?" He tucks a piece of hair behind my ear. "You don't think I know this is hard for you? I knew we were going to run into this moment." His eyes fall to my lips. "I knew you were going to want to kiss me and for me to take you quick and hard. But that's not going to happen today."

I nod rapidly, hating those words but trying to soak them in and accept them. Uncontrollable tears begin to flow because I'm afraid I may not be able to restrain my compulsions. I thought being away from Lo would be the difficult part, but learning how to have a healthy, intimate relationship with him suddenly seems impossible. He's a man that I want to take advantage of every minute of the day. If I'm not doing it, then I fantasize about it. How can I stop?

His breathing shallows, as though my tears are driving knots into his stomach. Mine has already collapsed. I feel utterly destroyed by guilt and shame and desperation.

His fingers dig harder in my sides, as though reminding me that he's here, touching me. "What's going to happen," he breathes, "is that I'm going to carry you through this door. I'm going to draw out every single moment until you're exhausted. And I'm going to move so slow that three months ago will feel like yesterday. And tomorrow will feel like today, and no one in this fucking universe will be able to say your name without saying mine."

And then he kisses me, so urgently, so passionately that my lungs suffocate. His tongue gently slips into my mouth, and I savor each and every movement. He kneads the back of my head, gripping my hair, yanking and sending my nerves on overdrive.

His hands fall to my ass, and he effortlessly lifts me up. I wrap my legs around his waist, squeezing tightly into a front-piggyback. He guides me inside, just as he promised. I hook my arms underneath his and press my cheek to his hard chest, listening to the unsteady beat of his heart. We're so close, but I still ache to be closer. My breath shallows for it.

He kisses the top of my head and carries me into my bedroom on the second floor. Well—*our* bedroom. My net canopy is pulled back, the comforter black and white with red sheets. Lo rests my back against the mattress, and I reach up to grab a fistful of his shirt and yank him on top of me. But he steps back and shakes his head.

Slow, I remember. Right.

My legs dangle off the edge, and I prop myself on my elbows as he stands in front of me.

"I'm yours," he tells me. "I will always be yours, Lily. But now it's time for you to say it."

I sit up and my eyes flit over all of him. In all our life, he has never once said to me, *you are mine*. He has never taken me the way I've taken him. He has *given* himself to me. And I realize, it's my time to make this right and give myself to him.

"I'm yours," I whisper.

The muscles in his jaw twitch, almost smiling. "I'll believe you when I see it."

I squint. "Then why'd you tell me to say it?"

He leans forward, his lips so close to mine. His palms set on either side of my body, forcing me to fall back a little. I hesitate to kiss him. He's testing me, I think. "Because I love those words."

My lips part. *Kiss me*, I plead. "I'm yours," I breathe.

His eyes drop to mine, watching me, drawing out the moment. The spot between my legs aches for him. I want the pressure of his body—to rock against me, to fill me, to say my name over and over.

Kiss me. "I'm yours," I choke, wide-eyed in utter suspense.

And then he sucks on the bottom of my lip, he teasingly bites it and then sinks his pelvis into mine. I buck my hips to meet him and he lets me.

Lo grips the hem of his shirt and tugs it off his head, tossing it aside. Before I run my palms over his taut chest and newly sharpened abs, he laces his fingers with mine. Simultaneously, he puts his knee on the mattress and pulls me higher onto the bed, my head finding the pillow.

He climbs on and keeps my hands trapped in his. Then he stretches my arms high above me, our knuckles knocking into the headboard.

His body hovers over me, no longer melded together. I squirm beneath the space I dearly hate, my heart thudding and raging to be even closer. "Lo . . ." I can't take it anymore. My back arches a little as I try to meet his body again, and he tilts his head, disapproving. So I stay still. I try to let him take control since I need to go slow. His lips lower but linger from touching mine. He keeps that distance as he unbuttons my jeans, relinquishing the hold on my hand. He uses his other to guide my palm to his zipper. *Yes.* It takes only seconds before I have him unzipped and unbuttoned, tugging his jeans off with familiarity. I wiggle out of mine and he lifts the shirt off my head, in nothing but a black lacy bra and panty set. I did know he was coming home today, after all.

He soaks in the curvature of my body with headiness, and he begins to remove his last article of clothing. "Eyes on me," he says huskily.

They are permanently fixed to the bulge in his boxer briefs. "They are," I mumble. Technically this is *a part* of him.

"My eyes, love, not my cock," he says, a smile behind the words.

I raise my gaze as he slips off his boxer briefs. Watching the way he looks at me nearly sends me into a tailspin. I swallow and can't help but catch a glimpse. Oh God, I need him now. He's hard and as wanting as I am, but yet, he has restraint.

I do not.

He could easily take advantage of my eagerness, most guys would. But in order to help me, he has to control my impatience and my compulsion to go again. And again. Because my addiction isn't entirely a one-way street the way his is. I need his body in order to satisfy these unhealthy desires.

So he must say no at some point. I just don't want it to be soon.

He leans forward again, and his lips begin their descent from my neck to my belly button, sucking, nibbling—teasing. My hands grip his back while I hold a moan deep in my throat.

He kisses my hipbone and gently slips off my panties, the cold air nipping the most sensitive places. I expect his lips to warm the spot, but he eases off me and unclips my bra, sliding the straps off my shoulders so, so slowly. The light touch taunts my nerves and my sanity. His tongue runs between my breasts and then dips back into my mouth. And that's when his arms scoop around me and lift me up in a tight embrace, my breasts melding into his muscles, my limbs nearly tangled in his. My legs wrap around his waist, and I ache to lower onto his cock. But he keeps his arms locked around my chest, forcing me above his lap.

"Sit on your legs," he tells me.

"But . . ."

He lightly kisses me and tears away while I try to go in for another stronger one. "Sit on your legs, Lil. Or I'll do it for you."

That sounds better. He sees the glimmer in my eyes, and he picks up my right leg and bends my knee so my heel is underneath my butt. As he goes for the left, his hand skims up my thigh and to the crease of my ass. Holy . . .

Okay, I'm sitting on my heels now, trying not to come before he enters me. What if my therapist wrote that I can only climax *once*? Besides that sounding like torture, I hope to have sex with Lo today. I will not ruin that by going crazy with foreplay.

I'm still sitting straight up, and his body has not drifted from mine. His heart pounds against my chest, and he cups my face in his hand.

"Breathe," he tells me. "Just remember to breathe."

And then with measured unhurriedness, he gradually rests my back onto my comforter and slowly begins to slip inside of me. The position allows for such deep entry that I cry out and grab onto his shoulder for support.

His forehead rests near mine, and he raises my chin, kissing me forcefully, just how I like it, before he begins to rock agonizingly slow. Each movement mimics our heavy breaths. My parted lips brush his as he digs deeper. I whimper, my toes already curling, my head already flying off my body.

His hand massages my breast, but his eyes never once leave mine. Hot tears seep from the creases, the intensity and emotion driving me to a peak so high that every time I breathe in, he breathes out, as though keeping me alive for this moment. I melt into his slow movement, the way he disappears inside of me, and the pace that causes my body to light on fire.

"Don't stop . . ." I cry. ". . . Lo . . ." I tremble, and his arms slip around my back again, holding me tighter.

He speeds up a little, and I feel the top of the hill. I see us climbing together.

And then he thrusts and holds inside of me. I buck and cry and claw at his back. My whole body pulsing, my heart thrumming—I am his.

I collapse back onto the bed, too exhausted to lift an arm or a leg. He takes care of me, bending my knees and stretching my legs out from the last position. He rests his hands on my kneecaps, and leans forward to kiss me again. I taste the salt from our sweat, and I raise my hand to grab the back of his hair, my eagerness suddenly replacing the tiredness from our emotional sex. But he laces his fingers into mine, stopping me.

I frown. "No?" *Only once?*

He shakes his head and then kisses my temple. "I love you," he whispers, his breath tickling my ear.

"I love you too," I tell him. But I do want to wrap my legs tightly around him, giving him no choice but to harden and take me again. He scrutinizes me closely, and he must see my impatience for round two.

His eyes narrow. "Not now."

I bite my lip. "Are you going to tell me what's in the envelope?" What did my therapist restrict? The answer is killing me right now.

"Nope," he says. "You'll just want it even more if you know it's forbidden."

I squint at him. "You're getting too smart."

He grins. "When it comes to you, I am." He kisses the outside of my lips. I love and hate when he does that. "Just so you know," he whispers, "I'd love nothing more than to fill you again. I'd do it a million times a day if I could."

"I know," I murmur.

He brushes my sweaty hair off my face.

And I inhale a deep breath. "I'm just glad you're home." I have Lo back. That's all that should matter right now. Not a round two or a three, but just him present, on the road to being healthy, and in love with me. That's all I should need.

I can't wait to reach that place. I just hope it's attainable.

He relaxes next to me, and I rest my head on his chest, listening to his heartbeat while he runs his hand through my hair. This is nice.

I almost drift to sleep, but the chime of a cellphone snaps my eyes open. "Whose is it?"

He reaches over onto my nightstand. "Mine." He flips the cell in his palm, and I crane my neck over his shoulder and see a text box.

I know your girlfriend's secret.—
Unknown

I shoot up, fear snapping me cold. Did I read that wrong? I snatch the phone out of his hand, and he grabs it back.

"Lil, calm down," he says, trying to shield the screen from me as he types a reply.

"Who is that?" I've been so careful. I've never told anyone I had a sex addiction other than Lo, and now Rose, Connor, and Ryke. Did they let my secret slip to someone else?

I bite my fingernail, and Lo clasps my hand while texting with the other. His eyes flicker to me, narrowing in disapproval.

When the *ping* sounds again, I basically climb on top of Lo so he can't hide the message. I read quickly.

> Who the fuck are you?—Lo

Someone you hate.—Unknown. Okay, that does not narrow anything down. Lo's enemies from prep school and college are numerous and vast. It happened when he retaliated against all the people who thought they could bully him into submission.

Lo tries to push me off, but I have my arm wrapped around his neck, close to choking him, so he lets me be. We're still naked, but I'm too frantic to be aroused.

> Fuck off—Lo

"That's your response?" I say, wide-eyed. "You're egging the person on."

"If you don't like it, then you shouldn't be reading my personal texts or spidering me like a koala bear."

True.

> And lose out on all the money the tabloids will pay me when I tell them Lily Calloway is a sex addict? . . . Never—Unknown

I blink. Reread the text. And gawk. No.

"Lil," Lo says, shutting off his phone. "It's okay. That's not going to happen. Look at me." He holds my face in his hands, forcing my eyes to his. "That's not going to happen. I won't let it. I'll hire someone to go find this asshole. I'll pay him off more than he'll get from the tabloids."

He's forgetting something. "You're broke," I say. His father took away his trust fund because he dropped out of college. Lo hasn't spoken to him since he left for rehab. He's alone and poor and all my money is tied up with my family. And they don't know about my addiction either. I'd rather not tell them. Ever.

His features darken, remembering. "I'll think of something else then."

The shame that my family will feel if they find out—the hurt and disappointment—I can't bear to even *think* about it. A female sex addict? A slut. A male sex addict? A hero. How much will I tarnish my father's company with the news? Sure, not a lot of people outside of our social circle know my name or who I am, but could this make tabloid headlines? Why wouldn't it? *Lily Calloway: daughter of the founder of Fizzle, a sex addict and a whore.*

It's juicy enough to satiate gossip columnists everywhere.

"Lo," I say as tears threaten to fall. "I'm scared."

He hugs me, drawing me close. "Everything is going to be okay. I'm not going anywhere."

I hold on to his words and repeat them over and over, hoping that will truly be enough.

BONUS

Notes to Future Selves

Lily's Note

Hello, Lily Calloway from the Future,

Please tell me aliens exist and they look like characters from Roswell. NOT the green scary kind.
　　Also, have your powers kicked in yet?

P.S. If time travel has been invented, feel free to come to the past and tell me what happens in the series finale of Teen Wolf. I NEED TO KNOW.
　　Also, the meaning of life and all that stuff. Rose would want to know. Okay, thanks!!

Goodbye,
Lily from the Present

Loren's Note

Lo,

I hope you think this is still lame.

From,
Lo

Rose's Note

Never lose your confidence.
And if you did, you can find it in your
closet amongst your heels.

Love always,
Rose

Connor's Note

Dear Me,

Congratulations on life.
You've won.

Best,
Connor

Daisy's Note

Dear Future Daisy,

I hope you're really happy. And when I mean really happy, I mean endless chocolate cake kind of happy.

I hope that all the shitty moments in your life are squashed by the good. And I hope that most of my cynical theories are proven wrong. And lastly, I hope someone finally spotted a unicorn. ☺

Love, Daisy

Ryke's Note

You fucking better still be there for Lo.

Ryke

ACKNOWLEDGEMENTS

The overwhelming support for *Addicted to You* propelled this book into its final creation. What was first supposed to be a short novella turned into so much more because of your enthusiasm for our work. So first, we're thanking all of you: readers and friends. For taking this wild, emotional journey with Lily and Lo.

We also have to thank all the bloggers who helped us promote *Addicted to You*. I'm not sure the response would have been even half of what it was without you all. Krista and I would love to name you personally, but honestly, there are just so many. As book bloggers, we knew the community was supportive, but the amount was just above and beyond what we expected. Thank you so, so very much.

A big thanks goes to our family for reading the series, most importantly to our mom, our aunts and our cousins. Without your constant praise, we might not have mustered the guts to share this sensitive work with the world.

And for anyone who suffers from an addiction or has experience secondhand that has thanked us, *we* thank you for reading. Someone recently said how people call it tragic when celebrities die from addiction, but they mock those who are currently suffering. We hope that this speaks to some people. We know it's not for everyone, but we do appreciate you even reading this far.

Krista and Becca Ritchie are *New York Times* and *USA Today* bestselling authors and identical twins—one a science nerd, the other a comic book geek—but with their shared passion for writing, they combined their mental powers as kids and have never stopped telling stories. They love superheroes, flawed characters and soul mate love.

CONNECT ONLINE

KBRitchie.com

KBMRitchie

Ready to find
your next great read?

Let us help.

Visit prh.com/nextread